Acclaim for Cristina García's

A Handbook to Luck

"Flashes with wit and color." —*The New York Times Book Review*

"Ambitious. . . . Vivid. . . . Those familiar with García's oeuvre will find old as well as new pleasures."
—*Austin American-Statesman*

"In this absorbing story, García once again uses her talent for description to conjure the melancholic half-memories of the places and people that immigrants leave behind. And García once again skillfully weaves together the stories of several people whose lives eventually intersect." —*The Seattle Times*

"The pleasure here is García's truffle-rich prose and expert handling of time's passage." —*Entertainment Weekly*

"García expertly braids each of [her characters'] stories together, tenderly tracing the passage of these 1960s children into 1980s adults as they begin to discover the often unavoidable gap 'between what you planned and what actually happened.'" —*People*

"*Handbook* evokes the poignant inner conflicts and emotional ambiguities of García's first novel, *Dreaming in Cuban*."
—*Sun-Sentinel*

"Rich and lyrical. . . . With a poet's ear for language and imagery, García breathes vitality into three ordinary characters who often perform extraordinary deeds."
— *Rocky Mountain News*

"Intriguing. . . . The fortunes in *A Handbook to Luck* display García's command of absorbing storytelling. You can't wait to hear what happens next to each of the characters."
— *The Miami Herald*

"Terrific. . . . [García] is a sensual prose stylist who writes characters from the body outward as good as any novelist in America."
— *Houston Chronicle*

"The familiar and exotic twine with ease — but, thankfully, not predictability — in *A Handbook to Luck*."
— *San Jose Mercury News*

"*A Handbook to Luck* shines with vulnerable characters, poetic language, and poignant epiphanies."
— *Ms.*

"Graceful. . . . Shows how fortune — good and bad — can spin life in a million directions."
— *Redbook*

Cristina García

A Handbook to Luck

Cristina García was born in Havana and grew up in New York City. Her first novel, *Dreaming in Cuban*, was nominated for a National Book Award and has been widely translated. Ms. García has been a Guggenheim Fellow, a Hodder Fellow at Princeton University, and the recipient of a Whiting Writers' Award. She lives in California's Napa Valley with her daughter and husband.

A Handbook to Luck

A Handbook to Luck

A Novel

Cristina García

Vintage Contemporaries
Vintage Books
A Division of Random House, Inc.
New York

FIRST VINTAGE CONTEMPORARIES EDITION, APRIL 2008

The Library of Congress has cataloged the Knopf edition as follows:
García, Cristina, [date]
A handbook to luck / Cristina García. — 1st ed.
p. cm.
Novel.
I. Title.
PS3557.A66H36 2007
813'.54 — dc22   2006048736

Vintage ISBN: 978-0-307-27680-3

Book design by Iris Weinstein

www.vintagebooks.com

Printed in the United States of America
10 9 8 7 6 5 4 3 2 1

For my husband, Bruce

But there are no kindly gods who will return to us
What we have lost, only blind chance . . .

—LUIS CERNUDA

PART ONE

A wondrous show of illusion can be created with a few simple elements: doves, cards, coins, music, and a fine top hat.

—ANONYMOUS MAGICIAN

(1968)

Enrique Florit

Enrique Florit climbed the stairs to the roof of his apartment building, which was eye level with the top of the street's jacaranda trees. It had rained that afternoon and dark puddles stained the cement and the peeling tar paper. When Enrique opened the doors of the wire-mesh cages, the doves fluttered to his shoulders and outstretched arms. Five months ago, he and his father had bought the doves and dyed their feathers a rainbow of pastels. Now Enrique poured their daily seed, freshened their water, listened to the low blue murmurings in their throats.

His father had introduced the doves into his act on New Year's Eve. He performed every other weekend at a cocktail lounge in Marina del Rey and needed the doves to compete with the top-billed magician's unicycle-riding parrot. Papi tried to upstage the parrot by having *his* doves ride a battery-operated motorcycle across a tiny tightrope. Enrique attended the New Year's Eve show. The doves performed unpredictably, sometimes riding on cue, sometimes cooing indifferently from the rim of his father's top hat. A couple flew out of the room altogether.

Yet each time Papi strode across the stage in his tuxedo and plum-colored velvet cape, Enrique's heart rose an inch in his chest. He overheard a woman with teased-up hair say to her table companions: *Ooooh, he looks just like that Ricky Ricardo!* In California, nobody heard much about Cuba except for Ricky Ricardo, the hijackings to Havana, and, of course, El Comandante himself.

Enrique coaxed the doves back into their cages one by one. The sunset reddened the hovering dust. A propeller plane took off from the airport to the south. It puttered high over the ocean before turning toward land. During their first months in Los Angeles, Papi had kept a suitcase packed in case they needed to return to Cuba in a hurry. He listened to the Spanish-language radio stations and played boleros every night before bed. He read *El Diario* for any news of El Comandante's fall and kept their clocks three hours ahead, on Havana time. After a while they grew accustomed to waiting.

Their apartment on Seventeenth Street looked out over an alley dominated by an unruly bougainvillea. They were only a mile from the beach, and the ocean air mildewed their walls and linoleum floors. Enrique liked to go to the Santa Monica pier on his skateboard and watch the Ferris wheel and the Mexicans with their fishing rods and empty, hopeful buckets. Papi slept in their one bedroom and Enrique curled up on the living room couch at night. Mamá's coral rosary hung on a nail over the television, next to a circus poster from Varadero. In the poster, an elephant with a jeweled headdress stood on its hind legs warily eyeing the ringmaster. An orange tiger roared in the background.

Enrique shared the bedroom's cramped closet with his father. Papi's frayed tuxedos were hung up neatly, massive and forlorn looking when emptied of his ample flesh. His shoes looked equally despondent, parked in a double row by Enrique's extra pair of sneakers. Only the white ruffled shirts, starched and at attention, gave off an optimistic air.

Once Papi had been famous throughout the Caribbean. He'd performed regularly in the Dominican Republic and Panama and as far south as coastal Colombia. *El Mago Gallego.* That was his stage name then. Of course, this was long before Enrique's mother died, long before the Cuban Revolution soured, long before they left their house in Cárdenas with its marble floors and its ceiling-to-floor shutters and the speckled goose named Pato who guarded their yard.

When Mamá was still alive, Enrique, in embroidered Chinese pajamas and pretending to water a slowly growing sunflower, sometimes joined his parents on stage. For a year after she died, Enrique barely spoke. He stayed in his Tía Adela's bedroom, where the fierce light shone through the curtains and the bedspread was embroidered with hummingbirds. Outside her window, bunches of bananas ripened before his eyes.

His aunt put a little bell by his bed so that Enrique could summon her whenever he wanted. She brought him *horchata* and miniature cakes with pineapple jam. She fussed over him, too, layering on extra sweaters and a woolen scarf to keep him warm. Tía Adela believed that everything wrong with the body could be treated with heat. In the mornings Enrique woke up breathless and sputtering, convinced that he was drowning. His aunt took him to see Dr. Ignacio Sebrango, a pulmonary specialist with carbuncled arms, who said that Enrique's condition was psychological and had nothing to do with the excellent health of his lungs.

Enrique's biggest fear was that he might forget his mother altogether. She'd died when he was six and that was three whole years ago. He replayed memories of her over and over again until they seemed more like an old movie than anything real. Everyone had told him that he was the spitting image of

Mamá. They both had small frames and fine black hair and skin the color of cinnamon. Only his eyes, a hazel bordering on blue, were like his father's.

Sometimes Enrique played with his mother's engraved silver bracelet, which he'd snuck out of Cuba in his travel satchel, or tossed it on one of her empty perfume bottles like a carnival game. Or he unfolded her fan from Panama, meticulously painted with an image of the Indian goddess of love. There were a few photographs, too. In his most treasured one, Mamá sat on their veranda in the shade of an acacia reading *A Passage to India*, her favorite book. Most of all Enrique missed her scent, a gentle mixture of jasmine and sweat.

There was leftover Chinese food and four heads of wilted lettuce in the refrigerator, remnants of Papi's brief attempt to improve their diet. Enrique grabbed the carton of milk and poured himself a glass. Then he sat at the kitchen table and tried to make sense of his social studies homework. He was confused by the variety of North American Indian tribes. The history of Cuba's Indians was simple in contrast: once there were Taínos; now there were none. Enrique suspected that his fourth-grade teacher, Mr. Wonder, deliberately mispronounced his name. He made "Florit" sound like some kind of tropical fungus.

After a year and a half in Los Angeles, Enrique spoke English perfectly. His mother, who'd grown up in Panama and was the daughter of the country's water commissioner, had taught Enrique the little English she knew. This gave him an advantage over his father but it didn't account for Papi's terrible trouble with the language. His father tortured each sentence, forcing English into the rapid staccato of Cuban Spanish. He called things *he* and *she*, instead of *it*, and pronounced his *j*'s like *y*'s. His vocabulary was good but his speed and pronunciation made it impossible for anyone to understand him.

Papi blamed his accent for stalling his career. A magician's sleight of hand, he told Enrique, was entirely dependent on his ability to focus an audience's attention. If people couldn't understand what he was saying—"Speak English!" some drunk invariably shouted during his performances—how could they be manipulated? Papi said that magic was largely a matter of making ordinary things appear extraordinary with a touch of smoke and illusion.

Enrique wished they had stayed in Miami with the other Cubans. At least his father could have performed for them in Spanish, not that the exiles were in any mood for magic these days. Their idea of entertainment would be seeing El Comandante hanging from a Havana lamppost. But everybody had told them that California was the place to go for a career in show business. Papi had begged him to join his magic act again but Enrique had refused. He comforted himself by imagining Mamá watching over his life from the sidelines, urging him to say no.

Lately, his father talked about moving to Las Vegas. He knew Cubans from the casinos back home who were working on the Strip as pit bosses, blackjack dealers, nightclub managers. Papi was also acquainted with a few mobsters who'd moved their gambling operations there after the Cubans kicked them out of Havana. Las Vegas was growing fast, he said, and soon would become the world capital of magic. Where else could a man start the day with fifty dollars in his pocket and end up a millionaire by nightfall?

Enrique turned on the television, forcing the thick knob from one station to the next. There were Abbott and Costello reruns on Channel 9, but he wasn't interested. They only made him laugh when he was sick. He had a slight cough and his neck ached. If he was lucky, he might catch the flu and get to stay home from school for a week. His ribs hurt after a scuffle in the playground. No big deal, just the usual uneven swap of punches with the bully from Ocean Park. It wasn't easy being the new kid (almost everybody else had known each other since kindergarten), and dark-skinned, and the second-shortest boy in the class.

The six o'clock news didn't change much. Whenever Enrique saw President Johnson on television, he remembered the American tourists who used to go to Varadero Beach before the revolution and rudely called everyone "boy." Every day more U.S. soldiers were being killed in Vietnam, fighting the Communists. Enrique lost track of how many thousands so far. Why weren't the Americans fighting the Communists in Cuba? What was the difference? And whatever had happened to the men who'd fought in the Bay of Pigs? Why didn't he hear about them? Enrique was suspicious of facts. As far as he could tell, nobody could be sure of anything except numbers, or something you could hold in your own two hands.

His paternal grandparents and his aunt had remained in Cuba by choice. Abuelo Arturo still strolled down Avenida Echeverría in his waistcoat and long-chained pocket watch and Abuela Carmen rode around town in a horse-drawn carriage, joining her friends for *guayaba* pastries on the tiled terrace of La Domínica Hotel. His Tía Adela managed to scrape by knitting baby blankets from old wool. They stayed in Cuba despite the shortages, despite the threat of another *yanqui* invasion, despite the hurricanes and the blackouts and the clashes with intolerant neighbors because for them, Communism or not, it was still home.

At school Enrique's best friend was a Japanese boy named Shuntaro, taller than him by an inch and with the same lanky hair. They spent Saturday afternoons at his grandparents' nursery on Sawtelle Boulevard, with its damp earth smells and its sleeping, lovestruck lily bulbs. The nursery specialized in bonsai—the rear greenhouse was devoted to them—and people came from all over California to buy their minuscule junipers and elms. This year they were growing a perfect dwarf pomegranate tree with golf ball–sized fruit.

Shuntaro's grandparents listened politely to Papi's stories

about magic. Enrique suspected they didn't understand a word he said. His father told them—looking around to include any customers within earshot—that magic was a noble, perilous profession. In the past magicians had been condemned as witches, sorcerers, and devil worshipers and frequently put to death. Only in the last hundred years had professional magicians been able to work without fear of persecution.

Papi's hero was Robert-Houdin, the French magician who'd inspired Houdini to adapt his name for the stage. In the 1850s, Robert-Houdin was sent by his government to calm the natives of Algeria with his wondrous feats. He did many things to impress the Arabs, including devising a chest too heavy for the strongest of them to lift and disappearing a young Moor from under a large cloth cone. By the time he'd completed his tricks, the Arab chiefs had surrendered, pledging their loyalty to France.

According to Papi, El Comandante had similarly fooled the Cuban people. After his victory march across the island, thousands of supporters gathered in the capital to celebrate. During El Comandante's speech—a deceptive concoction of propaganda and hope, Papi scoffed—top magicians were paid to send trained doves to fly over the crowd. When one of the doves landed dramatically on El Comandante's shoulder during the climax of his speech, the *santeros* and their followers took this as a sign that he was destined to rule Cuba.

To Fernando Florit, everything was connected to magic. When Enrique showed him his history report on Benjamin Franklin, Papi suggested adding a little-known fact to the biography of the inventor. In Franklin's day, he said, the famous illusionist Baron Wolfgang von Kempelen had devised an automated chess player that took on all challengers. "In 1783," Papi crowed, "Benjamin Franklin played against the machine and lost!"

Enrique opened the kitchen window and let in a woolly moth bumping up against the pane. A neighbor, cigarette dangling, was testing the engine of his big-finned '57 Cadillac, filling the alley with exhaust fumes. This was a nightly ritual, annoying to everyone in the building except Enrique, who found it oddly soothing. He set the table, heated the kung pao chicken, and put rice to boil, welcoming the familiar starchy smell. Then he finished studying for his vocabulary test and waited for his father to come home.

Fernando Florit burst through the front door just after nine o'clock with a box of chocolate éclairs and a pink silk scarf around his neck. He entered every room in the same way, swept in like a run of heat, overwhelming everything. Their cups and dishes, bought on sale at the five-and-dime, trembled in the cupboard. He scooped up Enrique and planted a rubbery kiss on his forehead. Then he took his place at the kitchen table. Enrique heaped the steaming Chinese food onto his father's plate alongside the fresh rice.

Their ritual never changed. They ate first, talked later. No matter how hungry he was, Enrique waited to eat until his father came home. It was two hours past their usual dinnertime and Papi was starving. He took pride in sharing a meal, no matter how modest, with his son every night. Some days it was the only time they saw each other. Papi was very busy: auditioning, rehearsing, recruiting talent agents, battling the competition, and, occasionally, performing.

Enrique studied his father across the table as if he were a natural phenomenon, a geyser, perhaps, or an erupting volcano. At school, Mr. Wonder was teaching science segments on geology and meteorology and Enrique couldn't help comparing Papi to one of the many violent assaults on the earth's crust. He imagined his father causing earthquakes, tsunamis, category 5 hurricanes. Enrique was more like his mother, quiet and thoughtful, preferring to read or work on an interesting math problem. He did advanced algebra and trigonometry for fun. It pleased him to think that mathematicians everywhere spoke the same language.

Papi finished the kung pao chicken and several helpings of rice. He settled back in his chair, spreading his huge thighs. *"¿Cómo estás, hijo?"* he asked. Enrique relaxed, knowing that no more than a cursory *Bien* was required. His father's question was merely the opening for him to talk about his day or continue planning their big move to Las Vegas. That was not to say that if Enrique did have something to share, Papi wouldn't have listened to him with attentive enthusiasm.

"Guess who I met today?" Papi asked, shuddering with excitement. "You won't believe it."

"Desi Arnaz?" Enrique knew that his father had it out for that conga-playing performer from Santiago. Señor Arnaz, Papi complained, insulted the dignity of Cuban manhood with his howling renditions of "Babalú." To even mention Arnaz in his presence was to guarantee a bitter outpouring of insults.

Papi grinned and waggled three plump fingers.

"Three names?" Enrique was surprised. Nobody in America had three names, at least not names they used publicly. Here, the more famous you were, the fewer names you had.

"Give up?" Papi's eyes bulged gleefully.

Enrique lifted his hands in surrender.

"Sammy . . . Davis . . . Junior!" His father dragged out the words slowly, clapping his hands in triumph. "He's looking for a new opening act for his show at the Sands and came to see my rehearsal, or half of it, anyway. This is it, *hijo*! What we've been waiting for!"

"When do you start?"

"You! You! You mean 'we'!" Papi stood up, shaking his colossal hips, and recited a line from a poem by José Martí: " 'In night's darkness I've seen raining down on my head pure flames, flashing rays of beauty divine.' "

Whenever he got excited Papi danced the maxixe, a Brazilian two-step he'd learned in Rio de Janeiro, and copiously quoted Martí. He knew by heart every one of his poems and most of his essays besides, including the prologue to the "Poem of Niagara," which began: "Contemptible times, these: when the only art that prevails is that of piling one's own granaries high, sitting on a seat of gold . . ."

As a child, Papi had memorized endless passages of Latin for his Jesuit teachers. The priests were fanatical for political oratory, too, forcing their students to recite the inspiring early speeches of President Estrada Palma (before the temptations of high office compromised his ideals). From a young age, Fernando Florit had been singled out for the priesthood, until his parade of gruesome tricks—one involving a stack of consecrated wafers and Padre Bonifacio's short-haired terrier—convinced the clerics that their star pupil, son of the richest dry goods merchant in Cárdenas, had been sent by the devil himself.

"Doesn't he have a glass eye?" Enrique asked.

"Yes, but it did not impede Mr. Junior's ability to assess my gifts in the slightest. He was particularly taken with my re-creations of nineteenth-century magic tricks."

"Great." Those were Enrique's favorites, too: restoring a playing card that had been burned to ashes; walking through a brick wall; pulling souvenirs from an antique cornucopia. "How much will they pay you?"

"The details will be worked out in due time, my little accountant. Haven't I taught you that a magician may disregard fortune, but never opportunity?"

Enrique didn't question his father's talents, but his business sense often left them penniless. "How long are they giving you?"

"I'm not certain what the standard warm-up act is for a man of Mr. Junior's stature," Papi said, somewhat impatiently, "but I would imagine it would be, at minimum, thirty minutes."

"You could do a lot in half an hour." Enrique tried to sound encouraging, not that Papi needed it. His father's optimism was not a fragile thing.

"*Mi hijo,* we will shake out our wings like butterflies!"

"Right." Enrique pushed the last of the kung pao chicken around on his plate. His insides were flip-flopping uneasily. He had inherited his mother's nervous stomach. His father, on the other hand, could have eaten the bark off a tree without ill effect.

Papi didn't like to talk about Mamá but he couldn't help himself sometimes. They'd been, he said, very much in love. Enrique remembered his parents holding hands and kissing a lot and slowly dancing to boleros. Sometimes they'd recited poetry to each other on the front porch, to the amusement of their neighbors. Now on his most despairing days, Papi paced the apartment trying to change history with "if only"s. If only he'd refused to let her do those dangerous aquarium tricks; if only he'd checked the weather report that day. If only this and if only that before he collapsed tearfully in Enrique's arms. These episodes exhausted them both and still explained nothing.

Last week Enrique had come across a library book called *The Odds.* In it, the probabilities of even the most seemingly random events were mathematically calculated. The odds of dying in a taxicab, of being born a quintuplet, or with only one kidney, or a sixth finger. Everything could be reliably predicted. The book also pointed out that the smallest carelessness, a hiccup of nature, could alter a person's life. On the day his mother died, a flock of storks, thrown off course by the strong autumn winds and looking like parasols, had landed in Colón Park, near the stage where his parents were performing. One of the storks got tangled up in an electrical cable and died at the same time as Mamá. What were the odds of that?

At the kitchen table, Papi retold the story of Sammy Davis Jr., but Enrique was only half listening. The last thing he wanted was to start over in a new place. In photographs of Las Vegas, everybody looked old and too tanned. Plus it hardly rained there. He'd read somewhere about the one time it snowed and thirty-seven people froze to death. If he and Papi went anywhere, it should be back to Cuba, where they belonged.

Enrique looked over at his father, happily chatting at him in Spanish. Papi was six feet tall and weighed an eighth of a ton, but he could still pass for a kid. With his broad waxy face and his babyish teeth, he would look right at home in a pair of short pants or licking a giant lollipop. For dessert, he offered Enrique a chocolate éclair, then ate the remaining three himself.

"What do you say we go out and celebrate with an ice-cream sundae?" Papi smiled, his hair shiny under the kitchen's single bulb. A bit of custard wobbled at the corner of his mouth.

Enrique took a bite of his éclair. He looked out the window for a sign of the moon. There was supposed to be an eclipse tonight but he wasn't sure exactly when. If he listened closely, he could hear the doves' gentle clamor on the roof.

Marta Claros

It was noon and the streets were quiet. Only the doves cooed and fluttered in the tamarind tree, wings blazing in the sun. Now and then Marta Claros overheard tired voices from behind the shutters and gates. She shuffled along the familiar, roughly paved streets of her San Salvador neighborhood and spotted the orange tree at the top of the hill. It was thick with blossoms, and the sweet scent of its fruit drifted toward her in fragrant wisps. The tree grew in the yard of the nicest house around. Marta didn't understand why everyone referred to the house as La Casa Azul when it wasn't blue at all but a hazy white, like when the sun shone through clouds on a winter day.

A drowsy-looking moth struggled up the hill beside her. Marta thought it might be injured and she wanted to adopt it. The moth was so tiny it wouldn't eat much, not like the skinny dogs and kittens she'd brought home and then was forced by her mother to abandon again. Marta put down her basket of used clothing—darned socks, blouses, skirts, and pants—and held out her finger.

"Come here, little moth," she coaxed. At least it wasn't a caterpillar. Caterpillars frightened her. Their miniature green horns made them look like devils. She avoided dragonflies, too, because everyone said that if you touched one, you would wake up with your eyes glued shut.

Marta was hungry but she didn't dare go home yet. So far today, she'd sold only two pairs of socks and a cotton blouse to the grocer's wife. Mamá had warned her not to return until her basket was empty and her pockets chiming with coins. If only Marta could make up customers the way she made up friends, like Caridad and Tomasina, who played with her whenever she wanted and didn't cheat at games the way her real cousins did.

She imagined her ideal customer: a fine lady with lace gloves and a wide-brimmed hat to protect her from the sun. The lady would live in a house by herself and invite Marta in for cookies and a glass of *horchata*. Then she would read aloud the way her teacher had read to the class, not to learn anything but just to hear a good story. The hour would unravel slowly, like a piece of frayed cloth. After Marta had a second helping of cookies, politely leaving a few crumbs on her plate, the lady would ask her: How much for your entire basket of clothes?

Recently, Marta had quit first grade (at nine she'd been the oldest in her class) because her mother needed help. Mamá was pregnant again and wanted Marta back on the streets selling used clothes—"barely worn" was what she was instructed to tell potential customers. Mamá had lost three babies in the past two years and didn't want to risk losing another. The one baby who'd survived lived only four days, his bones soft as clay. Then he got diarrhea, and his forehead sunk in, and he didn't cry anymore.

Shortly after Marta left school, her teacher came to their house wearing a flowered dress and white sandals. She tried to convince Mamá to keep *our Martita* in school, at least until she finished learning how to read. (Marta loved the way Señorita Dora said *our Martita*, as if Marta belonged to both of them.) Señorita Dora said that Marta had attended school for barely a year, and for a bright girl like her that wasn't nearly enough.

It was a shame, too, because Marta was finally figuring out the alphabet and running the letters together to form words. *P-a-l-o-m-a-s*. Doves. It seemed a miracle to her that entire stories were trapped in those haphazard scratches of black, stories that the best readers in the class could recite at the top of their lungs. The only thing she didn't understand was why the words in the books didn't sound the way real people talked.

"Will you pay for my daughter's food and her medicine when she's sick?" Mamá asked the teacher in a rude tone that embarrassed Marta. Señorita Dora remained silent. "Ah, just as I thought. Then this is none of your concern." The conversation ended there.

"Daydreaming again?" a lilting voice rang out.

It was Esperanza Núñez, coming down the street with a straw basket on her hip. Esperanza peddled ladies' underwear door-to-door, mostly to rich housewives who bought her fancy panties and baby doll pajamas. She said that her customers must be *putas* in bed, judging by their purchases. Lately, all they wanted were items imported from France that cost three times as much as the local products. Marta wondered how far away France was and why they made better underwear than the people right here in El Salvador.

Esperanza leaned forward and Marta glimpsed in her basket a tantalizing array of silk and lace underthings — scanty red and black pieces with minute hooks and ribbons that gave off an unfamiliar perfume. Could women go to the bathroom wearing all that?

A mariachi band blared mechanically from a radio, playing the theme song to a popular *novela*. Esperanza and her mother and every woman they knew listened to the radio show *Amor Perdido* at seven o'clock. It was about a spoiled, rich girl named Genovesa de Navarre, who, against the will of her family, snuck around with a tinsmith named Ambrosio Peón.

"What does it mean when your heart dries out?" Marta blurted out. Mamá had said this at breakfast while reheating tortillas and beans. For a heart to dry out, this must be a terrible thing.

"It means," Esperanza began, sad like Mamá, "that sometimes a woman has to learn how to pretend love."

But how could anyone pretend that? Maybe it was like pretending you weren't hungry when you really were. Marta wanted to ask Esperanza more questions but she kept her mouth shut. When people thought she wasn't so curious, they spoke more freely in front of her. Tía Matilde, the kindest and prettiest of her aunts, told Marta that sometimes a person had to chew on the truth like a tough piece of meat to get any satisfaction.

Now that she wasn't in school, Marta would have to learn everything by herself. Like why canaries sang and other birds didn't and could they all talk to each other. Or why her step-father hit Mamá so hard that she had to buy face powder on credit to cover the bruises.

Esperanza climbed the hill and rang the bell of La Casa Azul. It took forever for the iron gate to open. A plump woman appeared. Her eyes looked enormous, like a cow's, with thick fringes of lashes. She wore a sleeveless nightgown with a collar of feathers. If Marta had seen her after dark she might have thought the woman was an angel, or a snowy owl (there was a picture of one at school), or the foamy edge of a wave.

The sun felt hot on her head. If she didn't get in the shade soon, the sun could burn a hole in her skull and the words and ideas accumulating inside might leak out. Marta settled the basket of clothes on her head and started down the hill. A breath of wind stirred the hibiscus. She looked over her shoulder and saw Esperanza offering a glossy black brassiere, like a baby vulture, to the woman in white.

That afternoon, Marta went to her First Communion class at Holy Trinity Church. Sister Concepción only had to repeat a prayer twice for Marta to know it by heart. It was as if each word had its place in a procession, like the prancing horses in the Easter parade. In two Sundays she would walk down the aisle in her starched dress and veil, a bride of Christ, ready to receive His body.

The church was downtown, not far from her brother's tree. Evaristo had run away from home two months ago. After living in alleys and sleeping at the zoo (he liked the sloths and jungle monkeys best), he decided to move into an enormous coral tree near the Plaza Barrios. If Marta wanted to speak to him, she had to hoist herself up limb by limb and join him in the tree's uppermost branches. He'd wedged a wooden platform there and hung a scrap of plastic for a roof. It was a miracle he didn't fall and break his neck. Evaristo was stubborn, though. He'd suffered many thrashings from their mother but left the house after just one beating from their stepfather.

Marta brought her brother tortillas and beans wrapped in a banana leaf along with a tomato she'd stolen from Mamá's kitchen. She charged her customers a few extra cents in order to buy Evaristo treats. Once she brought him a chicken tamale with chili peppers, another time a slice of day-old *marquesote* that she got for next to nothing from the bakery around the corner. Evaristo loved lemon ice cones but it was impossible to carry these up to him in his tree.

"My Communion is in ten days, *hermanito*. I want you to come."

A river of sparrows noisily flowed above them. Her brother

turned toward the mountains, encircled with ash-colored clouds. From his perch, he saw many things: two purse snatchings; a prostitute servicing a customer in the heliotropes (her sour milk scent drifted up to him in his tree); a group of protesting students rounded up by the police.

"*Primero Dios*," Marta begged him. "You must forgive our stepfather, Evaristo. Remember our Lord's great sacrifice." She liked to repeat, word for word, what Sister Concepción said. This way her tongue wouldn't trip on sins by mistake. If Marta didn't know her brother so well, she would think that it was shame and not anger turning his skin pink.

"Why don't we work together?" She tried to sound encouraging. Marta knew that Evaristo shined shoes now and then. Once she saw him crossing La Avenida Independencia with his battered kit; another time polishing a businessman's boots outside La Mariposa, the famous steak restaurant. She didn't let on, though. Her brother was proud. Pride, too, she'd learned, was a sin.

"If you don't help me, who will? Maybe we could make paper flowers. I know where I can get some spine glue very cheap. Or we could sell oranges or brooms, it doesn't matter."

Evaristo looked away.

"Mamá's getting really big." Marta tried changing the subject. "I'm hoping it's a girl this time." Their mother's stomach was flatter than during her other pregnancies. Everyone knew that a high, round stomach meant a boy and a flat, wide one meant a girl. It seemed to Marta that their mother was happiest when she was expecting a child, as if her live children meant less to her.

She remembered Evaristo slipping out like a bloody tadpole from between Mamá's legs. He'd weighed barely three pounds and had sores on his head that looked like mosquito bites. "This one has a taste for death," the midwife said. She let Marta watch so that she wouldn't be afraid when her own time came. They were living outside San Vicente then, with their real father. The next morning, Papá left to find work in Honduras and never returned.

Everyone told Marta not to get too attached to her baby brother because he wouldn't live long. No amount of rubbing alcohol or *guarumo* leaves would stop his fevers. The village women were making his angel wings—better to pray for death than let a sick baby suffer—when Evaristo unexpectedly recovered. Mamá didn't report his birth at first, still convinced that he would die. Then she had to lie to the local officials about his birth date to avoid the five-*colón* fine.

Evaristo almost died again when he was two years old. They'd been walking along the muddy riverbank near their family's *ranchito* when he slipped and fell into the water. Down, down, down he sank, his eyes wide open, transfixed by the weeds and shiny fish. When he finally rose to the surface, Marta managed to pull him to shore by his hair. She carried him slung on her back like a sack of beans and staggered all the way home. That night, Evaristo woke up stinking of the camphor-coated banana leaves that covered him from head to toe.

"I miss you," Marta said, reaching for her brother's hand. It was dirty and calloused but he allowed her to hold it. She petted his knuckles, soothing him like she did their mother's chickens. At home the birds were everywhere, pecking through the rooms and the cement patio where the washing and cooking got done. Mamá let the chickens sleep in her hammock and had taken to raising a baby turkey in a woolen hat.

"Look at this," Marta said, pulling a pink plastic rosary from her pocket. "I won this for reciting the Hail Mary ten times without making a single mistake."

Evaristo took the rosary and examined it closely, fingering the edge of the crucifix. Marta swallowed hard. She felt something sticking in her throat, small and sharp as a hook. Long ago her father had hanged a rabid dog from their mango tree in the countryside so that the disease would float to heaven. Why was she thinking of this right now?

"I've been praying a lot to the Virgins lately," Marta said, coughing a little. "La María Auxiliadora. La Señora del Perpetuo Socorro. La Virgen del Carmen. I mean, I know they're the same, they're all one Virgin. But I like hearing their different stories, how they appeared to ordinary people in their villages."

"Do you think the Virgin could visit us?" Evaristo asked, his head resting on his knees.

"Maybe."

"Sometimes at night, I feel like there's somebody next to me."

"Do you think it could be *her*?"

"*No creo*. It's probably just some bird."

Why did people make such a fuss about virgins, anyway? Not the Virgin Mary, but regular women. In their own family, scandals erupted over women whose "pitchers" were discovered broken on their wedding nights. Tía Matilde had told her the story of poor Luz, whose husband marched her back to her parents the night of her wedding. He'd beaten the truth out of her: that the one who'd gotten to her first was the parish priest. Of course, Luz was to blame no matter which *picaflor* had trapped her. She left her parents' house in disgrace and nobody knew what became of her.

"Don't you miss listening to the radio?" Marta knew her brother was fond of sentimental *rancheras*, especially the one called "Look How My Heart Beats for You," although he would rather die than admit this.

"I have my birds." Evaristo pointed to a solitaire, whistling its lonely *fuiii fuiii* on a nearby branch. He told Marta that solitaires liked to admire their reflections and drank water from street puddles, like dogs.

A part of her secretly liked that Evaristo didn't live like everyone else. None of her friends had a brother who lived in a tree. But she feared that he might fall prey to the *Cipitío* or the *cadejos* or other goblins, unprotected as he was among the leaves. And what about La Siguanaba, with her frozen skin and hairy hand, who looked to grab boys by their nipples?

Marta watched two *garrobo* lizards chase each other around the trunk of the tree. In lean times people roasted the lizards, skewering them on sticks. Everyone swore that if you closed your eyes, the lizards tasted like chicken.

"Okay, I'll go with you for a while," Evaristo said, giving her back the rosary and shimmying down the tree. "Did you hear about that mechanic in Soyapango?"

How did her brother get the latest news? The night before, a friend of their uncle's was hacked to pieces by drunks with machetes in the center of town. Was it bad luck or God's will? This was the family argument whenever anybody died unexpectedly. Tía Patricia had lost two husbands in five years. Now everyone whispered that she was one of those white-spleened women who caused the violent deaths of their men.

"Do you know Jacinto López, the boy who sells firewood?" Marta blushed, linking her arm with her brother's.

"Is he bothering you?" Evaristo demanded.

Marta was pleased. If it came down to it, her brother would defend her. "He's declared his love for me."

"Do you like him then?"

"Not so much."

Marta enjoyed talking to Jacinto, though. He was smart and funny and he snuck into movies without paying. Afterward he told her the plots of the American westerns, playing out every scene. He was so good at dying that Marta often mistook his acting for reality. But Jacinto was too scrawny, like a stick in one of his firewood bundles. She preferred big, tall men like her father. Evaristo was spindly but he would probably grow as big as Papá one day.

"So where do you go when it rains?" Marta asked.

"Nowhere special."

Marta didn't stay much drier at home. The water seeped through the tin roof, which was patched here and there with wads of plastic. Marta stored her Communion dress (her cousin Erlinda's secondhand one) in her mother's cardboard suitcase to keep it dry.

"You know what Mamá did today?"

"What?"

"She spat on the floor and told me to run to the store and get her more face powder. She said that if I wasn't back by the time the spit dried, she would beat me."

"Did you make it?" Evaristo asked.

"*Sí,*" Marta said. "I did."

Evaristo

It rains all night long. The birds are huddled together on the thickest branch. At least there'll be worms in the morning, they say, plenty of worms. It's hard to sleep. Everything stinks. Flowers. Donkey shit. I can't see the stars through the clouds. The rain doesn't stop. Big fat drops. A lot happens under my tree. Only the birds see what I see. But they never shut up. This seed or that one. That bug or this one. The same stupid fights. Don't believe me if you don't want to, but I'm telling the truth. Up here, the water's still warm from the sky.

(1970)

Leila Rezvani

Before her mother imported the horticulturist from London, the garden was a friendlier place. Leila Rezvani walked along its manicured paths, past a showy rhododendron and a fountain painted with doves. A thin film of moisture coated every leaf and petal. The roses looked perfect, delicate and darkly veined. Yet to her the garden seemed decorous and static, like a roomful of her mother's friends. There was no comfortable place to sit anymore, nowhere to think or watch the clouds. She missed the date palms and the stubborn pomegranate tree and the old poplars and plane trees, too. Their previous gardener, a dwarf from Tabriz, used to coax peonies from the parched earth, laying down straw in early spring to protect them from frost.

When her family had first moved to the northern part of Tehran, her mother complained that their home was too close to the mountains, that the soil was spongy and wild rabbits came to graze on what little she grew. A proper garden was impossible. Leila hated their new home because there was no one her age to play with—only her older brother, Hosein, who disdained girls. That was six years ago. Now there were many more families in the neighborhood and Leila's best friend, Yasmine, lived right down the street. Together they listened to the Beatles and tried on their mothers' makeup and designer evening gowns.

The horticulturist, Mr. Fifield, had arrived in the middle of January. By May he had the garden blooming with exotic flora: boxwood hedges, blue hydrangeas, dogwoods, azaleas, periwinkles. He left no room for native species. Gone were the cypress and greengage trees, the narcissi and asphodels. Even the butterflies were driven away. Mr. Fifield's foreign vegetation drank enormous quantities of water, which was pumped in by a complex system of pipes and wells, prompting Leila's father to grumble, "How long do you think, Fatemeh, before we drain the country of water? Do you want to live under the sea then?"

Mr. Fifield inspected the English ivy along the garden's back wall as Maman rapturously watched. Leila didn't like the way her mother hovered around the Englishman, complimenting him, ordering that tea and sweets be brought to him on silver trays. Maman took extra care with her lipstick, too, a fierce shade of red that didn't suit her. And since when had she worn her skirts so short, flaunting her plump knees like a schoolgirl?

"Leila, go inside and bring Mr. Fifield a glass of lemonade," her mother insisted. "Hurry now. Don't keep him waiting."

Leila detested the Englishman. To her, he looked like one of those stiff-stemmed magnolias he'd planted. She especially hated the lilting way he spoke to her mother, elongating the first vowel of her name as if he were out of breath.

"Ah, my dear Faaatemeh," Mr. Fifield sighed, his hair damp from his toils. "*You* are the vital perfume of this garden."

Why couldn't Maman see through his flattering nonsense?

Sometimes Leila concocted dramas with the flowers to help take her mind off him and the fact that her brother was dying. Lilacs were definitely aristocratic and Leila cast them in regal roles. Petunias had an air of villainy about them, lovely and evil with their deceitful funnels. Lilies of the valley were excitable girls with an annoying tendency to swoon. Yesterday Leila had learned the word *virgin* from Yasmine, who'd heard it from an older cousin. It was curious to her that people could be defined as much by what they were as by what they weren't.

Her brother slept all day long. Not even the gusting winds woke him. Hosein was four years older and for most of their growing up had shown no interest in her. He hadn't been unkind, just indifferent. Mostly Leila had watched him from afar, as if he were a god. Since his illness, Hosein spoke to her more often, bestowing small compliments: the becoming blue of her blouse; her glossy hair pulled back in a single braid. His attentions pleased Leila, but they also made her uneasy.

Earlier today, Leila had brought him a bit of lavash and mint tea but Hosein wanted only sugar cubes to suck on. He said it was the last thing left he could really taste.

During Ramezan, Hosein had been exempt from fasting on account of his illness. He couldn't eat much without vomiting, anyway. Yet the scent of his meager portions of lamb and rice drove everyone mad with hunger and envy. Each day he drenched his bed with sweat, growing thin as a stalk of wheat. He missed the entire school year and wouldn't be returning to Switzerland to finish his studies.

Over Christmas, the doctors in London diagnosed Hosein with a rare form of leukemia. They prescribed their strongest painkillers and gave him four or five months to live. Out of desperation, Baba tried giving him experimental drugs. At first Hosein improved but then the treatments only made him sicker. By the time Baba turned for help to his superstitious sister, Aunt Parvin (who recommended an "egg breaker" to find out who'd cursed him), Leila knew her brother would die. No amount of medicine, or prayer, or exorcism would cure him.

Nobody in the family admitted that Hosein was dying, but nobody denied it anymore either. Leila wondered what it would be like to be dead. Was it a permanent silence, where nothing, not a leaf or the slightest breeze, ever stirred?

Next year she would leave for Switzerland to attend Hosein's old boarding school on the shores of Lake Geneva. She would receive a generous monthly allowance and perfect her English and French (she'd attended the trilingual International Academy since kindergarten). Children from the world's finest families were accepted to the Swiss school, Maman told her, and Leila would make many important friends. Eventually she would go to college in America, as Hosein would have done. But first, Maman insisted, Leila would need to have her nose fixed. ("We'll just have that nasty Rezvani bump shaved off and bring in the tip a little . . .")

Leila entered the kitchen, rousing the cook from her nap. "Maman wants lemonade for the Englishman," she said.

"Besm-Allah-o-Rahman-e-Rahim," Nasrin recited automatically as she sliced and juiced ten lemons. She looked continually weary, as if her very existence burdened her. Around her, the copper pots gleamed.

Leila found it irritating that Nasrin quoted the Koran for the most mundane of tasks. Polishing the marble floors and beating the day's dust from the rugs called for longer recitations. Nasrin put cookies and pistachios in gold-rimmed dishes and arranged them on a tray with the fresh lemonade. She wanted to deliver the refreshments herself but Leila insisted on carrying the tray.

"Silly girl, what took you so long?" Maman scolded her in English.

Leila watched Mr. Fifield pour gin from a silver flask into his lemonade. He offered some to her mother and she accepted, giggling. This would likely go on all afternoon. The Englishman's forehead was blotchy where his sunburned skin was peeling. Behind them, the sky spread its thick haze.

Leila wondered if the changes in the garden were confusing to the birds that had lived there before. Was one perch the same as another to the blue rollers and the gray hooded crows? Why hadn't the swallows built their usual nests in the eaves? And where were the nightingales? It was difficult for her to study the birds now, to watch their takeoffs and landings amid all this strange foliage.

"What can I do with a lazy girl like this?" Maman asked, as if Leila's shortcomings were a fit subject for conversation. "In the sun all day, turning her skin brown as a farmer's. And that nose! She certainly didn't get it from my side of the family."

Leila was tired of hearing about her mother's family — White Russians and Christians who'd immigrated to Iran after 1917 and thought themselves superior to Persians. Yes, their noses were smaller but so was everything else about them. According to Aunt Parvin, the Petrovnas had grown impoverished in less than a generation and Maman had had to support them with her nursing career. Naturally, Maman denied this. But nobody denied that Fatemeh Petrovna had been a great beauty in her day. It had taken Nader Rezvani, a young heart surgeon, the better part of a year to outmaneuver her other suitors.

Leila didn't understand what her parents had in common. At dinnertime, Maman complained about the servants' minor infractions, or reported the latest horticultural news — the camellias were taking root, the blighted hibiscus was finally rid of pests. Or she criticized whatever they happened to be eating: the underseasoned meatballs, the overcooked kebabs, the soggy eggplant stew. She never mentioned her son dying thirty meters away.

Whenever Baba asked Leila a question, Maman would dismiss it. "Don't waste your time with this sparrow-brain, my dear. She does nothing all day but daydream in the sun."

When Leila wanted to join the swim team at school, Maman

refused on the grounds that swimming built up too much unfeminine muscle. Leila appealed to her father but it didn't do any good. He left all domestic decisions to Maman. After dinner Baba would retire to his vast library of poetry, history, and the sciences, or go to Hosein's room and read him philosophy books until bedtime.

At family gatherings, Baba openly disputed the Shah's policies. He ridiculed the royal edict banning the plays of Molière because they exposed the vices of the monarchy. After his outbursts, the family whispered behind his back: *Nader is losing his mind. Imagine his firstborn, his only son, with an incurable disease of the blood.* A few maliciously speculated that perhaps the good doctor was a collaborator, waiting for his chance to turn in members of his own family to the secret police. No matter; his complaints made everyone, even his friends, feel unsafe.

Leila held the silver tray as Mr. Fifield nibbled on his cookies. Maman coyly nodded at everything the Englishman said, her pearl earrings swaying in assent. She liked to say that pearls brought good luck or bad, depending on the wearer. Her voice seemed distant to Leila, farther than the bee-eater lingering in the fig tree. The sun beat down on her arms, warming her skin. Leila studied the pomp of colors around her. If the sun helped things flourish—ripened the figs, coaxed the violets from their dank hiding places—then surely it could help her grow faster, reduce the time it took for her to grow up.

Mostly, Leila wished she could return to the Caspian Sea. Three summers ago her family had rented a villa there and spent a happy month swimming, hiking, and collecting rocks. In the evenings, Baba would sit in the garden and tell stories about the constellations. The sky seemed a mysterious expanse of velvet, pinpricked with promises. After their parents went to bed, Hosein would frighten Leila with tales of monsters like the Bakhtak (the chest crusher) or the Pa-lees (the foot licker) who murdered children in their sleep. Even Maman had seemed content that summer by the sea.

Nearby a magpie hopped on a branch of the lemon tree. During Ramezan, Leila ate lemons from this tree all month. She sliced each fruit in half, carefully studying its pulpy buttresses, and squeezed the sourness onto her tongue. Then she sucked on the rinds until they burned her lips and the insides of her cheeks. She did this every day during the endless fasting. Lemons, she rationalized, didn't count as real food.

Baba had suggested that she read to distract her grumbling stomach. He'd recommended Rudyard Kipling and Jules Verne, but their stories bored her. If the events they recounted hadn't really happened, why should she bother reading them? There was too much to explore in the real world.

The magpie stared at Leila and whined. The language of birds was something she wished she could learn. At times, Leila felt she understood them: their split-second hesitations before flight, their solemn meetings before migrations south. Baba told her that the bones of birds were hollow, that he could hear them whistling over the Zagros Mountains as they journeyed toward the Persian Gulf.

"Go check on your brother," Maman ordered. "Worthless girl, he's overdue for his injection. What would he do if I didn't remind you?" Then she turned with a shrug to Mr. Fifield, and let him kiss her hand.

Leila slipped into the house and down the marble hallway to Hosein's bedroom. A light flickered from the doorway, from the television, which stayed on whether he was watching it or not. Last summer everyone had seen the U.S. astronauts walking on the moon, but few people believed it was true. Yasmine said that her Uncle Mostafa, who worked for the minister of the interior, claimed that the whole thing was a hoax, that the so-called lunar landscape was nothing but a barren stretch of American desert. If you looked closely, Uncle Mostafa said, you could see lizards scurrying across the astronauts' boots.

Leila stopped in the bathroom to wash her hands with her father's green hospital soap. The lace curtains in Hosein's room fluttered. Leila approached her brother, asleep in his bed, and prepared his morphine shot. Her father had shown her how to calibrate the precise amount of the drug necessary to relieve Hosein's pain, how to inject him so gently that it wouldn't leave a bruise. Maman, the former nurse, couldn't bear to do this herself.

After moistening a cotton ball with alcohol, Leila pressed it firmly to the crook of her brother's elbow. Hosein opened his eyes and stared at her. His head looked swollen and fragile, like a too big blossom on a spindly stem. And his lips stuck out, as if they were clumsily pasted in place. She pictured his blood with its deadly froth of germs. Why had his body turned against him so viciously?

Last year at Baba's hospital, Leila had seen the body of a man, a traffic accident victim, lying on a dissecting table for the medical students to examine. On display were his heart and intestines, his honeycombed lungs, the wilted flesh between his legs. It jolted her to think that not long before, his organs had worked in graceful concert to keep him alive.

Hosein summoned Leila closer, his eyes pleading and wary. She put down the syringe and studied his face. Even sick as he was, her brother was more beautiful than she would ever be. He had Maman's fine features: a straight nose; a heart-shaped face ending in a dimpled chin. Once he'd had the rosy complexion of a pretty girl and was so tall—"a descendant of trees" was how Aunt Parvin described him—that it was difficult to see him clearly when he was standing up.

Leila leaned in and tried to decipher her brother's words. His upper lip was downy with hair and he smelled of Chinese muscle balm.

"I will die soon. You know that."

"Yes, I know."

"Please, Leila. This won't dishonor you, I promise."

She sensed a stirring behind her as Hosein struggled to pull away the sheets.

"Touch it. I beg you."

Leila didn't want to look, but it was impossible to turn away. The cylinder of flesh was buoyant and resolute, with a life the rest of her brother's body lacked. It made her curious.

"I don't have much longer, Leila. Have mercy."

The low rasp of his words cut the air. Leila smelled the yogurt soup and the spit-roasted chickens in the courtyard kitchen. A pot of geraniums flourished on the windowsill. As she reached for him past the folds of his bedding, she thought of something her father had told her: Nothing that is human can be alien. Hosein's flesh was warm and firm in her hand, and she gripped it harder than she'd intended. He moaned weakly. Was she hurting him?

"Don't stop. Please."

Leila held on. It was mostly smooth, like the trunks of certain saplings with knots where the faint blue veins stood out. Then with her thumb and forefinger, she encircled the knob at the end, a kind of snout, really, and squeezed it.

"Do you love me, Leila?"

She turned to her brother, but his face was unfamiliar. His eyes looked abnormally large and they held her captive, as if he were somehow anchoring himself inside her. A sticky heat spilled on her hand, like goat's milk, but thicker and more pungent. Did she do something wrong?

Maman called to her harshly from in the garden. Leila hurried to the bathroom and washed her hands with the hospital soap. This calmed her a little. She could hear the cook outside praising the Holy Prophet and his people with a clang of pots and pans. When Leila returned to her brother's bed, he was asleep. She picked up the syringe filled with morphine and slid the needle into his arm. This time, there was hardly any blood.

The rain came down unexpectedly, at a slant. In the garden the leaves crackled in the downpour. A taxi driver honked his horn and shouted *Son-of-a-whore*, no different than any other day. She could hear the call to evening prayers from the neighborhood mosque. There would be a party tonight at Aunt Parvin and Uncle Masood's house for their son's eighteenth birthday. (Their first child, a daughter, had died of diphtheria very young.) Aunt Parvin prided herself on throwing real Parisian-style parties with authentic French dishes and cream puffs for dessert.

Leila would wear her new dress, ivory colored with a pleated skirt and pearl buttons down the side. She would bring a bouquet of red tulips.

(1 9 7 2)

Enrique Florit

Enrique sat next to his father in the grand ballroom of the Flamingo Hotel, staring up at the stage. A hulking fellow in a lilac dress was auditioning to be Papi's assistant. The man's legs were clean-shaven, but his upper lip was stubbly and his falsetto unconvincing. Perhaps it'd been a mistake to advertise the job in all the local newspapers. Everyone within five hundred miles of Las Vegas who'd ever harbored ambitions of going into show business was strolling, bumping, flailing, shuffling, and sashaying across this stage.

The biggest problem, Enrique thought, was that Papi didn't know what he was looking for. After his fallout with Sammy Davis Jr. (Papi's ten-minute opening act had often stretched to forty) and his testy partnerships with lesser lounge singers, Fernando Florit had finally decided to hire an assistant. Or, as he proclaimed: "We must put to flight the maledictions that have been plaguing us!"

Last month, his father had tried out a six-foot-tall cocktail waitress named Betty Rouze, who'd been perfect in his latest trick. Betty strode onstage in nothing but a mink coat until Papi shot a fake pistol at her. As the coat blew apart, leaving the comely waitress momentarily in the buff, the pieces of fur turned into skittering minks. Unfortunately for Papi, Betty had run off with a car dealer from Muncie, in town for the Cadillac convention. Now Papi had only three weeks to prepare for his engagement with Vic Damone at the Flamingo Hotel.

"Next!" Papi yelled.

A dwarf wearing a faded clown outfit waddled onto the stage. She lit a cigar and blew smoke rings that turned into shadow puppets—a howling wolf, a tusked elephant, a chimpanzee with a baby on its back. Enrique nudged Papi appreciatively but his father's expression remained grim. He reminded Enrique, sotto voce, that he was looking for an assistant, not a competitor. The clown squared her hips in a combative manner, as if to say, See if you can top that, pal.

"My dear," Papi said in a conciliatory tone. "That was very impressive, but what else can you do?"

Enrique liked that his father treated each performer respectfully. In fact, the more execrable the act, the more impeccable his manners. His English was much improved, too, thanks to intensive speech lessons from a former Miss Arkansas turned blackjack dealer. Now he had a vaguely southern drawl, like everyone else. Enrique felt guilty for turning down his father's entreaties to perform with him again but he wouldn't go near a stage after what had happened to Mamá. He sensed that wherever she was, she supported his decision.

Papi decided to break for lunch, and they headed to the Flamingo's coffee shop. Enrique ordered his usual: a grilled cheese-and-tomato sandwich with French fries. His father got steak and eggs and a vanilla milkshake. They liked it here, not only because Papi got a fifty percent discount as the magician-in-residence but because — and this was a difficult thing to secure in a place as transient as Las Vegas — they were treated like family.

Their waitress, Doreen, showed Papi the new Chihuahua tattoo she'd gotten in Tijuana. Doreen adored Papi. Since Mamá's death, Enrique hadn't known his father to have a girl-friend, yet women flirted with him constantly. They stroked his cheek or tenderly rubbed his gargantuan knees — smooth as marble saints kissed for centuries, Papi boasted — and held his gaze with unmistakable longing. Did he spend time with them during school hours? As far as Enrique knew, nobody but he and his father set foot in their penthouse suite except for their housekeeper, a stout *boliviana* from Cochabamba who left them extra bath towels.

Backstage at the Flamingo, the showgirls shamelessly dressed and undressed in front of Fernando without a trace of modesty. Enrique, too, saw his share of unfettered buttocks and breasts and the neat strips of fur between the showgirls' legs. (His own body was unpredictable and mortified him without warning. The girls teased him, knowingly patting his crotch.) But he was perplexed about their bodies' specific mysteries and pleasures. His eighth-grade teacher, Mrs. Doerr, had shown the class a film that was supposed to fulfill their sex education requirement but was, instead, a documentary on the mating habits of prairie chickens.

Back at the ballroom, a dozen more aspiring performers were waiting to audition. The head bartender, Jorge de Reyes, stopped by to see the parade of hopefuls. One comedian performed his German shepherd jokes balancing on wobbly stilts. A Boulder City bail bondsman with a brick-red complexion billed himself a ventriloquist, although Enrique could read his lips from ten rows back. Discouraged, Papi postponed the remaining auditions until the following morning. A pale, freckled brunette holding a peacock intercepted them at the exit.

"Tomorrow," Papi apologized before she could say a word. "Tomorrow, I promise. Now let's go, *hijo*."

Enrique knew what their next stop would be: the poker pit at the Diamond Pin. The casino was located downtown next to the pawnshops and the motels-by-the-week, worlds away from the pretensions of Las Vegas as anything other than a place to gamble. At the Diamond Pin, there was no prettifying or pretending for tourists, no chandeliers or rooftop pools or valet parking, just slot machines and table after table of every imaginable game meant to separate a man from his money.

The giant thermometer at the east end of town read ninety-two degrees. Enrique took solace in the fatal sameness of the weather, in the spilled blue liquid of the sky. Papi had a theory about the weather, which he'd developed by studying old maps of the Americas. He believed that the monotony of climate tempered emotions, unlike the tropics, with their continual threat of change. Yet this theory didn't account for the drama they witnessed daily in Las Vegas. It wasn't a pretty sight to watch a man lose his last dime and consider the future. In spite of the steady weather Papi started getting migraines. He took to his bed with plastic bags of ice for his head, growing increasingly morose until he finally fell asleep. Invariably, the ice melted everywhere and he woke up irritable and damp as a baby.

The weather inside the Diamond Pin also stayed constant: cool and aquarium dim. The owner, Jim Gumbel, was a good friend of Papi's and made a fuss over him, ordering him frozen pineapple daiquiris (a ludicrous drink for the regulars) and setting him up at the best table. Fernando Florit wasn't one of the Diamond Pin's best customers—there were too many high rollers for that—but Gumbel respected him for his total disregard for money and the grace with which he lost it. If people were meant to hold on to money, Papi liked to say, they would have put handles on it.

Gumbel looked after Enrique as well, apprenticing him to professional poker players, most of them Texans, like Johnny Langston and Cullen Shaw, who taught him a lot more than how to expertly shuffle a deck. These men believed in poker the way other people believed in salvation. In the end, Enrique wondered, who would die surprised? The Texans said that Enrique was the best twelve-year-old player they knew. They told Enrique that poker, like life, was a zero-sum game: if you won, someone else lost and vice versa. To win, they said, you needed three things: a first-rate memory, an ability to read people, and heart—the courage to bet it all when the odds were in your favor.

Enrique loved playing poker but he preferred ordinary times with his father: eating at the Flamingo's coffee shop, sharing the newspaper and a pot of hot chocolate, listening to Papi recite his Martí poems ("I dream with my eyes open and always, by day and night, I dream . . ."). At night they unplugged their air conditioner, opened the windows, and let the aromas of the desert lull them to sleep.

At breakfast his father combed the newspapers for unusual crimes (he based his most macabre tricks on them), but he was disappointed by the tedium of vandalism and vagrancy in Las Vegas. The offenses were as monotonous as everything else, including the executions by the mob, who buried their victims in the Mojave Desert. In contrast, Papi said, Havana and Panama City were stupendous cities for crime. The combination of Catholicism, passion, and jealousy proved a potent recipe for the violent imagination. Every morning, Papi threw down his copy of the *Las Vegas Review-Journal* and complained that even a minor Cuban poet could commit more interesting transgressions.

❧

On the opening night of his father's show at the Flamingo, Enrique settled into a plush booth near the stage, which was draped with massive gold curtains. Waitresses circulated among the tables in miniskirts and beige stockings that made their legs look like artificial limbs. Enrique got aroused just looking at them, though he wasn't exactly attracted. The orchestra was playing up-tempo music, nothing he could distinguish. Search-lights scanned the crowd as the emcee announced the opening act: "Direct from Cuba, that infamous island of sin and Com-munism, descended from Indian nobility, renowned for his mind-boggling feats of magic from Havana to Buenos Aires, the Flamingo Hotel is proud to present the incomparable, the astounding, the unforgettable Fernando Florit!"

Papi appeared in a puff of psychedelic smoke and with great fanfare hurled a mirrored ball high into the air. Fastened to the ball was a rope ladder. He called over his assistant, the pale brunette with the peacock, whom he'd ultimately hired, and encouraged her to climb skyward. She did so, to the apprecia-tive hoots of the audience, and disappeared above the curtains.

"Lucille!" Papi called to her.

No reply.

"Lucille, *mi amor!*"

Silence.

He shook the ladder.

Still nothing.

Then he climbed up after her.

Soon body parts began thumping down to the stage: one leg, then another, a set of shoulders, a sequined torso, followed by an arched throat—all pieces of the missing assistant. The audi-ence murmured nervously. Even Enrique, who'd seen the trick countless times, grew agitated. Had something gone wrong? A moment later, Fernando Florit gracefully leaped from the ladder and started fitting the body parts together like a giant puzzle. With a twirl of his wand he called to Lucille one last time and, miracle of miracles, she stood up, erect and whole, looking somewhat dazed.

"What can we expect of the night but mystery?" Papi crooned to explosive applause.

He received three encores before Vic Damone took over the stage, singing a medley of hits, a frozen smile on his face. Five minutes later, Papi slid into Enrique's booth still wearing his tuxedo and cape. "So, how was I?"

"Pretty amazing." It didn't matter that he knew how his father's tricks were executed. In the moment Enrique, too, believed in the illusion.

Papi grinned and ordered two dinner specials: Caesar salads and lobster bisque followed by rib roasts with scalloped potatoes. He was in a festive mood. Fans crowded around their table, congratulating him on the show. Even Don Rickles stopped by to say hello. "You're a bigger sicko than I am," he joked and punched Fernando in the arm. Papi confided to Rickles that he was perfecting another trick, in which he would turn the hateful maître d' into a llama.

Suddenly, Enrique felt the spotlight on him. Vic Damone was addressing him as the Birthday Boy. "He's thirteen, today, ladies and gentlemen! Let's give the magician's son a warm round of applause!" Everyone turned to look at him. An army of waitresses marched over with a flaming baked Alaska. Damone sang "Happy Birthday" as the audience joined in. Papi laughed and laughed, proud of his coup. Enrique didn't know where he found the breath to blow out the candles.

After the hoopla, his father slipped him a crystal paperweight with an unfamiliar photograph of Mamá inside. She was very young, resplendent in a saffron-colored sari and wearing an orchid in her hair. Enrique was startled at his own resemblance to her. They could have been twins—except for the sari, of course. It turned out that the picture had been taken at the Hindu bazaar in Panama City on *her* thirteenth birthday. How long had Papi saved this for him? Why hadn't he shown it to him before?

Enrique stared at Mamá's photograph and remembered their last day together. It was a Sunday and he was sitting in the front row watching his parents' magic show in Colón Park. The wind was brisk and the flag next to the statue of Christopher Columbus noisily flapped. With Mamá's assistance, Papi swallowed samurai swords, conjured up goldfish and Dalmatian puppies, juggled hot coals bare-handed, and turned a bouquet of tulips into a parrot that sang the national anthem. Except for the wayward storks—everyone thought they were part of the act—the show went smoothly.

Enrique studied his mother during the performance. She was petite and shapely and wore fishnet stockings and high heels. Her thighs flared becomingly and her eyelids were painted a seawater blue. A silver bracelet gleamed on her wrist. Enrique caught her eye during the goldfish trick and she playfully winked at him, both pleasing and embarrassing him.

It wasn't until the finale that disaster struck. As usual, Papi bound Mamá's ankles and arms with rope and invited the flat-footed mayor of Cárdenas, who happened to be in the audience, to test their strength. Then Papi lovingly tied a white handkerchief around her mouth, which she emblazoned with an unrepentant red kiss. A snare drum rolled as he escorted her up the three wooden steps to the rim of the aquarium. In a show of muscularity, Papi raised her over his head and lowered her into the turquoise water. As Mamá sank to the bottom of the tank, her hair rose like a crown of branches. Her eyes remained impassive as she struggled against the ropes.

Enrique heard the crackling before he saw the sparks, and the entangled stork, and the thick electrical cable, like a curse from the sky, swinging off its pole and into the tank where his mother was nearly free of her bindings. Once more she caught his eye, this time with such a wilderness of feeling that it cut off his breath. Then she opened her mouth and slowly drifted to the back of the tank. In that instant Enrique knew without words or explanations, his hair bristling, his saliva turning to a bitter paste on his tongue, that no amount of bravery or longing could save his mother or return them to the path they'd lost. Mamá was trapped, like she was trapped forever in this birthday paperweight.

Enrique accompanied his father down to the Diamond Pin later that night. Papi was in his element, backslapping, buying this one and that one drinks. A couple of the regulars surprised Enrique with birthday presents: girlie cards, a set of erotic dominoes (pussy tiles, someone called them), and a five-pound sack of pistachios. One of the Texans, Cullen Shaw, who was funny and long-jawed and had a surprisingly strong singing voice, gave him an album of Enrico Caruso's greatest hits.

Before long, Johnny Langston staked Enrique a thousand dollars on a poker game for his birthday. How could he refuse? He took a seat and looked around at his middle-aged rivals: paunchy, pasty-faced men wearing Stetsons (except for Danny Seltz, a frozen foods impresario from New Jersey, who had on his lucky pom-pom hat). Enrique fingered his mother's silver bracelet, safely tucked in his pocket for good luck. The men were a circus of oddities and tics. Langston had chest hair so thick it seemed to swipe at his Adam's apple like a furry paw. Shaw licked his lips until it seemed they would vanish altogether. One by one, his opponents smiled at him in a way that made Enrique think of animals that ate their young.

Fifteen rounds later, though, he could do no wrong. Straights, full houses, a four of a kind. The mathematical probabilities of this kind of luck were staggeringly low, and Enrique knew it. But it was more than that—his brain had kicked into overdrive. He could remember every card on the table, effortlessly calculate the odds, read his opponents' minds as if they were whispering in his ear. The men cracked their knuckles, shifting uneasily in their seats. The cigar smoke stung Enrique's eyes but his mind stayed sharp. By five in the morning, he had more than half the chips on the table. Then he got a straight flush, his first ever, and won the pot: twenty thousand bucks.

It was daybreak when Enrique left the casino. The sun was weak and barely undercut the neon blaze. The ring of mountains stood guard over the city. Everything looked burned out. He hailed a taxi and got in, driving past pawnshops and sex shops, trinket and tourist shops. Crows were perched equidistantly on the telephone poles. The giant thermometer read fifty-eight. When the driver pulled up to the pink concrete fortress that was the Flamingo Hotel, Enrique tipped him a hundred dollars.

Outside his father's penthouse suite, a tall woman was waiting. Her hair was so blond it looked white. She wore vinyl go-go boots and a fishnet dress that displayed her enormous breasts.

"Where's your daddy?" she asked politely.

"Uh, still playing poker." Enrique felt himself getting warm all over. His hands dropped to cover the front of his pants.

"My name's Lori." She dragged on a stalklike cigarette and let the smoke accumulate over her head. "I heard you won some chips tonight."

Enrique shrugged. In Las Vegas, winning bought you instant privileges, but losing stripped you of them just as quickly. Really, it was a very democratic place.

"Want me to help you spend some?"

Enrique stared at her in disbelief. He imagined calling Shuntaro in Los Angeles to tell him. *No shit, man, she showed up just like that!* Lori's face was as white as her hair, except for her eyes, which were huge and brown, with eyelashes so long she looked like those matchbook drawings of a fawn. Her arms were hairless and smooth. Enrique remembered something his father had told him: Beauty is the advance payment on desire.

When Lori reached for him with her smooth white arms, Enrique trembled. This mortified him so much that he wanted to bolt. The hotel pool would open soon and for a moment he was tempted to go swimming. He could have the pool to himself, swim laps, clear his lungs. Instead Lori tucked his head against the cushion of her breasts and started slow-dancing. Enrique's cheeks still felt hot but at least his face was hidden. He breathed in her sweat beneath the layers of smoke and perfume.

Gently, Lori began kissing his hair. Then she brought his left hand to her mouth and sucked on his fingers. Enrique's whole body boomed with pleasure and fear. This was nothing like the film on prairie chickens. Would she know he was a virgin right off the bat? Why hadn't his father ever talked to him about sex? Enrique realized with a start that his other hand, the one not being sucked, was resting on the woman's hip. When he dared lift his head, she leaned toward him and whispered: "What's your name, sweet pea?"

Marta Claros

The marimba band started playing with fresh vigor after their break. The colored lights strung through the cypress trees competed with the stars for attention. In the distance, Marta could make out the hulking presence of the Izalco volcano. She was at the *quinceañera* of her cousin Anita, the daughter of Marta's stepfather's twin brother. People said that Anita could play cards and throw dice better than any man, that her fingertips were lucky. It was a good thing she was a girl or she might have become a professional gambler and disgraced her family.

There were over two hundred people at the birthday party near Lake Coatepeque, all related in one way or another. Anita's grandmother, Niña Cleotilde, oversaw the festivities from her wicker rocking chair on the porch. Marta smelled *chicha* on the breath of some of the men. She hoped a fight wouldn't break out and ruin the party. People used to say that her father could make cane spirits that ripped sense out of a man faster than a machete. When she was little, Marta had helped him squeeze the cane in the *trapiche,* the wooden press. The last Marta had heard, Papá had lost everything in the Hundred Hours' War with Honduras and was trying to cross the border into America.

The food at the party was delicious, better than anything in the capital, tastier and juicier, as if the fresh air made everything more flavorful. Marta gorged herself on rice with shrimp and roasted turkey from the banquet table. She eyed the platter of almond cookies next to the birthday cake, three tiers coated with fluffy meringue. Perhaps she could wrap up a slice to take to her brother.

Evaristo had returned home to live for a little while but he'd grown restless sleeping in a hammock and eating off a plate. Whenever a flock of doves whirred by, he would gaze at them with such longing that Marta gave up trying to convince him to stay indoors. Her brother was much happier in his tree. When the days were clear and bright, Evaristo felt a part of the hot, bleached skies. In the small hours of the night his tree's hush and sway soothed him, and its waxy leaves provided camouflage. Plus he loved the smell of the night jasmine, saturating the air like the *putas* downtown.

"Would you like to dance?" a young man asked Marta, catching her off guard. He had hazel eyes and was dressed more formally than the others at the party, with a button-down shirt and a skinny tie. His lips looked too pink for a boy.

"Está bien," Marta answered.

The dance floor was crowded with middle-aged people, unfamiliar aunts and uncles from her stepfather's family. The band rushed the hit song "Little Lies," and the accordionist hammed it up with a flowery solo. Marta spotted her stepfather dancing with Mamá by the avocado tree. His hair was fixed with a glossy pomade and his machete was holstered at his side. They looked happy together for a change.

Marta's partner was a good dancer, confident and steady. His name was Alfonso and he worked in the office of a textiles factory in San Salvador. A shipping supervisor was what he called himself but Marta suspected that he was inflating his position like so many men did to impress a girl.

"Are you wearing perfume?" she asked him, sniffing the air.

"It's cologne," Alfonso said, "from France."

There was that country again, Marta thought, the same one that made the naughty underwear the rich housewives wore.

"Where are you from?" Alfonso asked her.

"Near San Vicente, but I've been living in San Salvador since I was six." Marta watched him for any signs of arrogance. Country origins weren't appreciated by most city folks.

"I think your childhood is more like your country than your actual country," he said.

Marta stopped dancing for a moment to think about this. She liked the way it sounded, though she wasn't sure what it meant. Behind them, the moon rose over the volcano. The band shifted to a slower, more romantic tune. Around them, the couples drew closer.

Alfonso led her off the dance floor to a wooden bench where a young woman with a horribly swollen leg sat. Marta wanted to tell Alfonso how in the winter she and her brother used to make sleds from the leaves of the newly pruned coconut trees. The leaves were so smooth and wide that they whipped down hills faster than a sneeze.

"Have you ever seen a volcano erupt?" Alfonso asked.

Marta looked toward Izalco, big and purplish in the distance, and imagined sparks flying from its cone.

"Once I saw Conchagua go up," he said. "It was at night and the sky looked like it was exploding with fireworks. And the earth went *brrrrrr, brrrrrr, brrrrrr.*"

"Were you scared?"

"I was too far away to be scared. In school, I read about a city in Italy that was buried in ash. Archaeologists discovered

the people a thousand years later in the positions they died in—
working the fields, or sweeping the kitchen, or taking a crap."

"I wouldn't want to die like that!" Marta laughed. Then she
grew quiet again. She envied the schoolgirls in the capital their
blue-and-white uniforms and satchels of books. Why couldn't
she be one of them? There were so many things she wanted to
know. Her cousin Erlinda had told her that one in a hundred
girls was born without a navel *or* a womb. How could Marta be
sure this was true?

She reached up and touched her hair, wavy from the permanent Erlinda had given her. Her cousin was in beauty school
and had ruined her own mother's hair and the hair of several
aunts (they'd taken to wearing kerchiefs and cheap wigs until
their hair grew back) before persuading Marta to give it a try.
Luckily, the permanent took hold. Erlinda showed Marta how
to care for it with castor oil and a hair lotion called Bay Rum,
and warned her to stay away from ordinary soap and shampoo.

"My hair is normally straight," Marta said, twirling a dark
curl around her finger.

"So's mine," Alfonso chimed in, though it couldn't have been
curlier, and Marta giggled. "I have a transistor radio. Do you
want to listen to it?"

"There's music here."

"I know, but the band's awful. They play so fast everyone's
hopping around like rabbits. Besides, there's this show every
Sunday night that plays the Rolling—"

"What time is it?" Marta interrupted him. She'd noticed the
watch on Alfonso's wrist, its face shimmering with mother-of-
pearl.

"Almost seven."

"*La novela* is about to start!"

"Haven't those two gotten married yet?" Alfonso rolled his
eyes.

"No, that's what's so exciting. You don't know if they'll ever
be together."

"If I had a girlfriend, I wouldn't wait for her forever. I wouldn't care if she came from one of the fourteen families. You're either in love or you aren't. There's no in-between. You can't go through life being afraid all the time."

"But wouldn't you need her parents' permission?"

"We could run away to Los Angeles."

Marta's eyes widened. Mamá's oldest brother, Víctor, had left for Los Angeles ten years ago and never returned. Everyone said that Víctor worked all night cleaning office buildings and slept during the day, like an owl. They said he'd married a selfish Mexican woman, born there, who refused to have his children and made him wear rubber sleeves on his penis when they made love. At Christmas, Víctor sent the family money but they didn't hear from him the rest of the year.

Nobody talked much about Víctor anymore. It was as if he were dead, or worse than dead because at least you could visit the dead in the cemetery. How soon would her family forget her if she left?

"Are you thinking of leaving?" Marta asked.

"Yes, but don't say a word to anyone. I'm only telling you this because I like you."

Marta warmed with pleasure at his words, but she didn't show it. "Now, don't get any ideas about me. We've just met."

"It's not like that." Alfonso jammed a fist in his pocket.

"Mamá says it's always like that, no matter what the boy tells you."

"Did she follow her own advice?"

Marta didn't like the expression on his face, as if he knew everything and she knew nothing. Was he insulting Mamá? Maybe she should just get a piece of birthday cake for her brother and stay clear of this boy altogether.

A commotion broke out by the avocado tree. Her stepfather was lying flat on the ground with a crowd around him. A fat lady in a linen dress ripped a leaf off a banana tree and began fanning him furiously. Someone passed Mamá a handkerchief.

She wiped his forehead, but he didn't move. His twin brother hovered close by like a ghost.

"Throw some cold water on him!"

"Hit him on the chest!"

"Go find the doctor!"

Marta pushed her way through to look at her stepfather. His eyes were frozen open, like the fish she'd caught in Chalatenango two summers ago. Tía Matilde had fried up the fish, white and tasty, and served it with tortillas and pickled cabbage. Marta stared at her stepfather and felt nothing.

"*Se murió.*" She heard a voice whisper from the edge of the crowd.

It was Alfonso. His words quickly caught fire and everyone began repeating them—*se murió, se murió*—until they rose like smoke, higher and higher, mingling with the sounds of the cicadas, *chiquirín, chiquirín,* and reaching the mouth of the volcano itself. When the doctor arrived, he confirmed what everybody already knew. Marta studied her mother's face as she heard the news.

A month after her stepfather's funeral, Marta was working a second shift outside the fairgrounds downtown. The vendors were gossiping about the trapeze star of the traveling Mexican circus, a dwarf named Little Flea. Marta desperately wanted to catch a glimpse of Little Flea in his spangled costume, watch him do his triple and quadruple somersaults. People said that Little Flea flew from one end of the tent to the other, tucked tight like a baby in its mother's womb. Rumor had it that Little Flea, who was no taller than a grown person's knees, was quite the ladies' man, that not every part of him was pint-sized. They said that he'd sired sons, and normal ones at that, from Texas to Tierra del Fuego.

The circus tickets were expensive and only the wealthiest

people in town could afford them. Marta heard that the price would go down fifty percent on the last night of the show. But that was still two days' work. Was it worth it to see Little Flea? Despite her efforts, Marta made barely enough money to keep working. She thought it unfair that the circus sold its merchandise at three times the outside price, including stale potato chips and flashlights that broke after an hour.

A cluster of vendors waited for the circus to end, eager to sell the last of their toys and chili-spiced corn on the cob. Marta worked a second shift when there was a special event at the fairgrounds—the Argentine opera troupe, a Peruvian folklore band, even the sparsely attended book fair. After selling used clothes all day, Marta switched to her evening supplies: pinwheels, whistles, clown marionettes, whatever was popular. She'd stopped selling candy because the rain made her lollipops stick together.

Life had gotten more difficult since her stepfather's death. Mamá refused to leave her mourning bed except to boil water for coffee. All the cooking and cleaning and money-earning work fell to Marta. *Ái, que vea cómo hace.* See what you can do to manage. That was what Mamá said to her every morning. Was it any wonder that she was fantasizing about running off with a circus dwarf?

A full moon lit up the puddles from the afternoon rain. The smell of roasted peanuts and cotton candy mingled with the stench of mud. Marta wondered how her brother was faring in his new home, a banyan located three blocks from the charred remains of his old coral tree, which had been struck by lightning. Poor Evaristo was burned over most of his neck and chest. If it weren't for the *guardia* who'd rushed him to the hospital, her brother would likely be dead.

"What are you doing out so late?"

Marta was startled. It was the *guardia* who'd saved Evaristo's life. Could she have conjured him with her thoughts? Marta waved at him weakly, embarrassed by her frayed dress and poorly patched sandals. His uniform and boots were spotless.

"How's your brother?"

"Much better." Marta glanced at the pistol on the *guardia's* belt. Did he ever use it? Maybe it was true what people said— that you could judge a man by the degree of danger he courted. But what was the difference between danger and evil?

"Is he still living like a monkey in a tree?" the *guardia* asked.

"He's found better living quarters."

"Oh?"

"A banyan tree."

"Less flammable?"

"So he says."

Marta had heard terrible stories about the *guardias*. People said that dead bodies were appearing in the rivers, that the *guardias*—assassins in uniform—were responsible. A car swerved around the corner and its driver shouted: *"¡Chucho hijo de puta, el día te va a llegar!"*

"Do you know him?" Marta asked.

"Of course not," the *guardia* snapped. "It's just more of the garbage we have to put up with every day."

Marta wasn't sure what he was talking about.

"Don't you read the newspaper?"

"Not so much." Who had twenty centavos leftover in a day? The newspapers didn't print anything that concerned the poor either. Expensive toilet paper was what those newspapers were, but Marta didn't dare say this aloud.

"They're our worst enemy, Communists every last one." He spat when he said this, launching into a one-sided argument that meant nothing to her.

Finally, the *guardia* pulled a mirror from his shirt pocket and brought it close to his upper lip. Then he trimmed his mustache with a tiny scissors. It was the neatest mustache Marta had ever seen, an impeccable rectangle.

"My name's Fabián Ramírez," he said.

"Yes, I remember."

"I've been keeping my eye on you."

"I haven't done anything," Marta shot back. Who did he think she was?

"*Tranquila.* I don't mean under surveillance. I meant that I've been trying to find out what kind of girl you are."

"I've done nothing wrong!" Marta felt the fear energizing her.

"Listen to me. I've seen how hard you work. I want to make life easier for you. I hate to see you wasting your beauty like this." Fabián had small white teeth, neat and even, like his mustache. Marta noticed that his eyebrows were identical and his nostrils precisely the same size. There was something unnatural about him, like the flawless dummies in department store windows.

"You're not from around here?" Marta asked.

"I'm from Apastepeque, north of the lagoon. My father plants annatto trees and beans on a parcel there."

"And your mother?"

"Her family made grinding stones. But the stones lasted forever and after a while everybody had one. So they took up making *conserva de leche* instead." Fabián's voice dropped. "May I invite you to dinner?"

If she said no, would he shoot her? "There's no point in going out with me," Marta said. "I mainly eat tortillas with salt."

"That doesn't mean we can't have a steak now and then."

"Steak?" Marta felt a stream of cool air tickling the back of her neck. *Bueno,* maybe she could go out with this Fabián just once, slip a nice piece of meat into her purse for her brother. When would Evaristo ever taste steak? Marta thought of the paper flowers her mother kept in a rusty can, how much nicer real roses would be. Yes, the possibility of steak definitely appealed to her. Perhaps the *guardia* might even invite her to see Little Flea.

"Let me think about it," she said, nervously twirling a pinwheel.

"I'll take them all," Fabián said.

"*¿Qué mande?*" Marta heard a *clarinero* in the tamarind tree, noisy and insistent. What was it doing up at this time of night?

"Your toys." Fabián pointed at Marta's basket. "I'll buy them all."

(1976)

Enrique Florit

E nrique looked across the kitchen table at his father, who was scraping the last bit of pulp from his half grapefruit. Papi was dressed as the reincarnation of Ching Ling Foo, the Great Court Conjurer to the Empress of China. He wore a bald wig and pigtail, embroidered pajamas with a Mandarin collar, and silk slippers that curled at the tips. A month ago Papi had set their clocks to Shanghai time, switching day and night, and begun sleeping with an enormous Chinese dictionary on his chest. He hoped that the characters would seep into him and gradually change his identity.

Enrique poured himself a bowl of cornflakes with milk. He wasn't sure when the idea of impersonating the famous nineteenth-century magician had occurred to his father, but he suspected that it had something to do with all the kung fu movies they'd been watching since their eviction from the Flamingo Hotel. Younger magicians with fancy laser shows and foreigners with exotic acts (most notably a pair of Germans with Bengal tigers) were replacing the traditional performers like his father. At forty-eight years old, Papi was washed up.

At the height of his success, he'd earned ten thousand dollars a month—far from top billing but a decent living nonetheless, especially with the free penthouse thrown in. Now he was lucky to earn that in a year, working odd jobs and substituting for sick magicians on the Strip. Papi was aging badly, too, and suffered from a garish array of health problems: phlebitis, gastritis (no more fried pork rinds for him), prostatitis, gingivitis, and a desperate thirst he feared might be the onset of diabetes; not to mention his high blood pressure and irritable colon. His flesh, Papi complained melodramatically, was becoming a burden to his bones.

The two of them lived in a small apartment on the scruffy end of Paradise Road. Their building, flamboyantly named The Mermaid, had a nautical motif and dried starfish glued to the walls of the grungy vestibule. Their second-story rooms looked out on an abandoned gas station and a baby-furniture store that to Enrique's knowledge, was never open for business. After school, Enrique worked part-time at a meat-processing plant to help pay the bills. He ran probability theories in his head to stay sane. Only his and Papi's first year in the States had been more dismal.

A few of the high-rolling Texans still called Enrique, trying to coax him to play some more poker. Opportunity knocks but it doesn't nag, Johnny Langston scolded him. But Enrique didn't trust his playing the way he used to, not even with his mother's silver bracelet in his pocket. He didn't like living just to beat the odds anymore. He didn't want to believe, like their gambler friends, that anything legitimate was strictly for losers. Poker, at least the way it was played down at the Diamond Pin, was a ruthless business. After Enrique had won that big pot on his thirteenth birthday, the same men who'd lost the money had surrounded him in subsequent games like a pod of alligators and devoured his winnings.

Papi pulled a jar of maraschino cherries from the kitchen cabinet. There were a dozen identical jars behind it, lined up like a battery of soldiers. He twisted off the cap, plunged a finger into the crimson juice, and extracted a fat, dripping cherry.

"Have one," he said, offering it to Enrique. "It's good for you."

"I had a banana already."

Papi dangled the cherry over his mouth. "Did you know that Chinese women call their period 'the old ghost'?"

"Uh, no."

"I dreamt it. I'm telling you, *hijo*, that dictionary is working. How else would I know this?" Papi ate four more cherries in quick succession, then attacked the other half of the grapefruit. "Everything tends toward circumference. Things circle back, the good with the bad. The cycle is shifting for the better, I can feel it. Grapefruit?"

"No, thanks."

Enrique didn't particularly mind his father's rubber wig, or the pajamas that had replaced the tuxedos in their closet, or even his phony Chinese accent. (He was tempted to hang a warning sign around his father's neck: NEW PERSONALITY UNDER CONSTRUCTION.) This was show business, after all. What he couldn't stand was his father's obsessive dieting. The original Court Conjurer had been tall and thin and famous enough from old photographs that Papi had no choice but to conform to his image. He slavishly followed one weight-loss regimen after another, including the dreadful Riviera diet, which had him eating nothing but mussels for lunch.

Now, instead of reminiscing about his triumphant tours of the Caribbean, Papi rhapsodized about fine cuts of aged sirloin, platters of *chicharrones*, the marvels of crème fraiche and tiramisu. Should Enrique be insensitive enough to order dessert in his presence, his father would accuse him of outright sabotage. Papi even started smoking to curb his hunger. Really, he was becoming an unreasonable man.

"*Coño carajo*, look at this," Papi said, pointing to an article on page 26 of the *Las Vegas Review-Journal.* "Cuba's new constitution enacted. Ha!"

"Could you pass me the sugar bowl?" Enrique watched his father's anger spike perilously.

"*¡Qué desgracia!*" Papi looked as if he would split in two. Anything even mildly supportive of the Cuban Revolution had this effect on him. "Another hoax in the name of patriotism!"

"Remember your blood pressure." Enrique handed his father a glass of water and waited for the paroxysm to pass. "Besides, you need to stay calm. Ching Ling Foo never lost his temper."

Fernando's grand plan—beyond the fading dream of a democratic Cuba—was to unveil his Chinese persona and svelte new physique this summer at the outdoor arena reserved for rock concerts. The climax of his act would be the re-creation of Ching Ling Foo's notorious bullet-catch trick, a feat so dangerous that it had killed fourteen magicians in the hundred years since its debut. The publicity from its revival, Papi hoped, would jump-start his career and put him back in the limelight, where he belonged.

"Can you help me rehearse later?"

"I'm meeting Professor Smedsted at four." Enrique was being tutored by the math chair at the University of Nevada, who'd taken him under his wing. He finished buttoning his flannel shirt and gathered his books.

Next fall he would be applying to colleges. He was on the honor roll but he had no real extracurricular activities to offer admissions committees. Enrique suspected that they would be less than impressed by his poker skills or a recommendation, however effusive, from the owner of the Diamond Pin Casino.

Between school, his job, and watching out for his father, he didn't have time for much else. Not even a girlfriend.

Enrique dreamed of going east, to New York or Boston, somewhere far from the Las Vegas heat. He'd received brochures from MIT after he'd scored a perfect 800 on the math portion of the SAT. Enrique had taken the exam a year early, at Smedsted's insistence, just to see how he would do. The casinos were also courting him. They knew they could get him cheap. They dangled a few hundred dollars here and there for consulting jobs: fine-tuning the odds in their slot machines, figuring out the systems of gamblers winning too consistently against the house.

"Most of the Great Court Conjurer's tricks are simple, deceptively simple, but nobody has seen them for many years," Papi said, growing more animated. "Forget the empty pyrotechnics onstage nowadays. Audiences are so bewitched by second-rate magicians that they've forgotten the joys of simple wonder."

"I have to go now."

"Okay, give me a kiss."

Enrique hesitated.

"*¿Qué?* You're too old to give your father a kiss?"

"Bye, Dad."

The building manager, Mr. Smite, was outside watering the patch of dead grass that passed for a lawn. A crow fussed in a stumpy palm tree. The Mermaid was no better or worse than most of the buildings around it, eyesores with peeling paint and gashes of rust, their every blemish illuminated by the sun. Mr. Smite had been married to a former showgirl, a bronzed angel of a woman (he kept a photograph of her in his pocket) who'd returned to Minnesota after a year in the desert. That was back in 1963.

"How's the Chinee-man?" Mr. Smite asked.

Enrique waved and pretended not to hear him. He didn't

want to encourage Mr. Smite's morning lecture on the hidden connections between Communism and the rings of Saturn.

Enrique happened to like Papi's Ching Ling Foo tricks: spewing colored streamers that caught fire and exploded; extracting a five-foot-long pole from his mouth; producing plates and cakes from under the cover of an empty cloth. His father was experimenting with fire eating, too—Ching Ling Foo had been a master at this—but the kerosene was aggravating his gastritis and ruining his teeth. Only the bullet-catch trick, spectacular and risky as it was, made Enrique nervous.

At least, he told himself, this was an improvement over his father's short-lived attempt to break into the movies. Papi had managed by some convoluted set of negotiations—through a mobster friend of a producer's friend who took steam with him at the Flamingo's spa—to land a part in a low-budget Hollywood film. He talked it up for months, calling himself the Cuban Rudolph Valentino (no matter that Valentino had starred in *silent* films), taking potshots at Robert Redford ("A mere puppet of passion!"), picturing his name emblazoned on billboards across America. In the end, Papi was cast as a janitor in a teen horror film called *Black Fear,* in which he forlornly dragged a mop and bucket down a lonely high school corridor. He didn't have a single line.

It was a short drive to Anasazi High School in North Las Vegas. Enrique had bought his Maverick, red with a white vinyl roof, with money he'd earned at the meat-processing plant. He kept the chrome fenders gleaming. Enrique had won a scholarship to a local Catholic school run by the Marist brothers, but his father had refused to let him attend. After his run-ins with the Jesuits of Cárdenas, Papi didn't want his son having anything to do with, as he put it, those sadistic men of the cloth.

When Enrique got tired of school and work, he drove out to Red Rock Canyon, fifteen miles west of the city. He loved the sandstone cliffs, the thick stands of Joshua trees undisturbed by the wind. When the sun hit them just so they looked incandescent, as if on fire. Once Enrique drove to Red Rock in the middle of the night and saw a meteor shower. It seemed to him a private gift from the universe. Nobody he knew ever visited the Mojave outback. It was hard enough to picture Papi or any of the Texans in natural sunlight, much less the great outdoors.

These days, he and his father were avoiding the Diamond Pin. No matter that Papi looked and sounded like a crazy Chinese impostor. That wouldn't have stopped him for a minute. Papi avoided the Diamond Pin because he was ashamed of showing up with no money. Everyone in Las Vegas, down to the two-bit blackjack dealers, understood the golden rule: He who has the gold makes the rules. Nobody wanted to be around losers. It messed up their game, reminded them of bad times, killed the abundance they felt was rightfully theirs.

It was ferociously hot out. The orange trees on campus were flowering with phony-looking fruit. The cheerleaders practiced their routines in front of the main building, trying to drum up enthusiasm for the Friday-night basketball game against Henderson High. Enrique studied their kicking and shimmying, the sweat dampening their twitching thigh muscles. They aroused the envy of the other girls (even the smart ones on student council and the newspaper) as well as the lust of every boy on campus.

His taste, though, ran in another direction entirely. At the meat-processing plant, Enrique was fixated on his supervisor; the mother, in fact, of one of these cheerleaders. Her name was Janie Marks and she was in her thirties, divorced, with broad fleshy hips that undulated beneath her regulation jumpsuit. Her voice was a gravelly drawl that softened whenever she called his attention to an inadequately trimmed slab of beef. *Rico, honey, leave some fat on the sides or there won't be anything left to barbecue.* Enrique was usually up to his elbows in bloody chunks of meat. The sound of her voice combined with the smell of animal blood and all that raw meat got him so crazily hard that he could have made it right then and there with a hunk of rump roast.

Enrique remembered how in Cárdenas, every boy in the neighborhood had been in love with his mother. Not only was she beautiful — Mamá had lightly freckled skin and a tight little waist — but nobody else's mother could do a triple somersault or hypnotize a snake. The men on the corner spoke admiringly of Mamá. They celebrated her curves, her charming Panamanian accent, her petite hands and feet. Enrique didn't like it when they spoke of her like that but he couldn't have said why. Now he understood.

All day trudging from class to class, Enrique was reminded of the Stations of the Cross: stop, suffer, stop, suffer some more. The campaigns of Charlemagne. Irregular French verbs. Poems he couldn't make heads or tails of, expunged of punctuation. In the middle of a calculus test, he was called to the principal's office. Papi was in the hospital, seriously hurt, Mr. Hunter told him. Enrique didn't wait to hear the details. He ran to his car and raced off, accelerating through every red light in Las Vegas. At least his father was alive, he kept telling himself. Nobody could lose both parents before eighteen, could they?

At the Lord and Savior Hospital downtown, a nun in an old-fashioned habit escorted Enrique to the elevator, past the faded flower shop and the lobby's noisy row of slot machines. His father's room was in the intensive care unit on the second floor. Papi was bandaged from head to toe. A nylon dress sock dangled from one foot. His bald wig was off and his thin, gray wisps looked infinitely more doleful than the thick rubber. An arm and a leg were suspended with pulleys in lopsided flight, and his left eye was copiously padded with gauze.

Papi recognized Enrique at once, even with his other eye nearly swollen shut. "Thank God you came," he muttered. "I'm surrounded by Catholics." The words whistled through a missing tooth. He'd been brought unconscious to the emergency room three hours ago.

The police were calling it a hate crime and a local news station was investigating the incident. Nobody seemed to realize that Fernando Florit wasn't actually Chinese. The bartender from the Flamingo had already sent a get well card and a bottle of tequila. How had Jorge de Reyes heard about the attack?

"What the fuck happened to you?" Enrique whispered.

Papi tried to shrug but he winced from the pain. "As you can see," he said wearily, "my heart continues to beat out of long habit."

It turned out that he'd been on his way to Armando's Coffee Shop, where he often spent the morning reading, when a gang of teenaged boys mugged him in an empty parking lot. They were in drag, with Heidi braids and dirndls, and clearly on some serious drugs. Papi had only a five-dollar bill on him. They got mad and kicked him, pushed his face into a bed of shattered glass. Then they broke a few bones for good measure.

"The strange thing is, I can hear better now," Papi said, attempting to lift his head. "Ants walking across the windowsill. Jackrabbits in the desert. My whole body is one giant ear. The doctors say it won't last but I know it will. Think about it, *hijo*. There isn't a magic act like this anywhere."

Enrique stared at his father in disbelief. He was barely alive and all he could think of was capitalizing on some passing sensory freakishness to see his name in lights again.

"*Por favor,* can you get me a cigarette? They're over there."

His father looked so vulnerable that Enrique, against his better judgment, opened the nightstand drawer and found the pack of battered Winstons. He tapped out a cigarette and lit it with his father's plastic lighter. He thought of how the slightest mistake could kill a person. A wrong turn here, a misspoken word there, and boom—your luck ran out. Fortune wasn't something you could hold tightly in your hand like a coin. The smoke made Enrique nauseous but he dragged on the cigarette until the flame caught. Then he carefully held it to his father's lips.

"*Menos mal,*" Papi said, moaning. His lips trembled as he exhaled. "You're still my sweet boy."

"Maybe we should open the window?"

"Did you hear that?"

"What?"

"There's a moth on the ceiling fan."

Enrique followed the slow rotations of the metal blades. At first he saw nothing; then he spotted it—a white moth the size of a postage stamp with brown check marks on its wings. Jesus, nothing stayed ordinary around his father for long.

"How did you do that?"

"I'm telling you, I'm the human ear." Papi was jubilant. "I can hear the sound of sound. For an audience, the power of sight is relative, but hearing is another matter entirely. *Ay,* you just wait until I'm back on the Strip!"

Enrique held the cigarette to his father's lips for one last puff before flicking the butt out the window. The mountains in the distance looked fake. Everything in Las Vegas did. The names of things meant nothing here. A strong wind stirred up the dust. Enrique thought of the flag in Colón Park, and the storks thrown off course, and the single straw hat with a mourning ribbon that had flown through the air on the day Mamá died. If he could, he would stop the wind from ever blowing again.

A nurse barged in with a tray of compartmentalized food. There was a bowl of lumpy barley soup, chicken in some sort of gravy, unidentifiable side dishes. She turned on the radio without asking, moving the dial to a disco station.

"I see you have a visitor, Mr. Florit," the nurse said, sniffing the air warily. "How are you feeling?"

"I could use some more painkiller."

"You're already at your maximum."

"Just a bit more," Papi cajoled. "I need to rest."

The nurse turned one knob and then another, fiddling with the IV to make sure it was working properly. Enrique noticed the bruises in the crook of his father's elbow, where the nurse drew more blood. He was bulging in the middle, too, like a too ripe watermelon. The nurse pumped a hand crank at the foot of his bed that adjusted the angle of his mattress.

"Would you happen to have any maraschino cherries?" Papi asked her.

"Beg your pardon?"

"Cherries. I would be terribly grateful."

Enrique wished he could order up some real Cuban food for his father: roast pork and black beans, fried plantains, yuca in garlic sauce, pineapple flan. Each time Enrique's parents had returned from one of their tours of the Caribbean, his grandparents had thrown them a party and invited all their neighbors. The festivities always lasted well into the morning.

Mamá, though, preferred quiet times. She buried herself in novels, rereading her favorites. Enrique knew by heart the opening to *A Passage to India*: "Except for the Marabar Caves— and they are twenty miles off—the city of Chandrapore presents nothing extraordinary." Mamá liked to reminisce about her honeymoon, too, embroidering the events differently each time. But the facts remained: after a daylong courtship and a hasty civil wedding, she and Papi left Panama City on a little tramp steamer four days after they met. What had she seen in him that made her leave everything she knew?

Mamá's parents questioned the boat's seaworthiness, as well as their daughter's sanity. The little steamer had one battered smokestack and a Honduran flag at its stern. In exchange for a free berth, Papi provided the sailors with nightly entertainment and once made orange blossoms flutter down from a cloudy sky. For three months the boat sailed from port to port, carrying bananas and machine parts counterclockwise through the Caribbean, until it reached Havana.

"Turn that thing off!" Papi roared the minute the nurse left the room. "Not one of those ABBA-dabba Swedish nobodies—none of them, *¿me entiendes?*—compares to even the lowliest bongo player in Cuba."

Enrique switched off the radio and picked a small book off the nightstand, *Miracle Mongers and Their Methods* by Harry Houdini. It had been in his father's pocket when the teenagers attacked. He opened it to a dog-eared page and read aloud:

> "Norton could swallow a number of half-grown frogs and bring them up alive. I remember his anxiety on one occasion when returning to his dressing room; it seemed he had lost a frog—at least he could not account for the entire flock—and he looked very much scared, probably at the uncertainty as to whether or not he had to digest a live frog—

"Getting ideas for your act?" Enrique joked.

"I'm translating it into Spanish."

"Houdini in Spanish?"

"Why not?" Papi said, his leg swaying in midair. "His glory should burn in all corners of the world!"

Unlike his father, Enrique wasn't theatrically inclined. He'd performed with his parents only a few times. Papi kept a photograph of him as a toddler in blackface and diapers but Enrique couldn't remember what he'd done in that trick. He wondered sometimes if Mamá had performed just to keep Papi company on his travels. At home they were often inseparable, cooing to each other in a private language that Enrique didn't understand.

"I need to ask you something," Papi said. "But first, bring me the mirror from the bathroom."

Enrique dutifully tried to remove it from the wall but it was securely screwed in place. "Sorry, it won't budge."

"Tell me the truth, *hijo*," Papi said, attempting a smile. "How bad is it?"

Enrique didn't want to discourage his father but he refused to lie to him. "You've looked better."

"Am I still pretty?" Papi batted his one working eyelid.

"I don't think I would've ever called you pretty," Enrique laughed. "But let's just say I'm sure you'll be back to your old self in no time."

His father seemed greatly mollified. Then he cleared his throat and launched into a monologue about the beauty of working outside the system, unanswerable to any boss; how his life would've been impossible in Cuba; how sometimes good things were born from bad, from tumult and revolution, grief and ruination. He began to recite his all-occasion Martí poem: "I am an honest man from where the palm tree grows, and I want, before I die, to cast these verses from my soul. I come from all places—"

"How much do you need?" Enrique interrupted him.

"Forty."

"Forty thousand dollars?" Enrique was incredulous.

"I got myself in a little trouble down at the Diamond Pin," he said. "And this hospital won't be cheap. We don't have insurance, you know."

"Jesus Christ." Enrique sat on the edge of the hospital bed. He was sick of taking care of his father, of bailing him out of one scrape after another. But this was another order of fuckup altogether. Why couldn't he be like other parents? Why couldn't Papi take care of *him* for a change? Enrique looked at his father, helpless and mummified, and felt terribly guilty.

Last year, Johnny Langston had been down to his last hundred bucks. In thirty-six hours he'd built that up to fifty thousand dollars by betting all his money on every wager— blackjack, poker, professional football—calculating the odds, shrewdly, unsentimentally. He'd refused to touch anything as stupidly passive as roulette or the slots. If push came to shove, he would go down a lion. It was a matter of pride.

"The World Series of Poker begins in a week," Papi said,

cautiously enthusiastic again. His unbandaged eye followed Enrique around the room. "It takes ten grand to get in, but that won't be a problem if you decide to play. I know plenty of people who'll stake you." His breathing was labored, as if the air itself were straining his lungs.

Enrique poured his father a glass of ice water from the plastic pitcher on the nightstand. He poured; his father spilled. Enrique stared out the hospital window at the back lots and railroad tracks of downtown Las Vegas. Feathery clouds lined the horizon. He spotted palm trees and cottonwoods nearby, a flash of bougainvillea against the parched grass.

It was getting dark out. Enrique walked over to his father's bed and picked up the water glass, twisting it until it left a moist pink circle in his palm. It was all he could do not to shout at him, upend the tray of hospital food. Papi's delusions were crushing him, crushing them both. Yet his delusions were so much like faith it seemed cruel to take them away. How long was he supposed to keep his father afloat, anyway? What would happen if he just left Las Vegas? Wouldn't Papi have to figure things out by himself?

Enrique remembered the day he'd helped his father plant daffodils in the soft topsoil of Mamá's grave. She loved daffodils because they bloomed before the other flowers, because they were the first, she said, to imagine spring. Enrique set down the water glass and thought of a song his mother used to sing to him at bedtime, about a boat that tried, against great odds, to make its way across a treacherous current. *Había una vez un barquito chiquitito* . . . What choice did he really have? He decided, for now, to do whatever it took to keep his father alive.

Leila Rezvani

Leila strolled down the twisting back streets of the Tehran bazaar, where the lazy winter sun barely shone. The bookbinders occupied an alley to themselves, as did the haberdashers and tobacconists, the saddlers and tinsmiths and knife makers. The peculiar smells of each alley—glue, flint, leather, wool—leached into the skin of its practitioners. In the carpet aisles, the merchants were especially aggressive. One dealer offered Leila a gigantic rug woven in the likeness of President Kennedy. When she looked surprised, the merchant brought forth a rug of the Shah in his youth instead.

It was Christmas Eve and her father was missing. Six days ago, two men in double-breasted suits had shown up at his hospital and forcibly escorted him away before he could start a heart-valve operation. Leila had arrived on the Swissair flight from Geneva that same night. The director of the hospital, Dr. Karimi-Hakkak, was appealing directly to the Shah and had sent petitions to the courts and the central police station, but so far his efforts had yielded nothing. A ring of secrecy seemed to encircle her father's absence.

Maman complained that in recent months Baba had spoken out more publicly against the Shah, losing all prudence. If he didn't hold his tongue, he would put them all in danger. Who hadn't heard the rumors? Prisoners thrown into sacks of starving cats, burned alive on the electric "frying pans." Few ever returned home, dead or alive. But Baba hadn't been dissuaded by these stories. He'd countered irritably that if everyone succumbed to fear, the fear would win.

In the spices corridor, Leila picked up some cinnamon bark and held it to her nose. She thought of buying saffron and a bit of lapis to ward off the evil eye. How could the familiar seem so exotic to her after just a few seasons? A fortune-teller called Leila to her stall. "Advice for your heart, my beauty, advice for your heart!" she cried, waving a greedy hand. Her wrists clicked with bracelets of colorful gems. The fortune-teller promptly took out an astrolabe and a set of geomancy beads. Before throwing the beads, she held up a round mirror for Leila to gaze in.

"Look at yourself," she crooned. "See how pretty you are, *azizam*. You look like the very moon today!"

"No, thanks."

"Bale, bale!" She forced the mirror into Leila's hands. "Look at this feast! May I go blind if I'm lying."

For a moment, Leila was shocked to see nothing. Then slowly, her face came into focus: the high-arched brows, the shapely lips, the nose that seemed to belong to someone else — small and straight, with an upturned tip. True to her word, Maman had persuaded Dr. Ghanoonparvar, the best plastic surgeon in Tehran, to operate on her daughter. "I won't have her stigmatized in Europe," Fatemeh argued. On Leila's thirteenth birthday, her mother gave her a few pills to help her relax. This was the last thing Leila remembered until after her birthday "surprise."

The next morning, she woke up in the hospital, her nose packed with bandages and catheters in her nostrils to help her breathe. For two days she bled so profusely that she required a transfusion. It took another two months for the swelling to go down. The skin on her nose felt hard and stiff for a year. Her father had warned her that in life ten thousand people would try to tell her what to do, would promise her they could read the fine print on a star. But to know your own heart, he advised, it was enough to sit alone in the dark.

"You wait in vain for what you dread," the fortune-teller concluded. "For this you are chewing up your heart."

The mirror cost twice what it should but Leila handed over the money without bargaining. A toy seller ambled by with clay whistles. If only the dull ache between her legs would go away. A week ago she'd lost her virginity, she didn't know to whom. After waiting longer than any of the other girls at her Swiss boarding school, Leila had gotten exceedingly drunk on Finnish vodka the night of the Christmas party. She'd danced with lots of boys, something she hadn't done before, and kissed their bristly lips. Someone—who was it?—had begun stroking her breasts. When Leila woke up in her bed, the sheets were stained with blood and her mouth was sour. Her tongue tasted like someone else's tongue.

Now she prayed for three things: that she wasn't pregnant, that only one boy had done it, and that whoever it was wouldn't remember either. The morning after the party, everyone left for the four corners of the globe. Leila scanned the faces of possible perpetrators—Paul Trémont, Heinrich Ülle, Giovanni Scala—but their expressions betrayed nothing. There was one more thing she hoped: that her parents wouldn't find out. Already, Leila could hear her mother screaming: Worthless whore, why do you push us toward ruin?

Leila made her way to an Armenian café and ordered tea and rice pudding with rose water, hoping to soothe her nervous stomach. She watched as the waiter carelessly wiped the table with a dirty rag. After her brother had died, she'd inherited his sweet tooth. Every afternoon, Leila frequented the pastry shops near her boarding school—Le Petit Lapin, Patisserie Michaud, Café Vienna. All the bakers knew her by name. They saved her slices of Sacher torte and plum tarts, éclairs, mocha petit fours.

Classical Persian music crackled into the café from one ancient speaker. Leila listened to the sounds of the sitar and remembered a line of poetry she'd memorized in grade school: "How did the rose ever open its heart and give to this world all its beauty?" It didn't seem fair to her that a girl's virginity was so prized when a boy's was merely a burden to unload at the first opportunity.

Last night in her father's study, Leila had found a book by a woman poet, Forugh Farrokhzad. Leila read and read and didn't stop until she reached the last page. A note on the back cover said that the author had died in a mysterious accident at the age of thirty-three. This was only nine years ago. *Our old courtyard is lonely. Our garden yawns in anticipation of an unknown rain cloud, and our garden is empty.*

It was cold outside and the cypress trees swayed in the wind. The air snapped with electricity, with the possibility of lightning. Days like this were considered inauspicious by the tea-leaf readers and the interpreters of coffee grinds. Dusk would arrive suddenly, pressing from the mountains, crushing the light from all living things. Leila thought of Queen Soraya, the Shah's second wife, whom he'd divorced for not producing an heir. The money she spent shopping was legendary. His third wife, Farah Diba, was no different. Shopping was how most rich women in Tehran occupied their days.

A flock of them would be at Aunt Parvin's house tonight. Preparations were under way for the holidays, despite Baba's disappearance. (In their circles, both Christian and Muslim holidays were celebrated.) How could they throw a party with him missing? Her aunt's trademark silver bowls, filled with sprigs of winter jasmine, would decorate the banquet tables at discreet intervals. The guests would lie to Leila, offer her hope about her father. But the minute she turned her back, they would gossip: What was the use of his empty gestures, eh? Look what suffering he has brought upon his family! Where is the honor in that?

Down the street, Leila flagged a taxicab.

"To the police station," she said. Leila wasn't sure what she would do once she got there, but she couldn't very well just wander the city while her father was missing.

The central station was imposing and shabby all at once, like most government buildings. She wondered if the brutal decrees issued here had anything to do with the disdain the police felt from their countrymen. Fear was a terrible thing to have to live up to.

"Who's in charge here?" Leila asked the front-desk clerk.

"What is the nature of your complaint?" He barely looked up from a sheaf of musty documents.

"My father is missing." Leila heard the quaver in her voice and hoped it wasn't too evident.

"Down the hall, to the left."

Leila didn't have far to go. Filling most of the marble corridor was a long line of people holding photographs of their loved ones. Their silence echoed against the walls worse than any curses they might have hurled. Leila took her place behind a middle-aged woman in a chador cradling a school photo of a teenaged boy. He wore a crisp white shirt and the first wisp of a mustache.

"My eldest," she whispered and her eyes filled with tears.

"How long have you been waiting?"

"Since Wednesday."

"Surely not!" Leila exclaimed and everyone turned to look at her. She wanted to ask more questions but the crowd silenced her with their stares. Their positions were precarious and they didn't want some interloper spoiling their chance for a hearing with the Missing Persons Bureau.

Leila apologized to the woman, bowing slightly, and backed away. She tried to imagine describing Baba to the so-called investigators. Yes, her father was of ordinary build and height, ordinarily handsome, with ordinary-sized hands and feet, but there was nothing ordinary about him. To start with, Baba had no time for people who hadn't earned their station in life. Of course, that cut out most of their circle, with its who-knows-whos and its mutual back-scratchings. He avoided the royal family like the plague.

Did her father have a prayer against his enemies? If only he would keep his mouth shut or issue an apology, he might be saved. But what were the odds of that? The Shah himself would need to have a heart attack and personally call for Dr. Nader Rezvani to attend to him. Baba would never refuse to save a man's life, even one he despised. Only then would he be granted a pardon.

The glare of the winter afternoon made the trees appear drained of color. Where should she go now? With whom should she speak?

A taxicab pulled up next to Leila and the driver called out, "Where can I take you, miss?" He was elderly and clean-shaven, with a country accent.

"To the cemetery," she ordered.

The driver wound around the city, seemingly in circles, muttering to himself. Car horns blared along the crowded, too narrow streets. They moved so slowly that she might as well have walked. Leila rolled down her window and took in the late-afternoon smells of Tehran. "Build up your muscles with a liver-and-kidney kebab!" a vendor practically shouted in her ear. Another hawked oranges and sweet lemons from the north.

The city was growing so much that Leila barely recognized

it. Construction projects sprawled in every direction—power plants, electronics factories, brand-new hospitals. The Shah was importing countless experts, too: hydraulic engineers from Greece, electricians from Norway, mechanics from Italy, truck drivers from Korea. He paid for everything with oil money, while in the countryside the peasants still burned cow pies for fuel.

When Leila was last home, she'd accompanied her father on a drive to the Alborz Mountains. They'd passed new districts still smelling of paint and fresh cement. The hillsides were dotted with Swiss-style chalets. It took an hour to escape the city and finally breathe some clean air. Baba told her that the rich were boarding the daily Lufthansa jet in the morning, having lunch in Munich, and flying home in time for dinner. Others paid for the staff at Maxim's to cook and deliver their lunch from Paris. And the coast of the Caspian Sea was congested with garish new mansions and country clubs. Baba said that it sickened him to see even his formerly reasonable friends yielding to the frenzy of excess.

On Nejatollahi Street, the driver swerved to avoid a dead dog. Poor families from the countryside had set up tents near the local mosques. A bony gray horse pulled a rickety cart overflowing with junk and twine. The cab passed the Sarkis Cathedral, which the Armenians had built for themselves, its dome black with crows. The parks were empty except for the leafless trees and sparse grass, but the shops and cafés were packed.

Leila didn't realize until now how much she'd missed Tehran, the old city anyway, with its dusty side streets and everyday corruptions. In Swiss cities everything was as neat as a postage stamp. A month ago, a boy at her boarding school had been arrested for urinating against a tulip tree in the center of town. The boy, Ömer Özguc, was the son of the Turkish ambassador. Relations between the two countries were severely strained over the incident.

The cemetery, a confusion of tombstones and nettled paths, seemed larger than Leila remembered. It wasn't easy to find her brother's grave, even with the help of the crippled attendant. She hadn't been back since Hosein's burial six years ago. The wailing had been unbearable and Baba had refused to let go of the coffin's lid. Now there was only silence and a dry carpet of leaves.

Baba had aged visibly after Hosein's death. It was as if the years were waiting patiently in a corner of his body, then pounced on him all at once. At fifty-four, he looked closer to seventy. He began to speak like an old man, too, reliving his past through a magnifying glass. Before he was arrested, Baba had spent his nights reading histories of the Qajar era, retelling the tales as if they were his own. At boarding school, Leila was shocked to discover that Persian history didn't exist.

Thirty years ago, Baba said, peasant families used to bring their sick relatives to his hospital and camp out in the waiting room. The doctors and nurses would have to pick their way among rolled-out carpets, charcoal stoves, an occasional goat. Everybody would be smoking and talking loudly, coming and going as they pleased until all hours of the night. They wanted to see with their own eyes what they stood to lose. What would she give now, Leila thought, to hear Baba telling these stories again?

Maman also had changed. She'd given up on her garden, leaving it untended and wild. The wells went dry and the fountain painted with doves lay crumbling in the sun. These days, Maman lived for the mirror. She devoted herself to preserving her beauty with expensive creams and an occasional face-lift in London—and to finding a suitable husband for Leila. There would be an interesting young man at Aunt Parvin's party tonight, a physics student from the States who was home for the winter break. He was an identical twin, Maman said, a lucky trait.

How could she be matchmaking at a time like this?

A fig tree spread its meager canopy over her brother's plot, which was littered with rotten fruit. The seeds stuck out dully from the pulp like crooked teeth. An unruly vine was wound around the trunk, giving off an acrid scent that permeated everything. Leila imagined her whole family dead and buried beside Hosein, their bones slowly hollowing, submitting to the quiet claw of decay. For an instant, she longed to scratch each of their names in the dry earth.

"Are you still there?" Leila kicked the edge of her brother's grave, dislodging a clod of dirt. She remembered their last day together: the stir of Hosein's sheets, the taut warmth of him in her hand, the look from him that inhabited her still. Certain things, she decided, just couldn't be erased. At boarding school, Leila liked to dress in her brother's old clothes—his silk shirts and sweatpants, his sleek brown socks worn at the heels. In this way, she'd kept him close.

The wind blew hard against Leila's lamb's-wool jacket. *Leilaleilaleila.* A leaf floated past her face, dispersing the words. A thin lizard, encrusted with mud, waited at the foot of the grave. She listened for her name again, but nothing around her stirred. The insects mutely looted the last of the fruit.

"Help us, Hosein. Please help us find Baba," Leila prayed. "Tell me he isn't dead. Tell me he'll be returned to us soon."

Haq! Haq! Leila looked up, half hoping to catch a glimpse of the Bird of Truth. Instead she saw a dull brown thrush with thickset feathers singing off-key. What was it doing here in the bitter middle of winter?

A sudden excess of light scattered the sky's fragile blue, then disappeared altogether. Raindrops pricked her scalp. Leila unwrapped her cinnamon bark and placed it on Hosein's grave, securing it with a stone. The fig tree shed its final shadow. Then she hurried back to the waiting taxicab.

"Home," she told the driver. "I want to go home."

Marta Claros

Marta enjoyed the peace of Mrs. Sheffield's house after the incessant clatter of the shoe factory. For the past two weeks, the factory had been in full swing, trying to meet the army's deadline for a huge order of boots. Marta spent twelve hours a day, six days a week, staple gun in hand, affixing hundreds of leather soles to the stiff, shiny boots. She grew dizzy from the stink of the finishing glue, from the heat and the tedious repetition. It was a relief to spend some quiet time cleaning Mrs. Sheffield's home.

She'd met Mrs. Sheffield outside the British embassy, where her husband was the consul general. Marta was waiting for a bus when the Englishwoman tripped and fell beside her, breaking a heel. Marta came to her assistance and fixed her shoe with the glue she used for after-hours piecework. They spoke for a few minutes — Mrs. Sheffield's Spanish was excellent — and she ended up offering Marta a job cleaning her home every Sunday.

It was this extra day of work, paid to her in dollars, that made it possible for her to save enough money to leave the country.

Marta had wanted to keep selling used clothes and toys on the street, but her husband wouldn't permit it. Now that she was a married woman, he insisted, she couldn't go peddling her body along with her wares up and down every alleyway of the city. But she refused to stay in their apartment all day, waiting for him to come home and testily give her a few coins for the market. That was much more intolerable to her than the hand-cramping work at the factory.

Besides, she needed the money. If she'd learned anything from her Tía Matilde, it was to ensure her own keep. How surprised Fabián would be when he woke up tomorrow and discovered her missing. It wouldn't occur to him that she, or any woman for that matter, might leave him. But Marta had decided long ago to stop breaking her heart against his.

When she'd married Fabián, two days after her sixteenth birthday, Marta had said her vows in earnest, with every intention of staying with him forever. It was a simple church ceremony. Marta wore a crown of jasmine with her veil, and the hem of her wedding dress was embroidered with sequins and imitation pearls. Even Evaristo, reluctantly, had descended his banyan tree to attend. Marta thought that by marrying Fabián, her future was secured.

Nothing turned out the way she'd hoped. This wasn't to say that she didn't like her husband, at first—he surprised her with little gifts, buying her coconut ice cream or a pair of sneakers for her brother. Nobody had done that for her before. The fact was that Fabián had promised Marta two things she desperately wanted: to leave Mamá's house, and to have a child of her own. Tía Matilde warned her about marrying a *guardia* (only her mother thought him a good opportunity) but Marta didn't listen.

Today was their second anniversary. They were supposed to go out to dinner but Marta preferred going hungry to listening to Fabián complain about the price of a restaurant meal. To think that she'd once been swayed by his promise of a juicy steak. Marta decided that she was too tempted by easy comforts. Everything has a price, her aunt liked to say, and she was right. A woman's real dowry was the one she carried inside her.

Marta felt a heaviness in her abdomen. The arrival of her period put her husband in a foul mood, as if she were childless on purpose. Fabián had fathered twins in the countryside when he was a teenager—so the problem wasn't with him. Nobody in Marta's family had trouble conceiving, so it was a mystery why she couldn't get pregnant. Marta considered the children she saw living in the streets, urchins with no one to care for them, and wished she could adopt one. There was a gang of boys, no older than eight or nine, who rummaged through the factory's garbage bins for leftover glue. Who might they become if they were loved? But Fabián refused, as he put it, to bring mongrels into their home.

Last year, Marta had consulted an expensive gynecologist on the far side of town; Dr. Canosa told her that there was nothing wrong with her, that her infertility was all in her head. But how could *not* having a baby be in her head when all she could think about was having a baby? She made certain to have regular relations with Fabián, though he soon grew more interested in late-night wrestling on TV than in her. Love evaporated when there were no children to hold it together.

Marta didn't feel the giddy pleasures that made other women swoon, either. Fabián's mustache scratched her face and she felt bruised by him inside. He was covered in coarse hair and his penis swung so far to the left when erect that Fabián had to hold it in place with both hands. Marta was too embarrassed to ask anyone about this. The whole act seemed bestial to her, like dogs copulating in the street. For Marta, sex was uncomfortable but mercifully brief. If there was any pleasure, it was in the anticipation of conceiving a child.

Her aunt had recommended that Marta visit a healer in Ilobasco. Together they'd traveled by bus to Doña Telma's house, whose rafters were filled with squeaking bats. After a short consultation, Doña Telma told Marta that she had scars that were blocking the release of her eggs. She offered Marta a pouch of herbs to mingle with her bathwater but promised nothing—Yours is a delicate case, *hija*—and fondly wished her good luck.

❧

Marta liked Mrs. Sheffield's lemon-scented furniture polish, the way it foamed up quickly and made the wood shine like healing skin. She especially loved the toilet cleaner, a special blue liquid for use nowhere else. The tile floors were a cinch to mop, too, not like the dirt floors Marta was used to sweeping at Mamá's house, sprinkling them with water to keep down the dust.

Just last month, Marta had installed a linoleum floor in her mother's kitchen (the rest of the house still had dirt floors). It was the color of avocados with a stamped-on gold design. Fabián was furious that she'd wasted money on the floor but Marta didn't care. She was proud that it was her money, earned at Mrs. Sheffield's, which made the new floor possible. Her *patrona* had given her English-language tapes and a second-hand cassette player. The tapes made no sense to Marta, but she enjoyed the rhythm of the sentences just the same.

Outside, a flock of parakeets rushed by in a clamorous streak. Marta thought of her brother in his banyan tree. Evaristo was still shaken after having witnessed another abduction last Sunday. A group of soldiers dragged a young couple, shouting, into a van. The following morning, Evaristo found their mutilated bodies dumped behind the biggest department store on Paseo General Escalón. He recognized the couple by their clothes and the filigreed crucifix around the girl's neck.

Marta tried to make her brother swear that he wouldn't tell anyone about it. "Don't invite trouble, *hermano.* God will punish the murderers, don't worry." Bodies were turning up everywhere, he insisted, heads in one place, limbs in another. Evaristo saw everything from his tree, everything that was supposed to go unseen. But who could he tell? Who would believe him? On the news, the right blamed the left and the left blamed the right, but nobody was brought to justice. If the soldiers succeeded in killing all the poor, Marta thought, who would be left to clear the fields, or harvest the coffee, or grind the corn?

At the shoe factory, a woman named Sandra Mejía was trying to organize the workers to petition for shorter hours. What paradise did she think they were living in? Marta suspected that Sandra was a guerrilla—a Communist agitator, Fabián would have said—but they ate lunch together every day. Everyone called Sandra "Canary" because she stood ready to sing against injustices. When Marta revealed that her own husband was a *guardia,* Sandra spat on the ground.

When they were first married, Marta used to bring Fabián his lunch, traveling to the outskirts of San Salvador where his platoon was conducting maneuvers. Once Marta saw a pig trotting along a road with a human hand in its mouth and vowed never to eat pork again. Fabián couldn't explain where the hand had come from. Then her husband was transferred to the garrison in the capital. Mostly, the soldiers played cards there, or argued about sports, or listened to the same *cumbia* cassette week after week. Marta figured they were waiting for orders.

But Sandra Mejía said that the *guardias* tortured people in the back rooms of the garrison, that their methods grew more macabre by the day: people skinned alive, forced to swallow lye, choked to death with rags, slowly burned to ash. Fabián said that citizens who minded their own business had nothing to fear. Marta knew this wasn't true. Plenty of innocent people were being killed.

She couldn't imagine her husband torturing anybody. For all his bluster, he was a cowardly man. Yet he'd said that the only way for a real man to die was in battle. Men categorized things in ways Marta didn't understand. Fabián finally confessed that he'd been assigned to the firing squad. He said that fear excited the kidneys and nearly all the prisoners urinated in their pants before they died. Marta pictured the prisoners lined up against the *paredón*, young men and women, blindfolded, her husband taking aim. Those were his orders, his job, the way her job was gluing shoes and cleaning Mrs. Sheffield's house.

Marta opened the balcony doors of the Sheffields' bedroom. The sky was clear after so many rainy days. Perhaps the city would be free of mosquitoes this afternoon. The man who sold cloth bolts on credit passed by with his singsong *pregón*. Marta fluffed the pillows on the king-sized bed. There were photographs on the nightstands framed in silver, children and grandchildren back in England, each with the same pink cheeks. It was difficult for Marta to distinguish the adults from the children.

She felt a sudden cramp in her stomach and stopped sweeping, leaning on her broom. Sometimes Marta liked to pretend she was pregnant and eat enough for two (she'd gained forty-five pounds since her wedding). She drank so much milk it upset her digestion. Marta prayed to La Virgen de Guadalupe every night to help guide her child, her little wanderer, to her womb. *Ay, mi angelito, have you lost your way?* She imagined an assembly line of babies in heaven, asleep and waiting for delivery. When would her turn come?

The master bathroom was painted mint green. The tuberoses looked cheerful in their Chinese vase, brightly enameled with dragonflies. The gilded mirror was big enough for an entire family to gaze in simultaneously. Marta watched herself undo her girdle (a birthday present from Esperanza, the lingerie peddler) and settled on the toilet seat as the first trickle of blood began. She caught a small clot and smeared it against her thumb, searching for a sign of her child. Then she left a fingerprint on the mirror.

On her way home, Marta tried to commit everything to memory: the cobblestoned streets up the hillsides, the volcanoes standing guard over the city, the orphans on the corners begging for coins. She studied the swallows circling and diving around Evaristo's banyan tree. The north wind made the tree's canopy shiver and the nearby kiskadees—*cuio, cuio*—announced death with their bugle-loud songs. This was her very last day in El Salvador. The sooner she got out of the country, the better off she and Evaristo would be. Their father had tried to cross the border twice, but he'd been caught and deported both times. Nobody knew where he was anymore.

Marta parked herself beneath her brother's banyan and shouted into the leaves: "Come down, *hermano*! I need to talk to you!"

A moment later, Evaristo's head appeared upside down from a branch. His hair was sparse and what was left of his clothes was in tatters. His feet, black with dirt, curled around the branch like claws. Marta offered her brother a few tortillas but Evaristo wasn't hungry. He said the *guardias* had rounded up schoolgirls from a bus stop that day, called them Communists and whores. He said that he would do everything he could to find out who the girls were and memorize their names.

"Stay out of it, I beg you," Marta whispered, holding her brother close. Evaristo gave off a sharp, troubling odor, one she feared no amount of soap could wash away. "Look." She held up a key and pressed it into his dry, cracked hand. "This is for your post office box at the central station. The number is seven forty-one. Can you remember that?"

Evaristo's eyes were half-closed, as if he were listening to another voice far away. He scratched his chest and dropped the key to the ground. Marta pulled a square of gingham from her purse and sewed a pocket into the waistband of her brother's pants with thick black stitches. Then she tucked the key inside. Evaristo smiled at her with a corner of his mouth.

"Check the box once a month," Marta instructed, trying not to sound as impatient as she felt. "*Primero Dios,* I'll send for you soon." She embraced him, harder this time, and gave him enough money to last him several months. His whole body seemed to shrivel as he climbed back into his banyan tree. She hoped he would take a nap. If nothing else, it might give him an hour of peace.

❧

That evening Marta looked out the window of her apartment on Calle Sur. Political slogans covered the walls of the Catholic elementary school across the street. It was five minutes after curfew. The bread vendor from Santa Tecla was hurrying along the sidewalk with a last basket of loaves on her head. A single carnation enlivened her display. Marta thought of running downstairs to buy bread for her journey when—*Ra-ta-ta-ta-ta-ta-ta-ta-ta!*—the basket tipped and a cascade of loaves fell to the pavement, as if a hundred years were passing. *Ay,* what hapless string of days had led this poor woman to her fate?

Fabián returned at ten o'clock, smelling of *chicha* and beer. Fabián got drunk on the worst days of shooting. (His other job was whitewashing the firing-squad wall to erase the remains of the dead.) Getting drunk was more acceptable to him than crying, which Marta had seen him do only once, at his grandmother's funeral. Without a word Fabián pushed her onto the bed and lifted her skirt, ignoring her protests. When he pulled down her panties and saw the blood, he reached for his pistol and aimed it between her legs.

"Whore! You're killing my babies!"

Marta didn't react at first. She noticed a thin line of ants, like tiny black letters, marching along the wall toward the kitchen. She waited, calming her nervousness, then smiled at him. *Dámelo, dámelo, mi niño.* Marta reached for the gun, her eyes steady on his, and unfastened his fingers one by one. When she had both hands tight on the pistol, Marta took three deliberate steps backward. Then she aimed carefully, very carefully, and shot her husband in the foot. Marta brought her face close to Fabián's pained, sweating one: "From this moment forward, my legs are sealed to you. Do you understand? You can no longer use me for your filth."

She wiped off the pistol, gathered her things, and walked out the door. The overnight bus to Guatemala was leaving in less than an hour.

❖

Marta had never seen a sky this dark. There was no moon, and the stars seemed to hide in the black folds of midnight. The silence was so complete that Marta feared life itself had withdrawn from these parts. At any moment she might cross the border from one world to the next, imperceptibly, like death.

The *coyote* said that a night like this was good cover, that the *yanquis'* fiercest lights couldn't penetrate it. Marta reached for the rosary in her pocket and fingered another bead. It was the same pink plastic one she'd used for her First Communion. *Dios te salve, María llena eres de gracia.* Marta knew she would make it across the border. She had to. With La Virgen's help, she would make it across, establish herself in Los Angeles, then send for her brother. This was her plan.

The *coyote* led the way up a mountain that Marta could barely see. Its smells enveloped her. Sage and mesquite, the thirsting earth, the looming dust-dry cacti. Marta imagined the scent of rain. She pictured pines flourishing here, a *zapote* taking root. Tía Matilde liked to say that water rose to the skies by means of invisible rivers that later showered down on the land. The rivers had currents so powerful that they carried fish and frogs and snakes in their depths.

There were other people crossing over, like her. A Oaxacan couple with their sickly infant, slung from his father's serape. Brothers from Tapachula, both cross-eyed. A Nicaraguan woman, Dinora Luna, who looked to be in her forties but said she was fifty-three. Dinora's only concession to age was her limp, the result, she said, of her truck rolling into a ditch outside Panama City in 1966. She blamed the country's water commissioner—a jealous lover whose daughter had run off with a Cuban magician—for tampering with her truck. Epifanio Carranza had been her *amante* for years, she said, and used to keep a beachfront home with full-time servants just for her. But when Dinora told him that she was getting married, he tried to kill her.

"My leg was pinned under the dashboard for nine hours," she said with a shrug.

Dinora told Marta that she'd smuggled contraband from one end of Central America to another: liquor, tobacco, precious rain-forest woods. She, too, was leaving behind a husband, her third, and the violence that was ravaging her country. Marta couldn't see Dinora clearly in the darkness, only hear her voice. It was like talking with the dead.

On the steepest part of the climb, Marta stayed close behind the Nicaraguan woman. Their bodies leaned sharply into the blackness, their breath came hard, their blouses grew damp with sweat. Marta drank watered-down juice from her canteen but it barely quenched her thirst. She had to pace herself with little sips or she would make herself sick.

Despite her limp, Dinora was a sure-footed old goat. The *coyote* warned them not to dislodge any rocks that might start an avalanche. He said the border patrol had devices like giant ears that caught stray sounds in the desert, that it was dangerous even to sneeze. The slightest noise could bring helicopters, attack dogs, yellow-haired men seven feet tall.

Marta wondered what would happen if she died and became part of this land. Would her bones tick away slowly, like the fat heart of the mesquite? How long would night last if she were a stone, or a hawk lazily circling overhead? The air was chilly but she felt feverish. Around her, nothing stirred. A sudden coldness rose through her feet. Someone, Marta suspected, must have died on this very spot. She remembered the faces of the passengers on the bus out of El Salvador, the white banner of dust that ushered them into Guatemala. How many of them had made it this far?

When Marta's group reached the top of the mountain, the *coyote* refused to let them rest. Her legs were trembling from the climb and they weren't even halfway there yet. A part of her wanted to turn around but she was afraid to cross the desert by herself. The *coyote* explained that they needed to reach their checkpoint, seventeen miles away, before dawn. A truck would be waiting to take them to Mexicali, where they would be stacked three high in its false bottom container. Then on to California. *California*. Marta tried to pronounce it the way she'd heard it on her English-language tapes: "Peaches and oranges are only two of the many fruits grown in the fertile Central Valley of California."

"Hungry?" Dinora offered Marta a handful of almonds. The Nicaraguan woman ate them soundlessly, splitting them between her front teeth. "They keep up your strength."

Marta reached for the almonds, but her hand got tangled up in her rosary—it was coiled around a day-old sugar bun wrapped in wax paper—and the nuts scattered to the ground.

"Catholic or Evangelical?" Dinora asked.

"Catholic."

"Thank God for that. I'm so sick of Evangelicals." Dinora took a deep breath and pulled herself onto a rocky ledge. "They got hold of every one of my children. Now there's no talking sense to any of them. I can't light my candles or do my *pruebitas* without having them accuse me of doing the devil's work."

"Candles?" Marta chewed an almond, gritty and mildly sweet. She had an urge for *horchata* from the vendor at the Plaza Masferrer, the one who'd gotten caught in a firefight between the guerrillas and the army and died.

"To tell the future," Dinora said. "I learned as a girl."

"Could you tell my future?"

"Of course, *amorcita*. But I don't think our leader here will let us play with matches."

Marta laughed. She liked Dinora, in spite of her sacrilegious talk. Perhaps they could team up, share a room in Los Angeles to keep expenses down. Marta had a sudden vision of herself selling balloons, dozens of them tied with brightly colored string. Around her, everyone wore carnival masks.

"You'll be fine. I don't need a candle to see that," Dinora said kindly. "You have an instinct for dreams."

"Quiet over there," the *coyote* scolded them. "Do you want to spend the rest of your lives in hell?"

"We're more alone than death here," Dinora muttered.

It was freezing on the mountain and Marta drew her shawl more tightly around herself. What if it began to snow and they were buried alive? Last year she'd seen a show on television about an airplane crash in the Andes. Out of desperation, the survivors ate their dead companions' flesh. She couldn't imagine a worse sin. Marta rubbed her rosary beads again. *Bendita eres entre todas las mujeres y bendito es el fruto de tu vientre.*

The Mexican woman began sobbing on the ridge below, and Marta knew without asking that her baby had died. Against the *coyote*'s threats, they buried the boy on the hillside, fashioning a cross from sticks. His father dug the hole with his bare hands. Marta stood by the little grave and silently prayed. She wanted to cry, but no tears would come. For the next two hours, nobody said a word.

She could die here like this little boy, Marta thought, and nobody would know where to find her. Only Evaristo was aware of her plans and he'd promised to tell no one. Until Mamá got word, she would think that Marta had been abducted by the army or killed by her husband, especially if he recounted to her how she'd shot him in the foot. No, she decided, Fabián would be too embarrassed to admit what had happened.

It was remarkable how easy it had been to walk away from everything she knew: her family, her country, her habits, her belongings. Already, they were drifting away, like the balloons she imagined selling. But maybe remembering was just a form of forgetting, of choosing one thing over another, turning green into yellow, day into night. If it was true that she was leaving behind everything familiar, could she leave herself behind, too?

Marta heard the cry of crows in the distance. She envisioned their glossy plumage, the spread of their outsized wings. She searched the skies for the morning star, which she prayed would bring her good luck in the crossing. Then she recalled something Tía Matilde told her: Niña, it is always coldest before dawn.

Evaristo

The earth rumbles. Everything collapses. Buildings, trees, electrical lines, the sky itself. There's no more light. The birds are still. Not a single dog barks. I hold tight to the trunk of my old banyan and feel its roots tremble. I wait and wait for my sister but she doesn't come. She says she will send for me soon, that God will find a way. But I don't believe anymore. Marta believes. She believes with the soles of her feet. Pobre hermana. The world will end today. My arms are sore from hanging on. I don't know. I don't know how much longer I can wait.

(1979)

Marta Claros

It was eleven o'clock in the morning and Marta was tired from staying up most of the night with La Doctora. She pulled the dirty newspaper from the bottom of the biggest canary cage and cleaned out the food dish, rinsing it with warm water. Then she refilled the dish with minced spinach. Her employer had seven different types of canaries, each with their own dietary requirements. Singing in unison, they sounded like a dissonant church choir. Marta had been caring for the birds in Beverly Hills for over two years. They were supposed to be Marta's sole responsibility but La Doctora required more care than all her birds put together.

Her favorite canary, Benny, was the most enthusiastic singer by far. Marta had trained him to perform on cue. *A la una, a las dos, a las tres,* she instructed, waving her hands like an orchestra conductor. Marta loved changing Benny's bathwater and watched as he happily splashed himself. She laughed to imagine him with a miniature towel and bar of soap.

Marta continued her morning rounds in the backyard aviary. There was a hint of jasmine in the air and the wisteria hummed with bumblebees. The African gray parrot looked sullen. Yesterday he'd plucked out most of his feathers. When Marta spoke to him — his name was Homer — he lowered his head and deliberately shook it. How did he know that she was leaving him for good?

The new Gouldian finches were in love and chattered continuously, much to the annoyance of the scarlet macaw named Waldo. The peach-faced lovebirds' interminable squabbles agitated the other birds. Only the ringneck parakeets — there were eleven of them — stayed relatively quiet.

Marta had begun dreaming in the birds' different languages: warbles and trills, screeches and cries, all the signals of need and displeasure. It was something she understood now, as effortlessly as the mynah bird's imitations of everything — a slamming door, the neighbor's barking dog, a whistling teakettle. Marta chopped up a papaya and half a banana for the Tucumán parrot's breakfast and served it to him in his striped bowl. Then she clipped the wings of the green-cheeked conures and smoothed their ruffled plumage. For this work, Marta earned forty dollars a day. This had seemed a fortune to her at first, until she realized how little it bought here.

Shooting pains surged up the backs of her legs. She'd hurt herself on the crossing over, crawling under a barbed-wire fence near the Arizona border. Marta suspected a damaged nerve but La Doctora, a retired vascular surgeon, said there was nothing wrong with her. (Why did doctors always tell her this?) If only she could get her hands on some iguana lard and rub it into her legs, she would feel much better.

This morning, Marta noticed fresh cuts up the length of La Doctora's arm. She was left-handed and so the cuts — fifty or sixty gashes—appeared on the right. La Doctora had left the knife, smeared with blood, in the kitchen sink. Marta didn't understand why anyone would deliberately hurt themselves. She thought of the prisoners in El Salvador who were forced to wear *capuchas*, hoods coated with toxic chemicals, until they suffocated and died.

Today she read in the newspaper that a priest who'd spoken out against the violence was shot while saying Mass. His parishioners poured into the streets in protest, walking in circles, staring at one another in disbelief. First the bells of one church rang, then another and another, until the whole city was alive with the news. On the day of his funeral, Tía Matilde got in line at five in the morning to pay her respects and didn't file past the priest's body until two that afternoon.

Marta stood in La Doctora's kitchen and checked the contents of the refrigerator. The tortillas were gone and La Doctora had finished the last of the cheese. That was all her *patrona* ate: tiny squares of cheese, as if she were a mouse. La Doctora had separate dishes for dairy and meat, but the plates only collected dust in the cupboard. She said that it was a sin to eat anything that fed on garbage, which included pigs and shellfish. Marta agreed about the pigs but she wasn't about to give up her rice with shrimp.

Marta had lost thirty pounds working in Beverly Hills and was down to a size fourteen. Few things tasted good to her anymore. After caring for her birds she'd stopped eating poultry, too. How she used to enjoy a little roast chicken. Now what was left to savor? She was big-bosomed and curvaceous but her legs were thinning out. The owner of the dress factory, Frankie Soon, said she was beginning to look like those skinny *gringas* on television.

It was because of Frankie that she'd cut back her days with La Doctora. (Dinora worked at the factory and had gotten Marta part-time hours there.) At first Marta worked only on

Saturdays to make extra money. Then she started working nights and a few Sundays, too. Sometimes she and her boss were the only ones at the factory.

Marta was a good seamstress, fast and reliable, never a crooked stitch. Frankie was pleased with her work and found ways to test her skills and her loyalty. He gave her take-home projects and asked her advice about the other workers at the factory. He said she was the only one he trusted. Finally, after sixteen months, Frankie convinced her to work for him full-time. On Monday she would begin her new job at the Back-to-Heaven dress factory in Koreatown.

Marta was fond of her birds and hadn't wanted to give them up entirely. Besides, La Doctora had promised to secure a green card for Marta as a bird-care specialist. Marta liked the way that sounded, crisp and professional. But La Doctora wore her out with her demands—and still no green card.

One thing Marta planned to do when she left Beverly Hills was sign up for English classes. Whenever she tried out new words—*chair, yellow, tissue*—she felt as though she were fighting traffic with her tongue. It wasn't easy to find the time to study. Just like back home, the poor did all the hard work here. Without them the floors in Bel Air wouldn't get mopped, the gardens in Brentwood watered, the dinners in Pacific Palisades cooked.

Marta swept the patio of leaves and fallen feathers and wondered how El Norte had changed her. Would her street-vendor friends in San Salvador recognize her in a crowd? When she looked at herself in the mirror, Marta saw another version of herself. Yes, that was the shape of her face, and the mole on her throat was the same. *Híjole,* but the expression in her eyes. Something was definitely different.

Most of the time, she felt lonely in Los Angeles. Marta had worked day and night for nearly three years but she still didn't have enough money to send for her brother. Last week she'd visited Dinora, who lived with her sister's family in Lincoln

Heights, and they'd gone to the back porch to read her divining candles. Dinora said that she foresaw a great love for Marta, but when she lit a blue candle for Evaristo, it hissed with black smoke. That happens sometimes, Dinora said, waving the smoke away.

Dinora encouraged Marta to play the lottery but Marta was reluctant to gamble even a dollar or two. Her friend was lucky. Twice, Dinora had won fifty dollars. The one time Marta played she bet one dollar on a series of numbers that came to her in a dream—5, 17, 19, 28, 30, 41—but she lost her money just the same.

A hummingbird hovered near the bougainvillea, indifferent to the caged birds nearby. Marta wondered whether the canaries envied the hummingbird its freedom. Which would she prefer? To be well fed and comfortable in a cage or free to work herself to death? Marta studied the backyard aviary with its aimless rows of extravagant birds. They seemed like so many rich housewives, bored behind their metal bars. Perhaps she would choose to work, only not so hard.

The day was growing hot and the birds needed fresh water. The mynah bird imitated a plane flying overhead. Marta filled a pitcher with the expensive water the man in the spangled truck delivered in ten-gallon canisters. La Doctora spent a fortune on this water for her birds, but she made Marta drink from the tap. *Paciencia, paciencia.* To survive this day and every day that followed, patience was what she would need most.

It didn't make sense to Marta that her boss had invited her to dinner. Certainly, Frankie Soon wouldn't do this to fire her after she'd been working full-time for just a month. He'd dismissed others without warning—Yannett Hernández and Paquita Cruz, to name two. But she was his best employee, and he knew it. It was true that she'd been complaining to him about everything lately, from the stopped-up toilets and inadequate lighting to the meager pay. The other women were too afraid to say anything, so she said it for them. Would he get rid of her over that?

Marta suspected that Frankie might try to co-opt her, make her stop speaking out on behalf of the other workers. Well, he would soon learn that she wasn't so easily bought off. Marta remembered Sandra Mejía, the girl they'd nicknamed Canary at the shoe factory in San Salvador. According to Evaristo, Sandra had been abducted by the *guardias* in the central market and never heard from again.

At the Back-to-Heaven dress factory, the gossip flowed as the women rushed to complete an order for two thousand flamenco skirts. It was difficult to sew on the double tiers of ruffles just right. If the stitching was too tight, the bottoms puckered and impeded the swirl of the skirts; too loose, and the ruffles hung there lifelessly. At lunchtime Dinora tried on one of the skirts, black with red polka dots, twirling around and stamping her feet. "*¡Ándale!*" the women cheered, clapping their hands to the rhythm.

Frankie stormed over and put an end to their fun: "Enough dancing! Back to work!" Then he singled out Marta. "You!" he said in front of everyone. "You will come to dinner with me tonight." It was impossible to concentrate after that. Speculation about Frankie's motives ricocheted around the factory faster than a flock of swallows. As the afternoon wore on, a consensus grew among the women that their gruff, potbellied boss was in love with Marta.

"What nonsense!" she retorted. But she secretly wondered whether it was true. All afternoon, she snuck glances at Frankie through the glass partition of his office. If she didn't inspect him too closely, he appeared to her like any well-to-do Latino instead of *un coreano*. He wasn't bad looking for someone his age and he had a lot of money. She could do a lot worse than Frankie Soon. Best of all, he was an American citizen, which meant that anyone who married him would become one, too. How old was Frankie, anyway? Nobody knew for sure. Marta studied the unnaturally black color of his hair and determined that it was dyed. He must be about sixty, she decided, a vain sixty.

Her coworkers said that Frankie was a serious gambler and went to Las Vegas twice a month. That he was a ladies' man and insisted that his girlfriends powder the napes of their necks. No matter that he had a wife back in Korea. Marta was just his type, Dinora insisted, busty and with a beautiful face. Usually he went for younger women, then wrote them big good-bye checks when he was through. Guilt was a good thing for a man to have, the women concluded.

To Marta's knowledge, Frankie hadn't disrespected a single one of the hundred and forty-two women who worked for him. But that didn't mean he paid them very well. Before punching out for the day, a group of workers, led by Dinora and Vilma Colón, came up to Marta and asked her to use her influence to get them a raise. Their boss could certainly afford it. He lived in a mansion in Long Beach, they said, drove a gold-trimmed Cadillac, slept on a mattress filled with goose down—not so much as a single feather inside.

Marta remembered the time she'd helped her father restring a neighbor's bed with rolls of twine. Papá was good with his hands and people often came to him for advice. Everyone respected José Antonio Claros. Now she didn't know whether he was dead or alive. She wondered how different her life would have been if Papá hadn't left them. In the countryside they'd survived without electricity, grown everything they ate, carved their own spoons and bowls. A bicycle had seemed an unimaginable luxury. Nobody made much of it because everyone lived this way. How many lifetimes ago was that?

The restaurant was in a mini-mall on Olympic Boulevard. It looked no different than dozens of other eateries along this stretch. Marta studied the signs in Korean. She liked the angularity of the script, how each word appeared well built, like a brick house. The Spanish alphabet didn't look nearly as sturdy. It was getting dark and the sky was a plague of purples and oranges. The sunsets here were nothing like the ones in El Salvador. Back home, the air wasn't dirty enough for such chemical razzle-dazzle.

Frankie was waiting for her in a back booth, grinning widely. He stood up and invited her to sit down. Marta realized with a start that she'd never seen her boss smile. At the factory, he was all business. Still, his teeth looked too perfect to be anything but dentures.

There was a charcoal grill built right into their table. It was made of the hardwood that repelled termites. The waiter kindled the coals with a flick of his plastic lighter, then served them two bowls of pickled cabbage that tasted like *curtido de repollo*.

"Are you so unhappy working for me?" Frankie asked, pouring Marta a glass of unstrained rice wine.

"*We* could be happier," she said, deliberately including the rest of her coworkers. The drink was thick and bitter tasting. "Please, I prefer a Coke."

Frankie called over the waiter. Marta liked the sound of their Korean. She felt an urge to imitate it, to slide her own vowels up and down the same slippery slope. A moment later, her drink arrived with a dozen little dishes. Marta tried the soybean-paste soup with baby clams first. Everything was hot and spicy. A whole meal of this and she would surely need to call the fire department.

Frankie showed her how to hold the chopsticks and complimented Marta on her dexterity. Then he topped off her rice bowl with choice bits of meat.

"Why did you leave your country?" he asked.

His stare made her uncomfortable, as if he could read her mind. Marta had heard that there were people who could do this without your knowing.

"I've told you already. Why are you asking me again?" The heat from the grill was suffocating.

"Did something bad happen to you?"

"No," she said firmly.

"Then why don't you have children?" Frankie persisted, his mouth filled with marinated beef.

Marta's eyes watered against her will. "That's none of your business."

The smoke momentarily obscured Frankie's face. He put down his chopsticks and leaned toward her. His face was flushed from the wine and the heat. It looked like a lantern, one of the old-fashioned kinds lit with oil. "Then please allow me tell you a story."

Marta settled back and drank her Coke. Frankie said that he'd grown up on a buckwheat farm, working side-by-side with his parents in the fields. He was a good student, and eventually enrolled at the University of Seoul. There he befriended many writers and poets and fancied himself a writer, though he never wrote more than a few rhymed verses. He told her all this slowly, deliberately, as if he'd been rehearsing it for a long time.

Then, to Marta's surprise, Frankie wiped his mouth with a napkin and recited: "'I'll go back to heaven again with the dusk, together, just we two at a sign from the cloud.' My best friend wrote that. He was killed by the secret police. They thought he was a Communist spy."

Marta wasn't sure what to think. If this was a ploy for her sympathy, she wouldn't give in. Poem or no poem, she needed to stay strong for the women at the factory.

Frankie recounted how the police then went after everyone in the poet's address book, how they tortured him for seven months in the basement of their headquarters, using water and electric shocks.

"For this reason," he continued. "I could not have children. So perhaps we're not so different, after all." The sorrow rose off his skin like steam.

"But you have a daughter in Korea," Marta asserted. She'd heard this from the factory accountant, who wired money to his wife and child on the first of every month. Marta wasn't going to let him get away with lying to her.

"Yes, she's my wife's daughter from her first marriage. They came with me to Los Angeles, but they didn't stay. In less than a year they returned to Seoul. Me, I cannot return home anymore."

Marta felt sorry for Frankie. She didn't want to; there was still so much to complain about. The women were counting on her to get them a raise, to secure at least a nickel more per piecework. At the end of the week, the coins added up. But Marta didn't have the heart to bring up business just then. She filled a pancake with strips of meat and asparagus and ate it, taco style. It was delicious, not as hot as the baby clams, and she asked for some lime on the side. Frankie ordered more rice wine.

"I know you're saving money to bring your brother here."

"Who told you?" Marta didn't like the idea of him spying on her. Had Dinora been indiscreet? But it was true. She had nearly a thousand dollars saved for Evaristo's passage. She would need another thousand for a first-rate *coyote*. There could be no risks. Evaristo was fragile, shaken by everything he'd seen. After last year's earthquake had knocked him from his tree, he was barely hanging on.

Frankie reached into his pocket and pulled out a canvas wallet. He counted out ten one-hundred-dollar bills and slid them to Marta's side of the table. She stared at the money. Why was he giving this to her?

"To help you with your brother."

"No, I can't take it." Marta thought how easy it would be to slip the money into her purse, arrange for Evaristo to join her.

It was unthinkable that they'd been apart for three long years. How the devil knew her weakness! Her hands felt swollen with temptation, like stuffed gloves. Was this where her life was pointing? To this Korean *viejito* from half a world away? Tomorrow she would consult Dinora again, ask her to burn candles on her behalf.

"Where do things that don't yet exist wait to be born?" Frankie asked her.

"Excuse me?"

"How long have I known you?"

"Not that long, maybe a year and a half." Marta ate another stuffed pancake; it had grown lukewarm on her plate. She noticed the diamonds on Frankie's ring. Were they fake, too, like his teeth?

"You're a good woman. I think we can grow old together."

"You're already old," Marta snapped. If he was looking for a mistress, he could just forget about it.

"Not so old," he defended himself.

"How old?" she challenged. "Tell the truth."

"Forty-two," Frankie said without hesitating. Then he started to laugh.

Marta looked over at her boss—at the faded chestnut brown of his eyes, at his shoe-polish hair and the liver spots speckling his manicured hands—and she couldn't help laughing, too.

Enrique Florit

It was the Friday after Thanksgiving, the biggest gambling day of the year, and Enrique was playing poker at the Diamond Pin. Las Vegas was filled with out-of-towners, hometown champs ready to pit their skills against the pros. Enrique looked around his table at the other players and recognized nobody. This was a good sign. He hoped to quickly dispatch with their money and move on to games with bigger stakes. That was where the real fun was, not grinding it out with these weekenders. It was just past four o'clock. There was still plenty of time.

Across from him, wobbly as a sunflower, a long-necked man wore padded yellow gloves and sunglasses, trying to hide his tells. To Enrique's left was a guy in a maroon suit with velvet lapels and to his right, a woman sporting a felt hat and a rosy, ravaged face. The woman said that she was an orthodontist from Oregon and referred to her poker chips, ridiculously, as ching-chang.

Enrique entertained himself by thinking of the two and a half million possible five-card hands in a deck of cards. But it didn't relieve the depressing poker being played today. His tablemates called every raise, played mediocre hands, lost a few hundred bucks, then raced across the casino to try to recoup their losses at blackjack or craps. They didn't have a clue about the game. Most aggravating was when these two-bit players got lucky and mistook it for skill. But as Jim Gumbel liked to say, it was the little people who kept the poker economy running.

Gumbel was at the edge of the action, talking with his partner, who had a fat plug of tobacco in his cheek. Lately, tax auditors had been coming around to the Diamond Pin and there was talk of it closing. Gumbel calmly dispelled the rumors. Enrique wasn't too worried either. After all, the man was a former outlaw in Texas (a copy of the 1952 WANTED poster hung in his office) and it hadn't stopped him any. Gumbel wasted no time in pointless deliberations. If it wasn't about poker, it didn't interest him.

Enrique decided to skip the next game and get something to eat. He was up three thousand dollars and would need a lot more than that for school. He'd been accepted to MIT but Papi had begged him to defer for a year, and so Enrique gambled a little and taught math classes at the community college instead. *Why do you want to go bury yourself in the snow, hijo? You're a smart boy. Whatever you would learn there, you could learn just as easily right here with me.* One year had stretched to three—mostly because he had to keep bailing his father out of one financial disaster after another—and he still didn't have enough money to break away.

At the Diamond Pin coffee shop, Enrique was settling down to lunch when a commotion broke out at the craps tables.

Someone had hit a hot streak and a crowd was gathering around. Enrique got a glimpse of the lucky woman. She was stunning, unlike anyone he'd ever seen. And he saw his fair share of beauties in Las Vegas. A chant went up around her: Lei-la! Lei-la! Lei-la!

Enrique wandered over and watched her from a distance. The woman was petite and caramel-skinned, flawless from every angle, with a halo of loose, lustrous hair. She wore tight jeans, a beige cashmere sweater, and dangling earrings. He tried to decipher her accent but he couldn't place it. Normally, Enrique didn't go near the craps tables. The game was no better than roulette. Pure chance and zero skill. Craps players, for all their talk of "systems," simply got lucky, or not.

Leila rode her luck another ten minutes before the dice turned against her. Enrique joined the crowd that was rallying to keep her going. Everyone was feeling the heat. Only he remained silent. Enrique wanted to tell this Leila to stop and cash in her chips, but he knew it was useless. She was going down. It was like watching a pearl dissolve before his eyes.

"Gambling is a branch of mathematics," Enrique ventured as she walked away from the craps table. "Every time you doubled your bet you were doubling the casino's advantage."

"Thanks for the advice, but it's a little late." Leila headed over to a slot machine and thrust in a quarter. No luck. She followed with more quarters in rapid succession.

"I don't know if you've noticed, but these aren't fair random generators. Slot machines are programmed for one purpose only: to make profits for the casinos. I should know. I helped design them."

This got her attention, but Leila only put her hands on her hips and turned away. Enrique noticed how her cashmere sweater clung to her breasts like a second skin.

"Look, play the minimum limits until you get ahead, then cash out and move to another slot," he said, trying hard not to stare at her. "Your chances of hitting a higher prize will increase."

Enrique went to the cashier and returned with fifty rolls of quarters in a bucket. "Let's get started."

"Why are you doing this?" Leila demanded.

"Whose money is in the bucket?" Enrique could tell she was growing intrigued. All those years of playing poker—of reading faces, the betraying twitch of muscle—were paying off.

"Are you in, then?"

Twenty minutes later, Leila was eight hundred dollars richer.

"So what do you play?" she asked. A wild garden smell drifted off her hair.

"Poker."

"Do you ever get lucky?"

"Sometimes. But the point is to become skilled enough so that luck is less important. Poker's a lot more like race-car driving than gambling." Enrique remembered what Johnny Langston used to tell him: Forget the money in the pot, boy. It's not yours anymore. What you gotta ask yourself is this: Are the odds in my favor? Then don't let anything stop you.

"So what are the odds of me buying you lunch?" Enrique asked.

"About a thousand to one."

He laughed. "What if I throw in a magic trick?"

"Your odds are improving, but only slightly."

"And a tour of Las Vegas?"

"Let's start with the trick," she said, bemused.

Enrique stopped to think for a minute. What would his father do? "Don't go away." He dashed into the coffee shop, ordered a cup of tea, and brought it back to Leila on the casino floor.

"Sugar?" he asked.

"Sure."

He sprinkled two packets into the steaming tea. "Taste it.

Make sure it's not too sweet." The cup rattled against the saucer as he offered it to her.

She took a sip and handed it back.

Enrique swirled the tea slowly, holding the cup in both hands, and muttered a few lines of José Martí: *"¡Ve!—que las seis estrellas luminosas te seguirán y te guiarán, y ayuda a tus hombros darán cuantos hubieran bebido el vino amargo de la vida!"* Then he turned the tea in the cup into quarters.

"How did you do that?" Leila was astonished.

"For you." Enrique grinned and poured the quarters into her hands. For once, being a magician's son had come in handy. "Now can we have lunch?"

Leila yielded without saying a word.

"Fried eggs and toast," she told the waitress in the checkered apron, who inspected her closely.

"Over easy?"

"Yes."

"And you?"

"Grilled cheese and tomato."

"Again?"

"What the hell." Enrique waved her away.

The set of Leila's back stiffened and she leaned forward, as if about to take flight. Enrique thought of inviting her to Papi's early show at the Stardust. He had a new trick, in which he turned volunteers from the audience into a flock of geese. Instead Enrique told her about another poker player making the rounds, a cherubic fur trader from Saskatchewan whom everyone called the Fatal Angel on account of his gimmicky toga and deadpan stare.

"Did you see how that old crone was checking me out?" Leila interrupted. Her hands traced the air with fine gestures. "I get so sick of this. Sometimes I pretend to be an Indian to avoid the stupid questions."

"What questions?" Enrique loved the dark registers of her voice.

"About the Ayatollah. Or didn't you know he's declared you the number one enemy of Iran?"

"Me personally?" he joked, but she wasn't amused.

The waitress reappeared with their orders. Leila aggressively dipped her toast into an egg yolk, ignoring the charred bacon she hadn't ordered. One of her aunts, she said, had cured her husband's wrenched neck with applications of dried bread and egg yolk. Her Aunt Parvin had a remedy for everything: migraines, joint pain, gallstones, double vision. She was not beneath using leeches or cupping glasses when she deemed it necessary.

"Some people believe anything can be fixed," Leila said. "It's a mechanical view of life, don't you think?"

Before Enrique could answer, Leila dropped her bread in disgust. She said that neither the toast nor the egg had any specific taste, a taste that said, This is an egg, this is a piece of bread. "In Iran, bread is baked in a hole in the ground, ten feet deep, and it's shaped like a big, flat cake. It speaks, it shouts: I am bread!"

"Are you homesick?"

"Pah!" Leila was embarrassed. "How important is bread, anyway?"

Enrique took a bite of his grilled cheese. It was already cold and congealing to plastic. He wanted to say that he understood her perfectly. The smallest details—a Spanish street name, the taste of pineapple jam—could catapult him back to a life that no longer existed.

"Where do you pretend to be from?"

"An Arctic tribe called the Pedersags. In Farsi it means 'Your father's a dog.'"

"I should be flattered that you didn't try that on me," Enrique laughed.

"Yes," Leila said, staring right at him. "You should be."

Enrique got so flustered that he went on about some nature program he'd watched on Alaskan otters during one of the many nights he couldn't sleep, thinking about how he was wasting his life away. In the show, the otters floated on their backs leisurely cracking clams on their stomachs. What if everyone could be that self-contained?

"Your hair, it's beautiful," he practically shouted.

Leila scrutinized his fringed suede jacket and his western shirt with the mother-of-pearl buttons, which were his finest clothes. Then she looked down at his pressed jeans and rattlesnake-skin boots. She probably thought he was some kind of cowboy. Did she like what she saw? Enrique couldn't tell. His senses were in disarray under her gaze.

"Where are you from?" Leila asked, breaking the spell.

"Cuba. I'm from Cuba."

Then, for no particular reason, Enrique told her about the time he was three years old and jumped out the second-story window of his grandparents' house in Cárdenas, determined to fly. Word of the "miracle" spread and the whole neighborhood crowded into his grandparents' kitchen. Tía Adela predicted that Enrique would become the next pope. "*¡Imagínate!* A Cuban pope!" That same year, his aunt was forced to fight in the Bay of Pigs and got shrapnel in her stomach that lurched north like a compass after every meal.

"Do you ever wish you'd stayed?" Leila asked.

"Sometimes. But I'd probably be off fighting in Angola or someplace." Enrique felt his throat swelling up. "So where do you live?"

"Los Angeles."

"I lived in Santa Monica when I was a kid. What keeps you there?"

"School." Leila hesitated. "And my fiancé. We're getting married in two weeks."

Enrique tracked the rapid descent of his heart. "You're engaged?"

"We leave for Tehran next Friday. Hundreds of people are coming to the wedding. Relatives I didn't even know I had."

"What brought you here then?"

"I guess you could say I was testing my luck."

"And?" Enrique winced, anticipating more pain.

"So far, so good."

Coño, she was making him crazy. What kind of chance did he have with her? The same principles applied in love and poker, Enrique reminded himself, or so his Texan friends claimed. *When in doubt, opt for the bolder approach.*

"May I invite you to dinner?"

"We haven't even finished lunch," Leila teased him.

"The International Ballroom Competition is on at the Tropicana tonight. Do you dance?" He had to think of something to keep her near.

"Will you be performing?"

"I will if you come." Enrique issued a pleading smile.

"What's your specialty?"

"The maxixe. It's a Brazilian two-step. Not too many people know about it outside Rio. Actually, my father is competing. He's a hell of a dancer. I'd love for you to meet him."

"Meet him or dance with him?"

"There usually isn't much difference."

"I'd like to go, but I need to get home. My fiancé will worry."

"He didn't mind you coming to Las Vegas?" Enrique figured things couldn't be that great between them if she was here by herself.

"We made a deal," Leila said.

"Don't ask, don't tell?"

"Sort of. But he's still expecting me back tonight."

"Fear makes no exceptions then."

"What?"

"Let me take you."

"To L.A.?"

"Why not?" Enrique felt exhilarated all of a sudden, as if he were playing poker with wild cards. What were the odds of having her to himself for the five-hour drive? Low, he calculated, exceedingly low. A monkey typing out the word *Hamlet* (one in 15,625,000,000) had better odds.

"I'm not sure —"

"Look into my eyes," he insisted.

"Now what? Are you going to hypnotize me?"

"Trust your instincts."

Leila inspected him again, then offered him her arm. Enrique, exultant, escorted her through the maze of flashing slot machines, toward the exit. On their way out, they ran into Papi walking through the door dressed in full Ching Ling Foo regalia. What the hell was he doing at the Diamond Pin this early?

"*Mi hijo, ¿qué tal?* And who is this ravishing beauty at your side?" he crooned, dropping his many acquired accents and reverting to his original Cuban one. Papi held out his hand and took Leila's, planting a languorous kiss on her knuckles. "I haven't seen you around here, *mi amor.* It's a pleasure to make your acquaintance."

"I thought you said you were Cuban," Leila accused Enrique.

"We are. This is just his costume. I mean, my father's a magician and this is his stage persona." Enrique shot his father a desperate look. "Dad, help me out here."

"*Sí, preciosa.* Beneath the sophisticated veneer of the Great Court Conjurer to the Empress of China lies someone — believe it or not — even more intriguing. Here," Fernando said, pressing Leila's hand over his brocade-upholstered chest, "lies a heartbroken man, a man of exile, a man whose adventures throughout the uncivilized worlds could fill many volumes. Did I tell you, my jewel, that I have the hearing of a desert hare?"

This was too much for Enrique. His father's hearing had returned to normal years ago, even before he'd left the hospital. In fact, he was probably half deaf by now. No matter that Papi was obese or that his scars were visible through his thick stage

makeup. When it came to women, he was one hundred percent
Cuban.

"I'm driving Leila back to L.A. today," Enrique said tightly.
"She's getting *married* in two weeks."

"But you are much too young! *Ay,* I was married once to a
wonderful woman. My son's mother, in fact. Everything I do is
in her memory."

Enrique wanted to say: including putting the moves on other
women. But he kept his mouth shut. Maybe if he stayed quiet,
this would all be over sooner.

"My darling dove!" his father began to sob. "My rivulet of
honey! How I miss her so!" His tears left tiny tracks in his
makeup.

"You poor thing," Leila said, patting him on the shoulder
with her free hand.

"She was my mother, too," Enrique chimed in pathetically.
He couldn't believe that he was competing with his father for
this woman's sympathy. They were both sinking to new lows.
"We need to leave. Dad, please let go of Leila's hand."

His father looked up forlornly. "Perhaps I could accompany
you? I have some business to attend to in Los Angeles."

"No fucking way!" Enrique blurted out. "I mean, no. No,
Dad. You need to stay here. Remember the ballroom competition tonight?"

"Yes, of course." Papi straightened up. "Many people are
counting on me."

"Do gamblers bet on dancing, too?" Leila asked.

"Everyone bets on everything here," Enrique said glumly.
"Even the number of sugar packets in a bowl."

"I am favored to win third place," Papi offered modestly.

"But he'll probably place first. He usually does." Enrique
was feeling more charitable now that his father had backed off
from the trip.

"It requires gyrations of the utmost finesse," Papi added,

trilling his *r*'s and winking at Leila. "But I must be inspired. And you, bright light of the Orient, feast for my tired eyes, have provided it for me. Are you a Gemini?"

"Why, yes."

"I knew it! Just like my son. June twentieth?"

Leila looked surprised. "Are you an astrologer, too?"

"Well, my dear—"

"Pure coincidence," Enrique interrupted.

"Would you do me the honor of attending the competition?" Papi ventured. "With you in the audience, my nightingale, how could I not dance my best?"

Enrique began to protest, but Leila interrupted him.

"I would love to," she said.

"What about your fiancé?" Enrique stammered.

"He can wait one more day."

"How delightful! You know, my goddess, you are in the best of hands with my son," Papi threw in generously. "He is a man of character, an exemplary man. Above all, he is sincere. Trustworthy, kind, to be cherished—"

"No need to overdo it, Dad."

"You float over everything! Son of my soul!"

"Okay, we're out of here," Enrique said, quickly steering Leila into the bright shock of the afternoon.

"Be gentle with him, my beauty!" Papi called out after them. "He is my greatest treasure!"

"He's cute," Leila said once they were outside.

"Cute?"

"No, I mean it. He looks just like that—"

"Please don't say Ricky Ricardo."

After dinner at the Flamingo's penthouse restaurant, Enrique escorted Leila to the ballroom dance competition at the Tropicana Hotel. His father had arranged a ringside table for them. Enrique was used to glitzy events in Las Vegas but the jungle decor and the sequined-and-feathered contestants far exceeded his expectations. Papi looked more elegant than most in his white tuxedo with the plum-colored lapels. His shoes were black and blindingly shiny, the better to show off his intricate steps. His partner was a Brazilian woman four inches taller than him. Her stage name was La Víbora, and Enrique soon saw why. At the climax of their routine, she had a gyrating Papi suspended horizontally between her powerful thighs.

In the heat of a competition, his father's health ailments evaporated entirely and he moved like a man decades younger. He spun La Víbora across the dance floor, then lifted her high above his head as he executed a series of dizzying pirouettes. When they finally came to a stop—Papi was balanced sculpturally in the palms of La Víbora's hands—the crowd went wild, jumping on tabletops and roaring their approval.

Leila got caught up in the excitement and twisted an ankle trying to clamber onto a chair in her high-heeled gold sandals. Papi blew kisses in her direction, which she avidly returned. Enrique was impressed with his father, of course—how could he not be?—but he was flooded with a growing sense of resentment. When would *he* ever be the star of the show? Why was it so impossible to escape his father's shadow? What woman had ever jumped on a chair for him?

Enrique didn't want to wait until the end of the competition but Leila insisted on staying. Unsurprisingly, Fernando Florit and La Víbora won first prize with a special citation for their "extravagant creativity."

When Papi approached their table, still holding his trophy, Leila threw her arms around him and gave him a kiss.

"You were great, as always." Enrique tried to muster up some enthusiasm. Whatever his feelings, there was no denying his father's talent.

"*Gracias, hijo.* I couldn't have done it without you. And I was doubly inspired by the presence of our lovely desert rose from Arabia!"

"Leila's from Iran, Dad. It's not the same thing."

"*Bueno,* what are you two going to do now?"

Enrique hesitated. It was nearly three in the morning. Would Papi try to horn in on his date?

"Why don't you go swimming?"

"Swimming?" Enrique asked.

"To refresh yourselves before the long drive back."

"That's a great idea," Leila said. "I'm not sleepy at all. Won't you join us, Fernando?"

"No, no, my dear. My exertions have been sufficient for one evening. But I wish you a safe journey, and"—he leaned over to kiss her hand, his forehead still shiny with sweat—"my enduring veneration."

An hour later, after buying swimsuits in a twenty-four-hour gift shop, Enrique and Leila ventured into the Flamingo Hotel's swimming pool. It was closed but the guard, who'd known Enrique since he was a boy, unlocked the gate for them. Leila looked stunning in the remains of the moonlight, her face like mahogany, her dark eyes steady on his. Why did she make him so nervous? Why couldn't he be as easy with her as his father?

"Will you have to return home for good?" Enrique asked. They'd been talking about the revolution in her country.

"Maybe." Leila said her worst fear was that everyone would be forced to swim in a divided sea again, like in the old days: men on one side; women on the other, dressed in yards of black nylon. More than anything, she wanted to swim freely in the Caspian Sea. Her family had spent a happy summer there when she was nine. The best caviar came from the sturgeon in those waters, she said, and they'd eaten it daily for weeks.

"Caviar every day?" Enrique was incredulous, although he knew some high rollers in Las Vegas who boasted the same. He noticed the tan lines along Leila's neck and wrists and fought the urge to lick them. "Do you scuba dive?"

"How did you know?"

Enrique pointed to her wrists.

"I can see why you're good at poker."

"Where do you dive?"

"San Diego, mostly. Once in Baja. Everyone there spoke to me in Spanish." Leila shrugged. Then she told him about the time she'd seen a baby leopard shark off the coast of Rosarito. A huge school of baitfish also spotted the shark and turned together, as if on cue. "Do you think they take turns being leader?"

"Baitfish: democracy or dictatorship?" Enrique said in his best newscaster voice, but Leila didn't laugh. She seemed preoccupied. He would give up a year of his life to read her mind.

Enrique watched her swim back and forth along the length of the pool. She favored the breaststroke but she also swam on her back and side. She was more graceful than any human had a right to be. He could have watched her for the rest of his life. If only he felt confident enough to kiss her. But he couldn't get past the fact of her impending marriage. This was just the kind of wavering that Papi would have deemed defeatist, even unpatriotic. Every Cuban man, no matter his looks or his station in life, believed that even the most unattainable woman was within his reach.

❧

At dawn, they finally got on the road. Enrique opened the car door for Leila (he was relieved that he'd cleaned his Maverick the day before) and waited until she was settled before closing it. American girls made a point of commenting on his good manners — Papi said that it was the one thing that never failed a man—but Leila seemed accustomed to the royal treatment. They picked up cigarettes, beer, and some spicy tortilla chips at a nearby convenience store.

On the outskirts of town, Enrique was tempted to stop at Sol's Tattoo Parlor. He wanted to have Leila's name seared onto his shoulder in Persian lettering but he didn't want to scare her off. Would the Texans have risked it? Hell, yeah. So what did this say about him? Instead Enrique talked to Leila about mechanical engineering. It turned out she was majoring in it, specializing in factory robots. Leila was a junior at UCLA, where her fiancé was getting a double Ph.D. in nuclear and accelerator physics.

Enrique tried not to feel too wretched. Fact: Leila was sitting next to *him* right now. Anything could happen in five hours. He'd also managed to keep his father from coming along and ruining everything. That was a victory in itself. Enrique needed to concentrate on maximizing his possibilities. The rest he would figure out later. He suspected, though, that even the most accurate predictive systems could be wrecked by love.

It was a clear day. The clouds were piled high and spaced far apart. Nearby a train trundled by on its way to Salt Lake City, past a dusty clump of prickly pear. Dogs barked against the barbed-wire fence of a fallen-down house, all emptiness and neglect. Now and then tumbleweeds crossed their path. Enrique drove in the right lane, as slowly as he could without arousing suspicion. He wanted to make the trip last as long as possible.

Leila fiddled with the radio, trying to find a news station. She was curious about where the Shah and his wife would end up. She'd lost track of the countries that had rejected them since they'd fled Iran. Many of her relatives were leaving the country, too, unsure if they would ever return. Leila said that her father had been tortured by the Shah's secret police, that patches of his back were hideously scarred.

She said that her Iranian friends in Los Angeles wasted time endlessly comparing the two countries, in pointless debates fueled by cigarettes and tea. It got to the point that she could barely stand listening to their Persian classical music tapes. Too much nostalgia was like eating too many sweets, she said. It left you sick to your stomach.

Enrique drove past a diner with a huge American flag hanging limply on its pole. Several trucks idled in the parking lot, their tire flaps sporting the same chrome silhouette of a naked woman. A pile of gravel took up most of the lot's north end. Everyone talked about living the American dream, but what about its ravages? Wasn't that the more common story?

"Green card, green card. It's all anyone talks about here. But even if they hate it, they don't want to go home."

"Are they hard to get?" Enrique asked.

"The best way is to marry an American citizen." Leila lit a cigarette and blew the smoke out the window. Her mouth made a perfect pink O as she blew. "But that costs money."

"How much?"

"Two thousand dollars. Easier than falling in love, no?"

Leila turned the radio knob again, switching rapidly from station to station, singing along to random songs, moving to the music in her beige cashmere top. It was all Enrique could do to keep his eyes on the road. Remarkably, Leila knew many of the lyrics. Her voice wasn't worth a damn but her accent made the words sound elegant somehow.

> *Well, I woke up this morning, and I got myself a beer*
> *The future's uncertain, and the end is always near . . .*

Enrique felt himself falling hard. Hadn't his own parents gotten engaged in a day? Maybe brief courtships were a genetic thing. In 1956 Papi had been in Panama City for a week of performances at the Teatro Darío when he'd noticed Mamá at the Hindu bazaar downtown. It was unclear what happened next but that very evening, Sirena Carranza took Fernando

Florit home and introduced him to her parents as her fiancé. When they protested, Sirena threatened to burn herself alive on a pyre like the widows in India.

"I want to show you something," Leila said, taking a pair of worn brown socks from her purse. She said they were her dead brother's, that she wore them when taking her college exams. "I guess they didn't work too well yesterday."

Enrique was curious about her brother but he was afraid to stir up any grief. He knew how impossible it was to make the dead seem like they were ever alive. Time wore everything down. He wanted to tell Leila about his mother, about the look she'd given him before she died. But even that had faded to a vague memory.

This past year, Papi had tried contacting Mamá through clairvoyants and mediums of various ethnic persuasions, the latest a Croatian sorcerer with offices behind Caesars Palace. (The sorcerer claimed that Houdini had regularly contacted his beloved dead wife in this manner.) Nothing worked. Last Valentine's Day, Papi started writing baroque love letters to Mamá. He kept the letters chronologically ordered in manila folders should anyone—namely, Enrique—ever question his devotion. But Enrique suspected that the letters were like everything else about Papi, mostly for show.

"Do you want to go scuba diving?" he asked suddenly.

Leila rolled down her window to a blast of desert air. She popped open a beer and took a long swallow, making sure the paper bag camouflaged the can. Then she lit another cigarette. "Sure."

Enrique passed a pickup truck going forty miles an hour. He felt his blood moving at least twice that fast. He wanted to say something, anything, but he couldn't form the words. The radio turned to static then reemerged as a country station.

I walk for miles
along the highway

Well, that's just my way
of saying "I love you."
I'm always walkin'
after midnight
searchin' for you . . .

"It's pretty here," Leila said, dark strands of her hair lifting in the wind.

Enrique had driven this stretch of I-15 before with people who'd thought it a wasteland. They couldn't appreciate the subtle shifts of landscape, the way the light claimed the faintest shadow. They didn't notice the cactus wrens or the creosote or the quartz glinting off the cliffs. They didn't know that cloudbursts could drop an inch of rain in an hour, inciting flash floods, or that the desert bloomed gloriously in spring.

This woman was too good to be true. What would happen if he pulled to the side of the road and begged her to run away with him?

Leila fell asleep for the next hour. Enrique savored the simple luxury of staring at her. Twice he started to touch her throat, the gentle slopes of her shoulders, but he made himself stop. What would she think if she woke up? Leila stirred and looked at him, momentarily disoriented. Enrique told her stories about the ghost lakes in the region. Coyote Lake and Ivanpah Lake, to name only two. He liked the fact that mapmakers bothered to mention what was already long gone.

"How old were you when your mother died?" Leila asked tentatively.

"Six."

"What happened?"

"It was my father's fault." He was surprised at the vehemence in his voice.

"He killed her?"

"Not exactly."

Overhead, a pair of red-tailed hawks circled. They could

have made ribbons of the sky, sent down curling blue strips of it onto the white vinyl roof of his car. Enrique loved these hawks, the way their claws seemed to smoke with triumph whenever they got their prey. Unlike people, birds were uncomplicated. Everything they did was for a reason. Their survival depended on it.

In the split second that it took Enrique to point out the hawks to Leila, he heard the frantic honking. He spotted the eighteen-wheeler in his rearview mirror, barreling down on them with all its crude power, its brakes gone. The mirror seemed to frame the moment for later recollection. Enrique flashed on something his father had told him: Every beat of your heart has two possibilities, stop or go.

He stepped on the accelerator and twisted the steering wheel. The truck nipped the back of his Maverick—he felt the thick sleeve of air as it passed—sending them into an endless tailspin before spitting the car off the narrow road into the desert dust. Miraculously, they landed on four wheels. Around them was nothing but light and a ringing silence.

Leila was slumped against the passenger window. Her nose was bleeding and there was a cut along her cheek like a pink seam. She kept touching her nose with her fingertips.

"Are you okay?" Enrique took her hand and kissed it, tasting the blood.

Leila closed her eyes. Her face was pale and damp all over. It took every ounce of restraint Enrique had not to kiss her. He peered through the cracked windshield. The truck was toppled two hundred yards ahead of them. At that distance it looked like a toy, except there were flames and smoke billowing from its sides. Maybe the driver had died that instant.

Just then the truck's back doors blew open and dozens of monkeys clambered out, screeching and scurrying into the desert like a pack of deranged jackrabbits. One monkey, a little brown one, had a broken arm crazily angled at the elbow. Enrique kept staring at the monkey as it scuttled toward the car, screeching and chattering to itself. Then it jumped on the hood of his Maverick, baring its teeth, before joining the other monkeys in the desert. But where could they go? There were no trees for them to hide in, only the Joshua trees, which were impossible to hide in.

Enrique thought of how random energies approached a common point before exploding. Chance intersecting with history and logic and reasonable expectations. Forbidden knowledge made visible, effaced and divine, as the gods busily issued disclaimers. In the end, everything was measured against mystery. One hundred and twelve rhesus monkeys that should have been swinging in the jungles of India but were, instead, destined for research labs in southern California had been set free in the Mojave Desert. What were the fucking odds of that?

PART TWO

A white star fell into the garden,
Unexpected, unsought. Luck,
arrow, flower, fire . . .

— LUCIAN BLAGA

(1981)

Marta Claros

It was dark when Marta woke up and headed to her backyard chicken coop. The first hints of light stirred the sky, as
if the day were coming from far away. Marta walked past
her arbor of bougainvillea and the rosebushes she'd planted last
summer. She'd dug an herb garden, too, as Dinora Luna suggested, to have fresh remedies on hand against others' ill inten-
tions: rosemary, lemongrass, chili peppers, spearmint. Their
mingled scents made Marta feel safe.

It was against city ordinances to keep chickens in Los Angeles, but Marta wasn't the only one in her neighborhood raising
them. Those who didn't have chickens were bought off with
fresh eggs, so there was little danger of getting caught. Marta
cracked open the door to her coop and stooped inside to the
soft clucking of hens.

Buenos días, señoras. ¿Cómo amanecieron? She breathed in the acrid scent of the hay and shed feathers. If only she could settle in among them, know the sweet ache of laying an egg. Her body seemed so stingy in comparison.

Marta went from nest to dusty nest, gently checking under the hens for eggs. Nothing from Carmen or Elsa. Nothing from Malva, Hortensia, or Pura. Nothing from the usually prolific Verónica. Only Daisy was left. *No te asustes. Así, así.* Marta hated to disturb Daisy, but she didn't want her thinking she could forgo an inspection altogether. As Marta reached toward her, the hen pecked her hard on the knuckle. It didn't hurt but a speck of blood oozed forth, as if her skin had sprung a slow leak.

¿Tienes algo para mí, preciosa? Marta slid her hand beneath the reddish hen and felt the contours of one perfect egg. She picked it up, still warm from Daisy's body, and brought it to her lips. Carefully, Marta passed the egg along her face and neck, down her bosom and belly and between her legs. She prayed that some of Daisy's fertility might rub off on her.

Frankie complained to Marta about the number of eggs she collected. It wasn't normal, he said, to leave them on plump pillows around the house. Nobody he knew sewed clothes for them either. Eggs, he said, were for eating. Marta defended herself. At least she didn't sleep with the chickens, the way her mother used to do. What did it matter that she'd bought them a crib and a baby blanket?

"Crazy woman, what are you doing?" Frankie demanded when he saw the egg-filled crib. Marta refused to answer. Did she need to explain to him that the highest form of love was obligation?

In the prosperous neighborhoods of Los Angeles, the parks were filled with babies handed over to nannies to raise. Marta heard of one pregnant mother in Santa Monica who spoke openly of maybe aborting her child, her second. After her daughter was born, she went unnamed for six months. According to Celestina Pulayo, who worked two doors down from the family, the mother referred to her child simply as "the nanny baby."

Recently, several of Frankie's workers had quit to take babysitting jobs on the Westside. The hours were long, but the jobs were easy. It wasn't difficult to watch a child or two. Depending on the family, there was a lot of money to be made—three hundred dollars a week, or more, especially if you had a driver's license and spoke good English. Stories spread of families fighting over the best babysitters, bribing them with Christmas bonuses and vacations in Hawaii.

Sometimes unexpected problems arose. One woman Marta knew grew so enamored of her divorced boss that she stole his underwear and danced with his empty suits in the master bedroom. Silvia Camacho had bought a hat just like the one her *patrón* wore, and made her husband wear it when they made love. Marta couldn't imagine this happening to her. She wasn't nearly so romantic. In fact, she wasn't even sure she'd ever been in love. Only this much was certain: she longed to hold a baby in her arms.

"*Mamacita*, take it easy," Frankie said, discouraging her. "You've been working since you were five."

But Marta didn't want to stay home without a child of her own. Only Evaristo understood her. He asked her about her chickens and marveled at the size and sturdiness of their eggs. Thanks to Frankie's generosity, Evaristo had made it safely across the border. He was eating heartily and putting on weight, too. All cleaned up, he was a handsome man. At dusk he liked to climb the eucalyptus tree in their backyard. He stayed there for hours, quietly surveying the neighborhood.

From the time he was a child, people had said that Evaristo wasn't right in the head. But just because he didn't say much didn't mean he was stupid. Evaristo carried everything inside him. He'd told Marta about the fresh bodies littering San Salvador's parks and garbage dumps every morning, their faces slashed to pulp or burned with battery acid, their spinal cords exposed. Once Evaristo had come upon a pile of corpses, mutilated women stacked neatly behind a seafood restaurant, all wearing American jeans.

The first day Marta brought her brother to work at the factory, there was a near riot among the women. "You didn't tell us he looked like a movie star!" "He's just like that actor on *Today! Tomorrow! Never!*" Not a decent stitch of work got done for a week and Frankie had to let him go. Evaristo was oblivious to the chaos. Mostly, his gaze drifted toward the factory's one paned window, where the fronds of a palm tree beckoned more persuasively than the women around him.

Evaristo then tried cleaning offices at night, like poor Tío Víctor; "poor" because their uncle had fallen down an empty elevator shaft and been killed. The building's insurance company gave his Mexican wife two thousand dollars for his life. *¡Qué desgraciados!* Marta accompanied Evaristo on his rounds— emptying ashtrays, wiping down dusty desks, scrubbing toilets with disinfectants that stung their hands. Every night, he recounted more of the atrocities he'd seen.

Soon Evaristo grew depressed with this existence, eating little and sleeping all day. *Necesito estar afuera, bajo un cielo azul.* So Marta set him up with boxes of wholesale oranges and mangoes to sell on freeway off-ramps. She got him a Sunday job, too, handing out flyers for a fried chicken drive-through wearing a clown outfit and stilts. But Evaristo wasn't aggressive enough and he was fired. Finally, with Marta's encouragement, he began peddling crucifixes.

❧

It was hard to tell how the day would turn out. The sky was overcast and the spring winds were quiet. Only a sliver of blue shone through the upholstering clouds. Marta carried Daisy's egg in one hand and walked toward the house, a metallic taste on her tongue. She stopped to admire her sunflowers, which were nearly six feet tall. How optimistic they seemed, as if there would be no end of water and sunshine just for them.

Across the street, a bum was digging in the garbage bins for soda cans to recycle. Scrub jays screeched and fought in the laurel tree; another pecked apart a plastic bag in the gutter. The German shepherd next door chased the same stray cat. Today, Mr. Haley was painting his porch a bright orange. Marta waved at him and he swung his roller brush back at her, spattering paint. She picked up the newspapers — a Korean one for Frankie, the Spanish one for her. *El Diario* reported that three hundred people had been massacred near the Río Sapo in the province of Morazán. One nine-year-old boy had survived by hiding in a poinciana tree. There was a picture of him in the paper, looking small and scared. He reminded Marta of her brother as a boy.

The light in their bedroom was on. No doubt Frankie was doing his morning rituals: inspecting his gums, exercising his face muscles — to prevent their collapse, he said. Marta was convinced that he was a hypochondriac. Frankie swore he would die of a brain hemorrhage or a heart attack (his cholesterol *was* very high) or, worse still, some illness he couldn't pronounce. He revised his will regularly, spelling out his concerns: *Mr. Soon is to be ensured of a quiet death, not one with paroxysms of pain.* Frankie took to obsessively swatting flies, believing they carried lethal diseases. But Marta drew the line at his using insecticides in the house.

"You'll kill us both!" she protested.

For his last birthday — Frankie maintained it was his forty-fifth; Marta suspected it was his sixty-fifth — she bought him a baby Chihuahua to distract him. The six-pound Pablo turned out to be a big hit at the factory, where the women fed him lunch scraps and adopted him as Back-to-Heaven's unofficial mascot. Marta wished that Frankie would take the dog and leave for work early so that she could go shopping in peace.

Instead he intercepted her in the kitchen in his underwear and socks.

"Another egg?" Frankie asked warily. He'd been drinking and playing poker in Gardena the night before, and he looked unsteady.

Marta could always tell when Frankie lost money, although he didn't comment on his winnings or losses.

"*Sí, mi amor.*"

"Will you cook it for me?"

"You have your oatmeal." Marta was touched by Frankie's hairless, sagging chest. She could almost pretend he was her baby. "What did Dr. Meyerstein say?"

"I hate oatmeal."

"Remember your heart, *mi vida.*"

"*Hijo de la gran puta,*" Frankie growled.

Marta pretended to ignore him, smiling to herself. Her *chinito* certainly cursed beautifully in Spanish. She sat down to breakfast: corn tortillas, last night's beans, a helping of cream. After Frankie left for work, she climbed into the brand-new van he'd given her for Valentine's Day. It was light blue and had air-conditioning and bucket seats. Marta turned on the radio, switching to her favorite station. She drove in the slow lane of the freeway, the better to pay attention to the morning edition of *Pregunta a la psicóloga.*

It was a scandalous show. Ninety-nine percent of the callers were women lamenting their unfaithful husbands. Marta frequently argued out loud with Dr. Dolores Fuertes de Barriga, the on-air psychologist, who was a broken record on one subject: how secrets destroyed relationships. What nonsense! If Marta knew anything, it was how to keep a secret. To let a man know everything inside you was pure foolishness. Why give away your power for nothing?

When Marta got frustrated with the psychologist, she turned the dial to *¡Salvado!* on the AM Christian station. The show's host, a Colombian nun from the Sisters of Mercy, interviewed people whose lives had been turned around by the Lord. This morning Gonzalo Echevarría, a womanizing drunk and discount furniture clerk, testified how he'd gotten the heavenly knock last Easter morning. Gonzalo vowed that he was sober now, a good husband, and had been promoted to assistant manager of the furniture store, which, by the way, was having a big sale on leather recliners this weekend.

Marta headed downtown to the wholesale shopping district, to the alley that sold religious articles. She needed to stock up for all the weddings and First Communions in the spring. Evaristo peddled rosaries, crucifixes, evil eye pins, and dashboard saints (the bobbling Saint Anthony was especially popular) outside the churches of South Central. Marta bought things for him by the dozen, vigorously bargaining with the mostly Chinese vendors. She knew they respected her for not settling on too high a price. Come work for us, they joked.

The crucifixes in Sid Wong's display case were twenty percent off. Marta didn't care for the depictions of Christ with glow-in-the-dark blood but Evaristo insisted that these sold best, particularly after High Mass at Saint Regina's. (The pastor there was known for his gruesome depictions of hell.) Marta lamented that Frankie was an atheist and her brother hadn't set foot in a church since her wedding. The church in her neighborhood was especially pretty, with lilies at Eastertime, and the priests worked extra hard on their sermons. Maybe she could convince Evaristo to go again. It might help him heal. She could help him pick one saint to concentrate on, someone who would protect him.

Marta lived in fear that the police would arrest her brother. It happened on street corners every day. When Evaristo disappeared for two days last winter, she was convinced that he was dead or in jail. It turned out that a woman, now his girlfriend, had picked him up on Crenshaw Boulevard and taken him home. Marta suspected that despite his good looks, Evaristo had been a virgin. The woman, Rosita Cueva, was from

Juchitán and most likely a *bruja*. How else could she have so bewitched him?

There was a stall downtown that sold the best trinkets against the evil eye. Enameled medallions of the Virgin Mary were also on display and Marta decided to buy one for herself. If she wore it day and night, maybe La Virgen would take pity on her and bless her with a baby. No matter that Frankie claimed that he couldn't have children. Miracles happened every day. Look at that woman who'd gotten pregnant by her sterile husband an hour before he was killed in a drive-by shooting.

Frankie wanted a baby, too, but Marta knew that it was mostly for her sake. His only condition was that any child of his would have to attend Korean school.

"Who will help him with his homework?" Marta demanded.

"I will," he promised, and she believed him.

Since her first dinner with Frankie, he'd shown her nothing but kindness. He was far from perfect—an overgrown baby, if truth be told—but there was nothing malicious about him. Frankie was like the sugarcane he was cultivating out back: brittle on the outside but pure sweetness inside.

The women at the factory—except for Dinora, who defended Marta—jealously gossiped about their union. He couldn't marry Marta because he had a wife in Korea and a divorce was impossible. Well, she wasn't officially divorced from her husband either. (She'd heard that Fabián had remarried some country girl, which made him a bigamist on top of a *pendejo*.) Marta promised herself that she would send for the paperwork for a proper church annulment.

Last March she and Frankie had moved into their house. It was an old Craftsman, built in the 1920s, and falling apart. There was a hole in the roof and half the floorboards were rotting but Frankie had bargained it down to a good price. They decided to fix it up little by little. He'd put her name on the deed, too, though they weren't officially married. The official part didn't bother Marta. As far as she was concerned, Frankie was her husband. When he went off gambling and drinking with two condoms in his wallet, she didn't mind so much. Most of the time, the condoms stayed right where he put them.

Marta stopped at a luncheonette for a bite to eat. The mix of offerings on the chalkboard tempted her—cheeseburgers and *chilaquiles*, ramen soup, *pupusas*, chow mein, goat stew. "I'll have the chow mein and an *horchata*," she ordered. In Los Angeles, it was possible to become someone other than who you started out to be. You could go from poor to rich and back again, learn to speak another language, accustom your tongue to different spices. You could buy steak for eighty-nine cents a pound. This couldn't have happened back home. Who dreamed of going beyond what they knew? In El Salvador, each generation repeated the patterns of the one before. Even her brother had a chance at a new life here. If he could make it, she thought, anybody could.

Marta finished her chow mein and ordered a piece of apple pie à la mode. She was tempted to call the radio psychologist and ask about Frankie's dream. On Sunday, he'd woken up again with tears in his eyes. He'd dreamt that his mother was pounding barley in their backyard, her breasts swaying, her thinning hair white. The sun was setting like a rotten pumpkin, and her mud-walled hut had four doors. She offered Frankie a ball of salted rice. "You must leave now," she told him, but Frankie didn't know where he was supposed to go.

Frankie always dreamed of his mother on the nights he and Marta made love. He talked in his sleep, too, so loud and plaintively that Marta thought he might run outside and get himself killed. Frankie was a gentle lover, more of a boy than a man. He smelled of Philippine talcum powder. He had one acorn-sized testicle and his penis was scarred all over, like a once-shattered bone. *Mamacita*, he murmured to Marta, his eyes damp with emotion, nestling his face in her hair. *Mamacita mía.* But Marta felt more peaceful than aroused in his arms.

Usually a drop or two of blood and urine dribbled from the

tip of Frankie's penis. Marta consulted herbalists on Washington Boulevard for her husband's *maldeorín*, but nothing helped. When she listened to the radio and heard some hot-in-the-pants woman rhapsodizing about sex, Marta grew confused and resentful. Why didn't she feel those things? All she felt was a loneliness in her body that never went away. If only she could be more like Dinora. Her friend couldn't go long without sex—five days was her limit—and she managed to snag men who adored her and paid for her new kitchen cabinets. She juggled a couple of them at a time, keeping track of their comings and goings in a little notebook. When Dinora tired of them, she dismissed them without heartbreak or rancor.

Dinora had tried giving Marta sex lessons. "Do you ever take a man in your mouth?" she asked casually. Marta blanched at the suggestion. (Her aunt had told her only prostitutes did that.) "Does Frankie ever lick your pussy?" Was Dinora crazy? Marta would die of the shame. "Well, *mi hijita*, do you ever touch yourself then?" *Por favor.* If this was what good sex was about, then Marta would never have any.

On Maple Avenue, a warm wind tangled her hair and stirred a pile of newspapers tied with string. Two men walked by with bundles of long-stemmed roses from the wholesale flower market. A pair of fallen palm fronds scuttled along the street like oversized claws. Marta walked to the parking lot and stored her purchases in the back of the van. No more riding the buses for her. In Los Angeles, she knew, the buses separated the poor from everyone else.

It was true that Frankie wasn't as wealthy as the women in the factory said. There was no big house in Long Beach, no goose-down mattress, no gold-trimmed Cadillac, just an old Buick with electric windows. But their house on Forty-fifth Street was comfortable, and everything they planted in their yard happily took root. Marta settled behind the steering wheel and started toward home, *her* home. What more could she ask for?

Evaristo

It's hard to breathe here. The air is thick with smoke. The scars on my chest still burn. Nothing's familiar. Only the gray in the morning, the blue in the afternoon. I go north thinking it's south, west when I'm going east. Traffic speeds up the hours. Oranges taste of lemons from one minute to the next. The billboards torture me with their secret messages. How they shine with pretty lies. There's too much to tell, too much counting to do. This one dead, and that one, and that one. But where are the corpses? I find peace, at last, in the bed of a woman who smells of new leaves. Maybe she, maybe she alone will save me. In the folded-up wing of the night.

Enrique Florit

Enrique felt glazed and thick-eyed from the afternoon heat as he sat for another beer at the dockside bar in Kingston. The Xaymaca had bamboo walls, strings of anemic lights, and reggae so loud it seemed to shrink the place even more. A plastic skull decorated one end of the counter, which was glued with a thousand shells. The bartender, Tacky Watson, supplied his best customers with homegrown ganja. To Enrique's astonishment, Tacky told him that Ching Ling Foo was famous in Jamaica. Apparently, everyone had seen the Great Court Conjurer on television performing on the Johnny Carson show.

"Mon, how he catch dat bullet 'tween he teet?" Tacky asked. He insisted that Papi was Johnny's guest on the same night as Bob Marley, which was why the whole island had tuned in. To Enrique's knowledge, his father had never been on the Johnny Carson show, much less on the same night as Bob Marley. But

Tacky continued reminiscing as if it were *the* highlight of recent Jamaican history.

The discovery that his father was a celebrity here depressed Enrique, and he took to smoking a good amount of Tacky's dope. After his first cigar-sized spliff, Enrique grew convinced of his own visionary sight, his Far-Eye, and adopted the Rasta patois. "Yes, man, I-n-I move ina mystic, ina cosmic" was his response to Papi's long-distance question *"Hijo,* are you all right?" Enrique had called his father after being stranded in Kingston two weeks ago. He'd been thrown off a casino cruise ship and was biding his time, or at least trying to find a convincing disguise, before attempting to board another.

Meanwhile Papi had suffered his own debacle in Mexico. At the annual convention of the International Brotherhood of Magicians in Guadalajara, he'd been arrested for possessing the pelt of some kind of endangered guinea pig. Mexican authorities released him only after eighty-six magicians had protested in the Plaza de Armas, holding hostage the deputy mayor and his press secretary, whom they'd ceremoniously sawed in half.

Undeterred, his father was traveling to a magicians' conference in Buenos Aires next. After trying out a disastrous new act in which he'd impersonated a Prussian officer, Papi had decided to resuscitate his Ching Ling Foo routine and go international. No matter his worsening health and his widening girth. Armed with a battery of painkillers and digestive aids, he'd persuaded the best tailor in Las Vegas—Mario Buccellato catered to the city's top mobsters—to stitch in stretchy gold side panels to his Chinese tunics and take out the waist of his pantaloons. Thus prepared, Fernando Florit had hit the road.

So far, he was enjoying moderate success performing his bullet-catch trick in the rural theaters of Central America (except in Panama, where the Carranza clan made certain he couldn't perform) and planned to try his luck in Venezuela later this year. Papi had hung up on Enrique with an encouraging flourish of Martí: " 'Times of gorge and rush are these: voices fly like light: lightning, like a ship hurled upon dread quicksand, plunges down the high rod, and in delicate craft man, as if winged, cleaves the air.' "

At the Xaymaca, Tacky was trying to balance an egg on his forehead. He said the egg helped him remember his dreams. Enrique nodded sympathetically. One part of his brain was listening to Tacky; the other was trying to figure out a way back onto a casino ship now that he'd been blacklisted. The captains didn't appreciate having professional gamblers on board and were spreading the word about him. It bothered Enrique that they thought him a card sharp. He won his poker legitimately. There was no question that he was highly skilled—hadn't he apprenticed with the best players in Las Vegas?—but he benefited most from being underestimated.

For the past fourteen months, Enrique had hopped from one casino cruise ship to another (a flotilla of them plowed the Caribbean, mostly in winter), playing poker with some fairly deep-pocketed tourists. He'd demolished his share of high rollers in Santo Domingo, San Juan, and Martinique, too. He'd never made easier money. To him, the Caribbean was a lot like Las Vegas: a sea in which everyone was adrift, anchored by gaming tables.

On the casino ships, strange floating worlds all their own, Enrique's opponents were mostly retired midwesterners: pink, doughy men dragged aboard by their excitable wives. He'd cleaned out so many passengers on his last cruise—especially one ophthalmologist from St. Louis, who'd complained about him to the captain—that he had been given the boot at the nearest port of call, which happened to be Kingston. Kingston wasn't much of a tourist destination anymore; there was too much crime and hostility for that. Mostly the tourists went to Montego Bay, if they bothered with Jamaica at all.

Enrique was lying low in the one halfway decent hotel near the waterfront before hitting the poker circuit again. He would take a break and wait for the next cruise ship to come through. Tacky had told him that one was scheduled to dock late tonight, stopping only briefly. Enrique was in no hurry to go anywhere. The last thing he wanted was to return to Las Vegas. He was sick and tired of working so hard only to see his savings vacuumed up by his father's debts.

Papi could still make money opening for B-list singers, but it was more usual for him to go a year or more earning nothing (or next to nothing in Central America). Even when he did earn a few bucks, he couldn't hang on to it for long. Papi blew it on poker, or women, or another one of his get-rich-quick schemes. His latest: developing wigs for every ethnicity. Worst of all, Papi forgave himself too readily. *Ay, hijo, it was just a little misjudgment on my part.* It was amazing how goddamned enamored he was with himself.

If it weren't for Papi, Enrique thought miserably, he would've graduated from MIT by now, landed some big consulting job, been set up in a nice apartment in Boston or New York. Why couldn't he disavow his father long enough to get away for good? But thinking this only made him feel guilty. The fact was that he felt like a fugitive in his own life. A man in depressed self-storage. Only he couldn't figure out what he was saving himself for. Not even Tacky, who had an opinion on everything, could tell him. *Every day you goad donkey, 'im will kick you one day.* That didn't sound very hopeful.

On the morning of Leila's wedding, Enrique had gone and gotten his left biceps tattooed with a pair of dice intertwined with her name in Persian lettering. How pathetic was that? After their accident in the Mojave, they'd driven straight to Baja. Enrique was permitted to scuba dive after just one fly-by-night lesson and he eagerly accompanied Leila underwater. Giant squid were spawning in the area and clots of their white pulsating eggs were everywhere. Without warning, bat rays with huge wingspans swept in and started feeding on the eggs.

This infuriated Enrique beyond reason. If he'd had a harpoon gun, he would've shot the bat rays one by one.

In the middle of the commotion, his oxygen got cut off somehow. He tried to catch Leila's eye — his puckered hands waved at her frantically — but she seemed in a kind of trance. Enrique panicked and started to surface too quickly, feeling a terrible pressure in his chest. His legs felt like lead weights. Then Leila appeared before him, hooked their utility belts together, and pulled him more slowly to the surface. The last thing he felt was the brilliant weight of the sun hitting his face.

That night, they strayed far from their hotel and stumbled upon eleven giant sea turtles laying eggs on a deserted stretch of beach. Others seemed to be mating offshore. The females dug their holes with enormous flippers, then crouched and swayed as they laid their eggs. Without a word, Leila took Enrique's hand and coaxed him onto the sand. With the soft scraping sounds of the giant turtles around them, they made love for the first time. Leila stared at him so intently that it hurt to look at her.

On their fifth and last day together, Enrique slipped his mother's silver bracelet onto Leila's wrist. For good luck, he said, *y por siempre.* Then he asked her to marry him. But she refused him. Leila offered him the only reason Enrique understood: she couldn't bear to disappoint her family. *But do you love me?* He'd cupped her face with both hands and demanded an answer. Leila cast her eyes down and whispered, *Bale.* For months afterward, Enrique racked his brain, trying to figure out ways they might have stayed together. In the end, all he did was suffer and sulk. Five days with Leila and his life was ruined forever.

Enrique didn't want to think about what his Texan friends would have done in his place. It only made him feel worse. For their mutual birthday six months later, Enrique sent Leila a present at her old address in Los Angeles: a wet suit, sleek and beautiful, with a pair of matching flippers. He enclosed a brief note: *Please swim back to me.* He didn't know what Leila thought of his gift because he never heard from her again.

After leaving the Xaymaca, Enrique walked through the steaming streets of downtown Kingston. Jalopies careened around corners, barely missing pedestrians. A clump of deformed trees dominated William Grant Park. Enrique wandered into an old, octagonally shaped church girded with ornate columns. One of its stained-glass windows shone with a blue cross. Enrique took off his canvas hat and went inside, cooling himself with a splash of holy water. Then he sat down in a pew.

Enrique wanted to pray for something simple, like a nice woman to pass the time with in Kingston. Somebody he didn't have to pay. Shit, he was lonelier than an angel here. It'd been two months since he'd had sex with that plump roulette spinner in Santo Domingo. Margarita was older, in her forties, and her thighs had gone soft but Enrique reveled in her flesh just the same. When she asked him for fifty dollars the morning after, he was crestfallen. He paid her without saying a word.

He remembered the Flamingo bartender's abysmal luck with women. Jorge de Reyes was always falling for showgirls twice his size who abandoned him after cleaning out his bank account. Later he would admit that it didn't pay to be sentimental; then he would go and fall in love all over again. When Enrique stood up from the pew, his knees were sore and his hair sweaty. He lit a candle, jammed a hundred-dollar bill in the offerings box, and left the church.

On his last casino ship, they'd been traveling through the Windward Passage when the eastern end of Cuba came into view. For the better part of the afternoon the island hovered temptingly on the horizon. Enrique sensed its colors and smells drifting toward him, like an incoming tide. He stayed motionless on the deck, hungry, his mouth open and swallowing air. He'd never felt more lost.

It bothered him the way bits and pieces of his past surrounded him when he was sad. The little bell by his bedside in Cárdenas. His grandfather's '47 Chevy, belching smoke. His Abuela Carmen's deteriorating foam breast, which replaced the one she'd lost to cancer at thirty-five. The scarlet birthmark on Tía Adela's inner thigh that she occasionally let him touch. Once his aunt had taken him on a trip to the Colón Cemetery in Havana to petition La Milagrosa to shrink her uterine cyst. (It'd worked.)

Enrique thought of going to Panama and looking up his mother's family there. So many of the Carranzas had come to Mamá's funeral that their limousines had caused a traffic jam in Cárdenas. Enrique wasn't able to keep their names straight. He counted dozens of aunts and uncles and cousins, a ready-made family should he ever decide to find them. His worst fear was that they would blame him for Mamá's death. "You were there? You saw her die?" Enrique imagined them asking him again and again. And each time, burning with shame, he would say "yes."

If he ever got the chance, Enrique decided, he would tell them everything. How the snare drum had rolled as Papi escorted Mamá up the three wooden steps to the rim of the aquarium. How he'd carefully lowered her into the water. How her hair had floated above her as she struggled against the ropes. How she'd been nearly free of her bindings when the electrical cable struck. How he'd watched her drift lifelessly to the back of the tank.

❦

The sun glared down on the city as Enrique crossed King Street. He tried to picture the colonial town houses in their heyday, the balconies draped with hibiscus and coral vines, not degenerated into tenements pockmarked with bullet holes. At the far end of Ocean Boulevard, the rickety wharves were swarming with pelicans. Buzzards banked and wheeled in the distance, loose-stitching rips in the sky. Did they bring bad luck, like in Cuba?

Around him, everything breathed a futile abundance. Farmers, their legs pure sinew, toted their bundles of firewood and baskets of yams from the Jubilee Market. Goats nosed along the filthy alleyways, browsing in garbage cans. A pigeon with a ripped wing was dead on a doorstep, bruising the hour. The air was so viscous it felt three-dimensional. Enrique's lungs pumped hard walking just a short way. The tropical metabolism was simple: devour and grow.

The palm trees along the boulevard looked painted in place. Even the sea was unconvincing, though it couldn't have been more than a couple hundred yards away. Enrique clasped his head hard, then punched the air for no reason. He was still feeling stoned. Smoking a Cuban cigar—they were easy to get in Kingston—would clear his head. He thought of pirates' maps with big X's for where the treasures lay buried. He wanted a map like that for his own life, one that showed his precise location and what he had to do to find the gold.

Enrique settled into a wicker chair at another funky, open-air rum shop. He ordered a ginger beer, chasing it with a double shot of rum and a plate of salt-fish cakes. Rust had claimed most of the rum shop's tin roof. Last year's girlie calendar fluttered in the breeze. A transistor radio crackled listlessly. Enrique combed his hair with damp fingers and took a long swallow of a second beer. He leaned back and noticed the early moon, faint beyond the blue-green hills. Hurricane season wouldn't begin for another month.

Just before dusk, Enrique decided to visit Bob Marley's grave. He'd heard that when Marley had died earlier this year, his body had been laid out in his denim suit and tam, a Bible in one hand, his guitar in the other. The cortege stretched for fifty miles.

There were a couple of punk rockers at Marley's grave, alongside beggar kids, red-haired from malnutrition. Apparently, anybody who was anybody in punk was making the pilgrimage to Jamaica for inspiration. A stiff wind made everyone's clothes flap. A girl in a lavender miniskirt and tank top was laying a bouquet of calla lilies on Marley's grave. She was short and her legs were tightly muscled. Her friendliness caught Enrique off guard.

"Do I know you?" she asked.

Nobody had ever asked him that before. It turned out that she was Cuban, born in Pinar del Río, although she'd grown up in the States. Her name was Delia Barredo and she'd come all the way from New Jersey to pay her respects to Bob Marley. She credited his music with inspiring her to leave secretarial school and study modern dance. Enrique liked the artful way she paused between sentences.

The wind scattered Delia's lilies and Enrique retrieved them, tying them together with a length of vine. Then he returned them to the grave. He noticed orchids growing among the flamboyants, a hummingbird camouflaged by a clutch of torch ginger. Tacky had told him about a flower on the far side of the mountains that bloomed only once every thirty-three years. He'd been a teenager and in the first blush of love when he'd first seen them. " 'Twas boonoonoonoos!"

When Delia asked Enrique what he did, he surprised himself by answering, "I'm a gambler." Would it matter to her that he'd been accepted to MIT? That because of some computer glitch, they sent him a welcome-to-campus letter every August? He still flirted with going but the temptation faded more every year. Never mind. It felt good to be speaking Spanish with this *cubana*. Enrique tried to see inside Delia's eyes, but they didn't reveal much. Did prayers get answered so quickly or was this some kind of sick ecclesiastical joke?

On an impulse, Enrique invited Delia to check out the dance-hall scene later that night. But first, he asked her to dinner. She accepted calmly, as if it were no big deal. He liked this about her. The uptown restaurant served mostly continental cuisine but they chose the few Jamaican dishes on the menu: jerk chicken, coconut rice, cornmeal pudding for dessert. They shared a bottle of wine, too, the most expensive on the list. Enrique paid for everything with his gambling cash.

For a tiny woman, Delia ate a lot. Double portions of everything, with extra side dishes. She ate six fried plantains and a pint of Pickapeppa sauce. Delia told him that her father was a barber in Patterson and gave old-fashioned, straight-razor shaves. His real claim to fame, though, were his roast pork legs—marinated for six days with garlic and sour oranges— which he sold to other homesick Cubans at Christmastime. In his record year, 1977, he'd sold ninety-two legs.

Lady Cecilia was deejaying at the Crocodile Club and the place was jammed when they got there. It was like being inside an enormous mammal, hot and alive. The dress code for women was outrageous: as skimpy and as tight as possible. Delia looked positively Victorian in her lavender miniskirt. Enrique feared the force of his need and quickly lost himself dancing. Delia followed his every move. She was slight, like him, but had a curvy ass. He liked the feel of her pressed against him.

They danced every dance until they were soaked to the bones, until the soles of their feet ached and burned. At one point Lady Cecilia, her hair twisted with flashy gems, suggestively tried to swallow her microphone, rasping: *No soke wi' mi', no soke wi' mi'.* Enrique loved the way her words stacked up in one direction, then tumbled unexpectedly in another.

It was five in the morning when he and Delia left the Crocodile Club and found themselves laughing and kissing on the Kingston docks, their faces upturned to the last swirl of stars. Enrique could see the blue-and-white banners of his hotel nearby. He studied the peculiar beauty of Delia's face—the wide-set eyes and snub nose—now familiar in the cool, moist air. Soon the heat of the day would emerge from its resting places.

On the other side of the harbor, the casino ship waited, mammoth and looming from another world. "It sails in an hour," Enrique said. He thought of how Delia's hips matched his. How she calmed his loneliness, his tribal fever. *Coño,* why torment himself with doubts? "Please," he said. "Come with me." Delia stroked his face like his mother used to do. Her eyes were an inch from his, bewildered at first, then purposeful and gray. And to Enrique's surprise, and to hers, she said, Yes.

Leila Rezvani

They were still a hundred miles from home after a long weekend visiting the Grand Canyon. Little Mehri was asleep in her car seat and Sadegh was at the wheel. He hadn't said a word since they'd stopped for gas an hour ago. Maybe this was as good as it got, Leila thought, opening another box of sugar cookies: this deserted road; the sky heavy with stars; her hardworking husband and their nineteen-month-old daughter, who was a near carbon copy of him, only funnier.

"How's your headache?" Leila asked.

"Better." Sadegh's tinted glasses hid the lack of expression in his eyes and made his baldness more prominent. Since they'd moved to New Mexico, her husband had lost most of his hair. Earlier in the day, he'd walked to the edge of the Grand Canyon and been overcome by a fierce migraine. He'd fallen to his knees and might have rolled to his death (Leila was thirty yards away with their daughter, admiring the view) if some war veteran's wheelchair hadn't inadvertently interfered. He said the pain had felt like a hatchet to the back of his skull.

Lightning flared in the clouds as they sped along the two-lane highway back to Los Alamos. Leila wasn't permitted to turn on the radio. It was another one of her husband's edicts. She was willing to listen to anything as long as it filled the gloomy air between them, but Sadegh hated music. He said it prevented him from thinking. He avoided alcohol and refused to dance, too. Leila joked that he was worse than the mullahs back home but her husband wasn't amused.

At their wedding, Maman had been radiant. Her daughter was marrying a fine young scientist with foreign degrees and a big future, someone she'd chosen herself. It was her greatest moment, the chance to show her friends and family and the remnants of Tehran society that, revolution or not, she'd done her job well. Sometimes Leila thought that the real choice hadn't been between Sadegh and Enrique but between pleasing her mother and pleasing herself.

During the ceremony, a happily married great-aunt on Sadegh's side of the family rubbed a sugar loaf over their heads to ensure prosperity. And Sadegh's father quoted loudly from *The Book of Kings*: " 'Sufficient unto women is the art of producing and raising sons as brave as lions.' " His parents showered them with fancy gifts—carpets from Kashan worth a fortune, a pair of rare lovebirds to celebrate their union, leather chests filled with linens and brocades. Only Sadegh's twin brother, Ahmed, didn't wish them well. His American wife was divorcing him in Ohio and taking custody of their children. Everyone said that he was depressed. All Ahmed said was that this couldn't have happened to him in Iran.

The reception was held at Aunt Parvin's house. Candles illuminated the garden's flower beds. Tables were decorated with ribbons and cascading roses. Liveried waiters served vintage wines and piled everyone's plates high with barbecued lamb. There were cream cakes and grapes, which were truly the color of emeralds. Fat goldfish swam in the fountain and the pool was covered with a wooden dance floor. A jazz band played old standards late into the night. It was, everyone agreed, the best postrevolution wedding ever.

On their honeymoon to the Caspian Sea, Sadegh wanted to make love to Leila all the time. But she felt the slightest excitement only if she imagined that it was Enrique giving her kisses, caressing her thighs, circling her nipples with his tongue. Sadegh had the hotel prepare romantic picnics for them, which he spread out on rugs under willow trees and near streams. Whenever he tried to coax Leila back to their room, she begged him to stay outdoors. Sadegh lovingly indulged her at first, but he soon grew impatient with her disinterest.

After graduating, Sadegh had accepted a research job at Los Alamos National Laboratory, the first Iranian-born physicist ever to do so. Everyone said that this was an extraordinary coup for a new Ph.D. Sadegh had been tempted to stay in Tehran—everyone treated him like a big shot—but the scientists he knew urged him to seize the opportunity, to learn everything he could, then return to Iran and share it with them. Before they left for New Mexico, Maman took Leila aside and warned her: *Women are like fruit trees; they have to bear children or they'll wither.*

In no time at all, Leila was pregnant.

Leila turned to look at her daughter in the backseat. It was impossible to tell that she'd been born seven weeks premature, wrinkled and irascible as an old rug merchant. Mehri was plump and round-faced now, and had the same beauty mark on her cheek as her father. Her hair was thin and straight, like his used to be; her hands precise replicas of his. Only her nose was like Leila's—her old nose, with the bump in the middle and the too long tip.

It was said that a baby's future was written on its forehead by an angel with invisible ink. This happened at the moment of birth and nothing anybody did could change it. If this was true then perhaps Leila was meant to have married Sadegh after all, meant to have his child, meant to live in this lonely corner of America. Perhaps it was written on her brow that she never really had a choice at all.

Today, Mehri was dressed in little overalls and a rainbow T-shirt, as feminine as she ever got. She didn't wear the frilly dresses her grandmother sent her from London except for the five minutes required for a family portrait. Leila feared that her daughter looked too masculine but Sadegh dismissed her concerns. He always defended Mehri, questioned Leila's judgment. He said he didn't want his daughter growing up to be another empty-headed woman.

Most of the mothers Leila knew in her neighborhood didn't work and had no interest in careers. Several had gone to college but not a single one had graduated. Leila was a semester shy of graduating herself. The summer after her junior year, she'd interned at an American company in San Diego, trouble-shooting factory robots. There was something deeply satisfying about the order and logic of the work. In the first lonely months after Mehri was born, worn down from the round-the-clock baby care, Leila dreamed of running away, of returning to the robot factory. But Sadegh wouldn't hear of her working.

Leila reached for a can of warm cola and more sugar cookies. She'd gained fifty-two pounds during her pregnancy and hadn't lost an ounce of it. It was a relief to be so voluptuously invisible. What did she care what Sadegh thought of her shape? They passed a few saguaros, ghostly in the dark, hoarding their water for centuries. Leila loved the desert but it held no interest for her husband. Nothing in the natural world did — not the mountains, not the oceans, not any kind of flora or fauna.

She remembered how Enrique had appreciated the desert —

the noon heat like a disease, the weight and respite of its endless dusks. If you let it, he'd said, the desert persuaded you of its hallucinations. Like him, she was intrigued by the extreme adaptations of plants and animals living so close to their own survival: the battalions of cacti; the lizards that shot blood from their eyes when alarmed; snakes so still they looked like sticks. What was the minimal amount of moisture any of them needed to stay alive?

"Long day tomorrow?" Leila asked Sadegh. Why did she still bother making conversation with him?

"Same as always," he muttered.

Her husband was unhappy at Los Alamos. Although he'd tried to fit in, Sadegh didn't feel comfortable with the other scientists. Whenever he pointed out their mistakes, which was often, they jokingly called him Ayatollah, or worse, and ridiculed his accent. They blamed him for everything wrong in the world: the hostage crisis; the high price of gas. They made him feel ashamed of being Iranian. Sadegh started calling himself "Persian"—Persian like the poetry, and the miniatures, and the rugs.

Often, he complained to his twin brother, who was equally miserable in his job as the night supervisor at a Cleveland electrical plant. Leila overheard her husband reminiscing with Ahmed about the opium they'd smoked when they were teenagers. It was a family pastime, Sadegh maintained defensively. His parents still smoked opium every day. Obviously, it hadn't done them any harm. Then he turned to Leila, softening his tone: "We should try it sometime, my love. Maybe it would help you relax."

Lately, Leila had been avoiding sex with her husband altogether. Perhaps it was her own fault that she found no pleasure in bed with him. Perhaps Enrique had spoiled her for good. In Baja they'd held each other belly to belly, thigh to thigh until the sun came up. He loved her smell, everything she said, the way she held her teacup. Was that love? Leila sadly remembered a fragment of a poem by that Persian poetess: *Those days of wonder at the body's secrets* . . .

But there'd been more than her own feelings to consider, Leila reminded herself. She tried to imagine telling her parents about Enrique Florit, a gambler without a college degree, a man whose mother was dead and whose father was a Las Vegas magician. Impossible.

"How can you be so logical?" Enrique had pleaded with her on their last night together.

"I need to consider my future."

"*I'm* your future."

"Darling, please."

Wasn't it better that she'd left Enrique while she still could? No matter his voice and his elegant wrists, the softness of his lips, the way he gently rested his head on her breasts. The odds of them lasting weren't good. So why was she still thinking about him?

Last Christmas she'd worked up the courage to ask Sadegh to go down on her. She told him she'd heard that most women climaxed this way. This enraged him. What real man would fall to his knees to please a woman, he demanded, licking and lapping at her like a dog? Who did she think he was? After listening to a sex therapist on a radio talk show, Leila suggested that they see a marriage counselor. He grew even more incensed. Talk to a stranger about such private matters? Was she mad?

It was midnight when Sadegh reached their turnoff. Their house was in a fast-growing development on the outskirts of Los Alamos. The community was laid out in a grid with three styles of homes, variations on a theme, costing within five thousand dollars of one another. The lawns were measured down to the inch and the aspen saplings were planted equidistantly along the streets. The maple tree in their backyard was growing tall from Leila's obsessive watering. Last summer, a new elementary school had opened down the road.

Leila recalled how her father used to criticize the Shah for setting apart a private school for his children. "The crown prince should have gone to public school. He should have kicked and he should have been kicked." Maman defended the royals, insisting that the prince went to school with the children of the palace gardeners and cooks. Baba countered: "He must meet real people. He should have friends who are not from the court." Why was she remembering this right now?

Shortly after she married Sadegh, her parents separated. Naturally, nobody was calling it that. Her mother had moved to London "temporarily" to escape the war and soothe her raw nerves. Rumors flew that she was seeing that English horticulturist from years ago, but who could prove this? To everyone's surprise, Maman took up painting watercolors. Leila hated to admit it, but her mother's still lifes weren't half bad. She'd sent them one of a dead pheasant for their first anniversary.

Baba was staying on in Tehran, bitterly alone. He ate only fried eggs with a little salt for dinner. He'd lost his appetite after an explosion at the local post office killed thirteen people. Body parts had flown everywhere, draping lampposts and automobiles. One man's hand, complete with a Swiss wristwatch, had landed on Baba's shoe. Baba had been carrying a sack of pomegranates from the market. He dropped them with such force that they burst open on the sidewalk, scattering crimson seeds.

The lights were on inside the house. A pickup truck with Ohio plates was parked in the driveway. The only person they knew from the Midwest was Sadegh's twin brother, Ahmed. Leila got out of the car and unbuckled Mehri's car seat. Sadegh shuffled up the walkway with their luggage and put the key in the door. Leila followed him, carrying their sleeping daughter.

A fedora was perched on the edge of the china cabinet. There was a gun on the carpet alongside an overturned vase of lilies. Clots of blood like dull cherries studded the mirrors and walls. What was left of Ahmed's head was shaven, like a prisoner's. He must have put the gun in his mouth and pulled the trigger. Leila stared at her brother-in-law's hands, which were lying peacefully at his sides. His oxford shoes were clumsily tied together. There was no note, no explanation but the implied one: Take me home.

Sadegh covered his face with his hands and cried so violently that it frightened Leila. His suffering was unfamiliar, stark and separate from hers. She was much more transfixed by the sight of her grieving husband than by her dead brother-in-law. Mehri woke up and saw her father crying, then started wailing herself. She dropped to the ground and ran around the dining room, tracking tiny footprints of blood.

"No one must know of this," Sadegh said hoarsely, wiping his glasses.

"What are you talking about?" Leila asked. Her jaw hurt, as if she'd been chewing for days.

"No one must know of this," he repeated.

Leila ran to the telephone but Sadegh grabbed her wrists and held them behind her back. His mustache scraped her lips as he spoke, deliberately, flattening her resistance. She felt utterly trapped by his stare.

"If you breathe a word of this to anyone—anyone, do you understand?—as God is my witness, I'll take Mehri from you."

"But why?" Leila whimpered. He was twisting her wrists so hard she feared he might break them. She remembered what Sadegh had told her when they'd first met: Everyone watches a man for his weakness.

"Red! Red! Red!" Mehri shouted.

"What do you want me to say?" Leila rasped.

"That he was murdered."

"Murdered? But the police won't believe it."

"To hell with what they think. I'm talking about the family."

Leila knew instantly that their relatives back home would believe his story. It would confirm their worst fears about

America, save them from scandal, from the malicious gossips that picked at others' miseries like vultures. Sadegh would preserve his family's *aberoo*, his honor, at all costs. He would make certain that Ahmed would be portrayed as a great martyr, sacrificed to the evils of the West. But to the police in Los Alamos, he would be just another suicide.

Leila envisioned the procession of men carrying her brother-in-law's coffin to the cemetery. How the mourners would keen and weep, caught up in the euphoria of grief. Overhead a parade of dark clouds would follow them through the winding streets. And the lies. The lies about Ahmed's death would multiply until they covered the truth like graveyard dirt.

"I'm going to call the police," Sadegh said. "Let me do the talking—and don't interrupt me. Answer only if they speak to you directly and repeat everything I say, word for word. If you do or say anything else, I'll kill you."

"You're crazy."

Sadegh twisted her wrists tighter and pushed his forehead into hers.

"Please, you're hurting me," Leila cried. "At least let me put Mehri to bed first."

"Make it fast," Sadegh said, releasing her.

Leila collected their daughter off the sofa, where Mehri had found a dusty licorice stick behind the throw pillows. Her hands and knees were smeared with her uncle's blood. What would Mehri remember of this night? And Sadegh? Could they ever find an excuse for ordinary happiness again?

"Bedtime, Mehri *joonam*." Leila held out her arms and her daughter climbed into them, her small heart ticking hard inside her chest. The night air slipped in under the door. A sudden wind stirred the saplings, bringing a fresh scent of green. How nice it would be to sleep, Leila thought, a deep forest of sleep. Tomorrow was Monday and she would stay in bed all day. "Sleep well, my darling," she whispered in her daughter's ear.

(1 9 8 3)

Enrique Florit

Enrique looked out over the poker pit and was satisfied
with what he saw. Every customer was deep in play.
Nobody was wandering around, restless or waiting for
a table. The dealers were crisp and sharp looking, and there
were enough of them to keep the players happy. Anyone who
came to his pit knew they could expect the best service. No
riffraff. No hangers-on. No maniacs or disruptive drunks.

During his first months at the casino, everyone had tested
him—the general manager, the customers, even the busboys
and bartenders. It was natural. They wanted to see what he was
made of, how far they could push him. The word was that he
was too friendly to be fierce. They were wrong. Oh, he took
good care of everyone all right, high rollers or low. But certain
things weren't tolerated. There were rules. Enrique wasn't
above using a little in-house muscle to enforce them. For that
he'd hired Jensen, six feet four inches of solid persuasion. One

nod to him and the offender was out the door. Enrique was tired of poker's low-life image. He didn't want his children growing up feeling ashamed of him.

Enrique surreptitiously checked his watch. There were no clocks in the casino and the temperature was a steady sixty-eight degrees. The one concession to decor was an aquarium teeming with tropical fish. Enrique didn't want his customers reminded of anything else—not wives, not mortgages, not jobs or errands or anniversaries. Last summer he'd gone to Saint Bartholomew's church across the street and convinced the pastor, with a sizable donation, to stop their hourly tolling of bells. Profits at the casino went up twenty percent after the bells were silenced.

Enrique had been hired to run the Grand Casino's poker pit in Gardena a year and a half ago. He wasn't sure he was going to like it. He was more accustomed to being at the center of the action than on the sidelines watching others play. People used to buy *him* drinks, mob *him* after he'd won those poker tournaments, told *him* he should write a how-to book like some of the hotshots in Las Vegas. Enrique didn't think he'd reveled much in the limelight—certainly nothing on the order of his father— but he'd gotten used to the attention all the same.

It was eleven o'clock on a Saturday night. Enrique was keeping an eye on Madge Gowan at Table 14. The woman was in her fifties, petite, a chain-smoker, and a formidable opponent. When she won, which was often, she vibrated like a hummingbird. There were complaints from the regulars that Madge was a cheat but Enrique watched her closely—he'd had a video camera trained on her for weeks—and found no evidence of foul play. The fact was that men didn't like losing money to a woman. It turned them into spoilsports.

Sammy Nguyen walked through the double doors of the casino with his cronies. He wore a thick gold chain around his neck, and his fingers glittered with diamond rings. Usually Sammy wore a jade pendant of the Buddha that festively clashed with his red silk shirts, but not tonight. Tonight he was looking more subdued. What did he have up his sleeve?

"My man, how's it going?" Enrique asked, clapping him on the back. He spoke into Sammy's left ear because his right one was deaf. What Enrique understood about his Vietnamese clients was this: they'd already lost everything—family, businesses, their whole fucking country—so poker was no big deal to them. They played full out, took no prisoners. What kind of chance did some furnace repairman from Reseda have against them?

Enrique distributed the Vietnamese guys to various tables. When he sat the Nguyen gang together, customers complained that nobody could understand what they were saying and suspected them of cheating. The losers complained the loudest. They flourished like weeds in a casino. Enrique could smell them, stale and bitter like everything old, with wet-cement complexions. Their rare lucky streaks didn't last long either. It only encouraged them to lose some more. One of them, a stuttering car dealer from Mar Vista, sat at Table 29. Nobody liked playing with him because he slowed up the game so damn much.

It was quieter than usual. Nothing but the murmuring of the dealers, the clicking chips, the shuffle and tick of the cards. The stillness seemed to be waiting for something, but Enrique couldn't figure out what. Newcomers were surprised by how peaceful a good casino was. They expected fistfights, hell-raising, which happened less than anyone might guess. Or else somebody got lucky and everyone crowded around for the excitement. Mostly, though, the playing was sullen and intense. Not even a good-looking woman—and there were generally a few lingering around—could distract a serious poker player; forget one with a winning hand.

Waitresses in hot pants and shiny stockings trundled across the floor with their food trolleys. The offerings were at the opposite ends of the nutritional spectrum. The Vietnamese ordered fruit plates, staying lean and sharp through the night. The big-bellied Americans relied on chili dogs and fries to keep them going, and more beer than was advisable. Customers griped that it took an hour or more to get a cup of coffee, but this was a top-management decision. Coffee was the casino's enemy. Alcohol, on the other hand, you could get with a snap of your fingers.

A few of the regulars were losing money to Freddy Silva at Table 42. Freddy came from a casino family in Havana and drank only weak Ceylonese tea from tea bags he brought himself (he suffered from paranoia). His father had run the gambling operations at the Tropicana for years before he was murdered. His grandmother, Carolina Diamante de Silva, had been considered the best blackjack dealer on the island. Gamblers had come from around the world to play at her table. Freddy had left Cuba with the Mariel exodus on an overcrowded boat that capsized off the Keys; he'd headed straight to Gardena, where he'd heard there were new card parlors opening up.

Enrique was busy organizing the Grand Casino's second annual poker tournament, scheduled for next month. He was pleased when his father had shown up with their Las Vegas friends to compete last year. It was a veritable Diamond Pin reunion. All the regulars were there: Johnny Langston, Cullen Shaw; even Jim Gumbel put in an appearance. Papi surprised Enrique by coming with a huge bankroll (where had he gotten the money?) and wanting to play with the pros.

His father was hopeless at poker. He'd always been hopeless at poker. He would always *be* hopeless at poker. A blind person could read the expressions on his face. But Enrique knew it was useless to argue with him, and decided to let him play. Papi lost five grand in the first round, betting wildly and making a general spectacle of himself. To make matters worse, he went back to his hotel room, returned as Ching Ling Foo, and insisted on rejoining the tournament.

"You can't play again," Enrique said, trying to stay calm. "You've been eliminated." How could his father embarrass him in front of everyone like that?

"Fernando Florit was eliminated," Papi began in his phony Chinese accent. "But I, dear boy, am the reincarnation of the Great Court Conjurer to the Empress of China. Now step aside and let me play."

"Papi, please."

"I beg your pardon. Have I made your acquaintance? My name is Ching Ling Foo. And you are . . ." He held his hand out politely. His rubber wig shone dully under the fluorescent lights.

"Goddammit." Enrique flung out his arms in frustration. It was all he could do not to pull that fucking wig right off his father's head.

He looked around helplessly as a crowd began to gather. Everyone had an opinion. A couple of the players threatened to put on Halloween costumes, debating the merits of one superhero over another. Others questioned the tournament's organization—and Enrique's handling of it. Ching Ling Foo continued to vigorously defend his right to compete with everyone else. (How his father could convince anyone of anything in that getup was a mystery to Enrique.) Soon the general consensus was clear: Let the Chinaman play.

Enrique sucked in his breath and showed Papi to one of the center poker tables. His father played a lot better as Ching Ling Foo, and managed to stay in character for the next two hours. His opponents found it difficult to read his face under his thick makeup, much less understand a word of his pidgin English. This time Papi made it as far as the fourth round, winning a modest pot. Then he lost it all on a foolish bluff. His father seemed more pleased with himself than was rational for someone who'd just lost a large sum of money. The art of losing graciously, Papi liked to say, was much harder to master than winning.

After the tournament, which Johnny Langston handily won, the gambler ribbed Enrique about becoming a pit boss, giving up the game to go legit. "Now when you gonna come back and play some poker, boy?" For a couple of days afterward, Enrique felt listless at work, contemptuous of his steady paycheck, itching to sidestep his routine. He didn't know anymore what he was doing and why. It was pathetic to keep using Papi as an excuse.

After bumming around the Caribbean fleecing retirees, Enrique had headed to Las Vegas with Delia, whom he'd married off the coast of Barbados. (He'd lied and told her that the Persian tattoo on his shoulder was the name of his favorite Sufi poet.) Back home he won several major tournaments before deciding to retire from professional play. He wanted to go to bed at night with steady money in the bank. Was that such a bad thing? He was a family man now with twin baby girls and a ranch house less than a mile from his and Papi's old apartment in Santa Monica. (Enrique had a recurring dream that his house had no roof, just a floor on which ash was continuously falling.) Plus Delia was pregnant again.

Enrique looked down at himself. He was twenty-four years old and developing a paunch. He'd never gone to college. He had a family, a mortgage, responsibilities. His future, it seemed, was set. Only his past remained unsettled. Between work and the twins and the endless domestic emergencies (they'd needed a new water heater last week), there wasn't much time to wallow in the past. But now and then, his thoughts drifted back to Leila and he smelled her wild garden scent on his skin. This made him feel guilty, as if he was cheating on his wife.

❦

At midnight, Frankie Soon came in to the casino looking like a luck-hungry bird. Frankie dropped thousands in a night, and not just on poker. Booze. The occasional hooker. Illegal side bets of every kind, especially college football. When he was on a roll, Frankie could hold his own at the best poker tables. Enrique didn't know much about him except that he owned a dress factory in Koreatown and was said to be living with a Salvadoran woman decades his junior, which probably accounted for Frankie's passable Spanish.

"Good to see you, Frankie! Getting younger every day, eh?"

"I'm trying," Frankie laughed, showing off his new dentures. There was something in his demeanor, in his refusal to bow to aging (witness his jet-black dye job and manicure), that reminded Enrique of his father. Frankie always wore a guayabera, light blue and freshly pressed. None of his other customers looked this good.

Enrique steered Frankie to the bar and ordered him a double scotch on the rocks to loosen him up. Some nights he preferred tequila, the expensive kind with the pale worm in the bottle, and Enrique kept some in stock just for him. Frankie played better with a couple of drinks in him, although his behavior didn't change—upright, a gentleman, never belligerent or morose. In the years that he'd been coming to the Grand Casino, Frankie had developed a reputation for equanimity, win or lose. In short, he didn't make a nuisance of himself. Enrique couldn't point to another man in the house that he could say the same thing about.

An hour later, Frankie was winning big at Table 9, his lucky number, and ordering plate after plate of scrambled eggs. He joked that because his cholesterol was high, his woman wouldn't let him eat eggs at home. What he really wanted, Frankie said, were some fried chicken feet. When would the casino start serving those? Enrique secretly cheered Frankie on, although he knew it was unprofessional of him. He wasn't supposed to have any favorites among his customers. Yet something made him want to confide in Frankie, ask him for advice.

It was four in the morning when Frankie got up to go, eleven thousand dollars richer. Enrique walked him to the front doors, a red lacquered affair with dragon handles.

"My wife is pregnant again," he said.

"*¡Felicidades, hombre!*" Frankie looked genuinely pleased for him. "When?"

"A few months."

"Maybe you need a babysitter?" Frankie offered Enrique a cigar, then lent him his gold-plated lighter. "Where do you live?"

"Santa Monica."

"That's good."

"Good?" Enrique blew out a mouthful of smoke.

"I have the perfect babysitter for you."

"Who?"

"*Mi mujer.* She won't take any money, though."

"Of course I'd pay her," Enrique insisted.

"She loves babies but she can't have one of her own. You'd be doing me a big favor."

"I'll talk to my wife."

"*Sí, claro.*"

A truck rumbled by, making the earth tremble. Enrique let his cigar die out. He was sweating profusely, he didn't know why. Papi was coming for another visit next week. They hadn't seen each other since the disastrous tournament last year. Enrique had finally lashed out at his father in front of everyone: *You killed Mamá and don't have the courage to admit it! You call it terrible luck, or a huge tragedy, or a curse from God-knows-where but it's never your own damn fault!* Papi was so stricken by this accusation that he staggered backward, knocking over a food trolley, and scurried out of the casino without saying a word.

The next morning Papi showed up at the casino in his civilian clothes, freshly showered and shaved, and greeting everyone. He took Enrique aside as if nothing bad had happened. *Gracias, hijo. I couldn't have asked for a better son.* Then he gave

Enrique a photograph of Mamá standing on the deck of a ship, her hair flying everywhere. *She was your same age here, hijo. We were just married and she was already pregnant with you. She looks happy, no?* This made Enrique even more furious with his father—furious for making him feel guilty; furious for not having shown him this picture before. How many more of these did he have hidden? But it was impossible to stay angry with him for long.

For one thing, Papi's health was plummeting. On top of his usual ailments he had an ulcer, suspicious new skin tags, and grew tired walking across a ballroom. Fernando was becoming what seemed unthinkable to them both: an old man. This afflicted Enrique more than anything. He tried encouraging his father to eat healthily ("Give up steak, *hijo*? Have you gone mad?") and exercise ("What do you mean 'walk'? Walk to where?"), but Papi dismissed his suggestions. He considered aerobics—the word irritated him beyond reason—a pastime ill-suited for cultured men.

Papi's only form of exercise was women. It didn't surprise Enrique that his father's latest girlfriend was thirty years younger than him. Violeta Salas was a Nicaraguan waitress at the Sahara Hotel and a former Sandinista guerrilla. (Papi made political exceptions for beautiful women.) He went to great pains to keep his age a secret from Violeta, avoiding senior citizen discounts and early-bird specials, which he'd formerly patronized with gusto. (It must've killed him to pay full price.) Afternoons in Las Vegas, the Great Court Conjurer announced to his sexy new love, were for the already decrepit.

One of his impresario friends was financing Papi's latest project: marketing the Ching Ling Foo Magic Kit. Enrique often caught his father pitching the kit on late-night television, between the oldies albums and the automatic vegetable peelers. Papi reveled in the idea of millions of anonymous, insomniac eyes on him and he expected to make a fortune. Didn't people retire on more ridiculous things? The last shot of the commercial showed Papi spewing fire from his mouth, then grinning at the camera with blackened teeth: "For only $29.95 plus tax you, too, can become world-famous like Ching Ling Foo!"

❧

Outside, a moist breeze stirred the palm trees lining the casino entrance. Colorful pendants fluttered on crisscrossing lines. The grass was still wet from the sprinklers. A helicopter rattled over South Central, swinging its cone of light. It was impossible to see any stars beyond the low-slung clouds and the competing glare of casino neon. At this hour, Enrique felt the absence of everything. He missed his mother especially, and tormented himself that he'd done nothing to save her life. It didn't matter that he'd only been six years old.

What he understood now was this: the night was black and blanketing, soft on his neck, gathering him in, revealing nothing. It was as if he existed alone, in a vacuum, untethered to anything real—sunlight, or grass, or his wife's dwindling embraces. He couldn't hear his breath, or his heart, and he felt the silence go through him like a freight train. The day's first light seemed to him unbearably sad. Enrique longed to protect his wife and daughters, but so much could go unpredictably wrong. Sometimes his fear kept him awake at night, hanging like a bat in the back of his brain. He tried to calm down by thinking of round things: beach balls and pita bread, hula hoops, the smallest coins. It didn't help.

He got in his car, a brand-new Buick, and put the key in the ignition. The radio blasted a song he immediately recognized: *Well, I woke up this morning, and I got myself a beer. The future's uncertain, and the end is always near.* He could see Leila vividly again, singing off-key, the sweet encasement of her beige cashmere sweater. Enrique felt the lyrics stirring in the back of this throat, but he held off singing them. If he started to sing, he might not stop—and where would that leave him?

Nothing was ever the same twice, he decided, not happiness, not hurting. Enrique turned off the radio and rolled down the window. Then he sped toward the highway, his headlights illuminating dust motes and moths. A waft of night jasmine gave him a jolt. Was he smelling the jasmine or merely remembering it? It didn't really matter. In fifteen more minutes, he told himself, he would be home.

Leila Rezvani

It had been a mild winter in Tehran. Despite the air raids, the vendor on the corner grilled his corn over an electric heater and the walnut man peddled his shelled nuts in salted water. Birds started appearing in gardens and on telephone poles, unsettling the beds of red tulips. A flock of parrots chattered restlessly in the budding maple trees between the British embassy and the Hotel Naderi. All this made Leila believe again in the promises of spring, although it never did her any good.

It was nearly midnight. Mehri was asleep, snoring like her father with her lower lip caught on the edge of the pillow. The house was peaceful without Sadegh. Leila preferred it when he was away on business. There was more oxygen in the air, even with the windows shut tight. She was less afraid of everything, too—of the *komiteh,* and the patrolling vice squads (who'd taken to throwing acid in the faces of women who wore too much makeup), and the threat of bombs from Iraqi planes. Yes, her husband's absence made even the war with Iraq more bearable.

Leila lit a candle and toured her home in the dark. Tuberoses filled every vase, giving off a vague scent of death. The crystal chandelier refracted the flame in the dining room mirror, reminding Leila of the lights of merry-go-rounds. As a child, she used to sit in her father's lap at the circus and eat cotton candy and pistachios. They both loved the elephants and the tiger tamers best. Baba had told her something then that Leila hadn't understood until this moment: It's human nature to love even what doesn't return love.

In the kitchen, Leila startled the maid, who was sitting with a cup of tea and a hunk of that morning's *sangak*. The television was on. On the news, a group of veiled mothers whose boys had died in the war were celebrating their martyrdom, crying with joy and holding one another. Were they mad with grief?

"Excuse me, madam, what can I get for you?"

"Nothing, Zari. I just thought I heard a noise."

"It's my stomach grumbling. You know I need to eat a little something before bed or I can't sleep." Zari peeled a hard-boiled egg and stood up to reheat some sour cherry rice from dinner.

"Yes, of course. No more moths?"

"Thank God, they're all gone."

Yesterday there had been a strange infestation of moths in the kitchen. Nobody could figure out where they'd come from. Dozens of them, small and luminous with brown markings on their wings, fluttered in the damp air like so many petals. It took the maid and the gardener, an amateur lepidopterist, an hour to round them up with his butterfly net.

Leila climbed the stairs to the second-floor landing. There were four bedrooms along this hallway. The guest room for Sadegh's parents was first, with its astronomer's map of the heavens painted onto the ceiling. The map had been Leila's idea. She liked to imagine following the long trail of Eridanus to the other side of the universe, or sitting on Polaris and watching the slowly rotating planets. Sadegh objected to her decorating as an unnecessary extravagance, but he showed off the ceiling to every visitor.

It wasn't easy adjusting to life in Iran. As if the war weren't dangerous enough, she and Sadegh had gotten into nine car accidents between them their first year back. Red lights, friends had warned them, were meant only as suggestions. There was no such thing as traffic lanes either, much less staying in them. A blare of the horn or a clenched fist took the place of turn signals. It was a miracle they hadn't been killed. The government had finally agreed to provide Sadegh with a full-time chauffeur, the very one who'd driven him to Arak on Tuesday. Not that the chauffeur drove better than anyone else.

An American-trained nuclear physicist like Sadegh was in great demand in Iran. This was why he'd decided to stay after his brother's funeral. Everybody kissed his feet, especially once he began reporting directly to the head of the Nuclear Energy Commission. Sadegh basked in the attention and special privileges. For all the talk of freedom, he'd felt imprisoned in America. Here he could be a real man again.

Leila wanted to find work as well, but her husband refused to give her permission. He liked seeing her in a chador, voluminously entombed in black, captive and invisible. Was this what men really wanted? Sadegh hated the tight jeans Leila had favored in the States, which, he said, exhibited her whorish tendencies. *Jendeh*. How many times had she been called a whore, first by her mother and now by her husband?

Leila missed Los Angeles, missed the peculiar gray of the Pacific, the seabirds plunging into the waves at dusk, her weekend scuba diving trips. Mostly, she missed the sense of possibility, of one day being different from the next. Why had she given up her freedom to marry Sadegh? What had it brought her except the world circling around her deadening heart?

The second room along the upstairs hallway was her husband's. It was painted a deep blue and had gold-plated accents: doorknobs, faucets, bureau pulls. Sadegh liked to joke—it was his only one—that everything he touched was gold. Mehri's room, with its sunflower-stenciled walls and giant microscope, was next. Sometimes Leila randomly opened the atlas on her daughter's desk and tried to picture the places beneath her fingertips. Leipzig. Harare. Brunei. She never got further than the taste of the names on her tongue.

This afternoon, Leila had taken Mehri to the amusement park on the outskirts of the city. It was less crowded than she'd expected for a Friday. Mehri begged to go on the Ferris wheel and Leila relented, against her better judgment. The contraption was fifty years old, straining and screeching with each revolution, and a heavy smell of oil drifted off its engine. High above the ground, Leila tried to discern the Ferris wheel's melody but it sounded generically carnival. Overhead, jackdaws shredded the feathery clouds.

The Ferris wheel lurched to a halt as they neared the top. Mehri was delighted and rocked their gondola back and forth, leaning into the gray light. It began to drizzle, though not enough to wet anything significantly. Down below, a couple of umbrellas gloomily bloomed.

"Maybe we'll stay up here forever!" Mehri shouted.

A red balloon floated past them, just beyond their reach. A girl wailed inconsolably at the base of the ride. Leila and Mehri watched the balloon drift higher and higher until it was no more than a speck of blood in the sky. Then it was gone.

"Did the balloon go to heaven?" Mehri asked.

"Only people go to heaven."

"What about fish?"

"Fish don't go to heaven." Leila turned to her daughter. Her round face was flushed and happy, and her nose flared like a mongoose pup's.

"What if they did?"

"You don't have to worry about that, Mehri *joonam.*"

When the Ferris wheel started up again, the jerky movements made her daughter laugh. How Leila loved Mehri's abandoning laugh. These days, it was the only thing that sustained her.

The last room on the hallway was Leila's. It was closet-sized, intended for a servant, with no windows and a cupboard for storage. On her nightstand stood an empty bud vase. Leila went inside and locked the door. Most nights she slept with her daughter, except when her in-laws visited. Then Sadegh would insist that they sleep together for appearance's sake. Once a month he came looking for her in Mehri's room. Leila would feel the rough tug of his hand on her shoulder and follow him, dutifully, to his bedroom.

If she was lucky, Sadegh would be sound asleep within minutes. If she was unlucky, he would blame his impotence on her. Sometimes he would force her to suck him for an hour or more. All the while he would tell her how ugly she was, how her skin had lost its suppleness, how her ass was flat as a serving tray. Sadegh complained that she offered him no encouragement and threatened to supplement her attentions with a *havoo*, a temporary wife, a juicy woman to stir his manhood. Leila prayed that he would.

Leila had left the hospital only a few days ago. On the night of Baba's sixty-fifth birthday, she'd collapsed at her Aunt Parvin's house. The clandestine party had reminded her of pre-revolutionary times: platters of caviar, designer evening gowns, seventies disco music. One minute Leila was dancing to "Staying Alive" and the next thing she knew, she was waking up in a hospital room choked with a funeral's worth of flowers. Even her mother heard about the incident and sent a telegram from London, reminding her that a lady refrained from making a public spectacle of herself.

Dr. Banuazizi, her attending physician and a close friend of Baba's, told Leila that she was suffering from nervous exhaustion and advised her to give up cigarettes. It was true that her lungs ached from smoking and the chronic pollution. But what else was she supposed to do for her nerves?

Leila didn't want Sadegh visiting her in the hospital, but nobody could deny him the right to see his wife. Every evening he barged in carrying a box of dried apricots (he knew she hated them) and demanded to see her charts. Leila trembled so badly that the tubes in her arm made the IV bottles clatter. Sadegh was furious with her. People were whispering that he couldn't control his wife. How dare she embarrass him like that?

Leila sat on her narrow bed and considered the ways the weak lied to the strong. How many lives were like hers, based on capitulation, on the threat of violence and disgrace? She retrieved the book of Farrokhzad's poetry she'd borrowed from Baba's library and found, as always, a sad solace there: *I cried all day in the mirror. Spring had entrusted my window to the trees' green delusions.*

Her childhood friend Yasmine had found her own solution to the mullahs: never to marry. She rejected every suitor who came calling (though they were fewer in number these days) and lived in a wing of her parents' house. She worked part-time as a computer consultant, coming and going as she pleased. She refused to participate in what she called the "culture of lies." On weekends, Yasmine went hiking with her girlfriends in the Alborz Mountains and cooked in the open air. To her, surviving in Iran was all a game.

Yasmine harshly criticized Leila's marriage: "You are like a drum, a *tabl*. He beats on you and you produce a sound." Leila knew that her friend was right.

There was black-market Turkish vodka in the cupboard, tucked in among her fancy underthings: silk teddies, push-up bras, garter belts from her more sexually optimistic days. It was a miracle she'd managed to smuggle them into the country. Leila poured herself a double shot of vodka and unbuttoned her blouse. She looked down at her wilted breasts, ruined from nursing Mehri, against her mother's advice. Absently, she rolled a nipple between her thumb and forefinger. The puckered skin of her stomach looked like orange rind.

Her bottle of tranquilizers was kept hidden in the nightstand drawer next to the silver bracelet Enrique had given her. He'd said the bracelet had belonged to his mother, that she'd worn it on the day she died. Leila had thought him morbid for giving her his dead mother's jewelry. Only recently had she begun to appreciate the great sacrifice of his gift.

Leila shook out two peach-colored pills and swallowed them with a gulp of vodka. The pills, Dr. Banuazizi promised, would help her take care of Mehri and become a better wife to Sadegh, would help her keep her mouth shut, help her cope with the war and the lack of color everywhere, with the streets renamed for martyrs. Perhaps the pills would help her, ultimately, forget who she was.

After a second drink, Leila dimmed the lights and tugged off her skirt and panties. She thought of her mother's garden long ago, of the silent company of the flowers and the fragrant fruit trees. The leaves and petals lay scattered on the dirt paths and the summer winds would gust them into low-swirling eddies of pinks and greens. It seemed to Leila that she'd been truly happy then. She had no idea what happiness would look like to her now.

Often, she fantasized about returning to California. She wanted to scuba dive again, finish her degree. But what sort of life would be possible? To support herself, she would need to work twelve hours a day. More and more, she wondered about Enrique. Was he married? Did he have children? Was he still in Las Vegas playing poker? Tomorrow, Leila decided, she would write him a letter and find out.

But what was she thinking? Sadegh would never grant her a divorce and the laws were all in his favor. She could fight him in court, but even with the considerable influence of Baba and his friends, she might still lose Mehri entirely. Then where would she be? Trapped in Iran, without her daughter, or prospects, or work (Sadegh would make certain of this), and utterly dependent on her aging father.

Leila licked her forefinger and slipped it between her legs. The moistness surprised her, as if a separate life existed there, far from her worries. Perhaps the body knew more than the mind about what was good. Most days, she was so removed from her flesh that it startled her to rediscover it. She remembered how Enrique had kissed her hand after their accident in the Mojave. How soft his lips had been, how tender. Later, his lips had memorized every inch of her skin. If only she could stretch her loneliness to reach him.

The image of Enrique was interrupted by another one: a circle of stern-faced mullahs eagerly watched Leila touch herself, whips in one hand, Korans in the other. *Marg bar Amrika.* Death to America. It was necessary for them to make an example of her, to administer many lashes for her transgressions. *Allah-o-Akbar!* Together they shouted this again and again. One of the mullahs reached for Leila and tried to force his finger inside her as the others urged him on. *Bale! Bale!* She felt herself opening like a violet in the rain.

Leila lit a cigarette and lay in bed thinking. She needed to find peace here, if only for her daughter's sake. To everyone in their social circles, she and Sadegh were the perfect couple: educated, enviable, with key protectors in the government. Not even her father suspected how unhappy she was. Leila didn't want to worry him, and it was unthinkable to confide in her mother.

Last year Sadegh had bought a country house for them two hours from the city. Mehri rode her donkey there and picked lemons in the orchard. Now Sadegh was building a villa overlooking the Caspian Sea. Leila was excited to return to its shores, but she feared that the memories of her family's one happy summer there might be ruined forever. When Leila told Sadegh that she wanted to start scuba diving again, he laughed at her: "Scuba diving in your chador? That would be a sight."

At first, Leila attributed her husband's black moods to Ahmed's suicide. After his burial in Zahir-o-dowleh Cemetery, Sadegh never mentioned his brother again. Then Leila blamed his depression on his opium smoking. Whenever his parents visited, they cozily smoked their hookah and pipes together. (Leila had to bribe Mehri with video games to stay away from them while they smoked.) After they left, the sweet, sickly smell permeated the house for days.

It seemed to Leila that Sadegh's family had willed themselves into a state of amnesia after Ahmed's death. Sadegh's father hadn't finish high school but he started insisting that everyone—family, servants, bank tellers, friends—call him Dr. Bakhtiar. (Only Leila's father called him by his first name, Hassan.) Sadegh had a double Ph.D. in nuclear and accelerator physics and wore his degrees like a suit of armor. He complained that he should be called *Doctor Doctor*, but nobody paid him this respect.

Leila tossed and turned but she couldn't sleep. She had an urge for hot beetroots and porridge, like when she was pregnant. She got out of bed and rummaged in the cupboard for her bathing suit, the navy blue one with the transparent midriff, and put it on. There was a tan suitcase in the back of her closet. Inside was the wet suit Enrique had sent her for her twenty-second birthday, a present she'd never acknowledged. Leila pulled out the wet suit now. It was black, and sleek, and musty as old rubber.

It was chilly when she opened the glass-paneled doors to the downstairs patio. The flowers were just beginning their spring bloom. Leila was proud of her courtyard garden, its redolent whispers, the refuge it provided to weary birds. The sky was muddy looking. There were no stars to speak of and the moon had disappeared hours ago. The leaves of the fig tree waved to her like a thousand hands in the dark. Without a sound Leila dove into the deep end of the pool. When she was a girl, she'd wanted to dive into pools with barely a ripple. She practiced and practiced but never got it right. Now she could do it without effort, erasing herself completely.

Leila opened her eyes and swam the length of the pool underwater, counting the turquoise tiles. Her body felt muted and cool. She came up for air, long enough to breathe in the night jasmine. Her mouth was filled with old names, dead numbers, a taste of fried eggs and toast. Could she describe her life to Enrique? Would he understand what she'd become? It began to rain lightly, more promising drops after the winter drought. Leila recalled again those pure afternoons in her mother's walled garden, how the ecstasy of each bird's flight had begun and ended in stillness.

(1984)

Marta Claros

It was her tenth swimming lesson in a month and Marta was weak from ingesting so much pool water. In the nearby bottlebrush tree, three sparrows noisily hopped from branch to branch. Marta found it difficult to concentrate. She regretted the day the Florits had moved into their new house in Santa Monica Canyon. It wasn't so much that there were four more rooms to clean (with no accompanying raise) but the fact of the pool: it was like having another child to take care of, only without the rewards.

"You must put face in water and exhale!" Mr. Karpov shouted impatiently.

Señora Delia had hired the Russian swimming instructor to give Marta and the twins private lessons. The baby, Fernandito, was still too little to swim. Marta adjusted her bathing cap with the rubber sunflowers and thought about how the lesson was costing her employers $1.25 a minute. Breathe in, sixty-three cents. Breathe out, sixty-two. How could she focus throwing away money like that? Marta had bought her bathing suit for six dollars on sale downtown. Orange wasn't her favorite color but she'd refused to pay twice as much for the navy blue one. When she'd tried it on at home, topped with her fifty-cent bathing cap, Frankie had pronounced her beautiful.

Marta felt guilty that it was taking her so long to learn how to swim. Señora Delia had told her not to worry about the cost of the lessons, that she wanted her to be a good swimmer by summer so everyone would be safe in the pool. But it wouldn't end there. After she learned to swim, Marta was supposed to take a lifesaving course at the YMCA. She'd gone to see the lessons in progress. The students had to drag each other, gasping, from the biggest pool she'd ever seen. Then they took turns blowing air into the mouth of a discolored, inflatable dummy. She'd signed up to be a nanny, not a dolphin, Marta thought miserably, dunking her head in the water once more.

What if some people weren't meant to swim, their bodies unfit for anything but land? She'd consulted a *curandera* on Normandie Avenue, who'd prescribed ground fish powder to help her float. The stuff tasted awful and hadn't helped her one bit. On the black sand beaches near San Salvador, the currents were so strong that they whisked even excellent swimmers out to sea. The rivers were no better, treacherous and unpredictable, mainly good for washing clothes. That was why she'd never learned how to swim—it was much too dangerous. Why take unnecessary risks?

"Now move arms like this," Mr. Karpov said, vigorously demonstrating his windmill technique.

Marta imitated him, paddling her arms like the old-fashioned boat she once saw churning its way across Lake Ilopango. Mr. Karpov was arrogant and made swimming seem like a matter of intelligence. If he was so smart, what was he doing teaching swimming to the children of the rich? It was true that the Russian made a fortune, though. Mr. Karpov earned in four hours what it took Marta forty hours to make. Maybe she *should* learn how to swim and give him a little competition.

Already, God had granted her so much. Didn't she have a good husband and work she loved? Wasn't her brother in the States? It was heartbreaking that Evaristo might be deported but this was his own fault. If she prayed hard enough, perhaps He would forgive Evaristo, soften the heart of the judge, give her brother one last chance. Yes, Marta was confident he would be saved. Only her wish for a child hadn't been granted. But you couldn't always be asking, asking, asking God for everything. He needed to see that you were ready to suffer for Him, that you prayed regardless of His response. Marta tried to remember the name of that saint who'd survived an entire season of Lent eating sixteen Moroccan figs. Now, *that* was sacrifice.

Caring for the Florit children had made Marta want a baby all the more. On the weekends especially, when she couldn't revel in their sweet flesh. Marta felt as if she was living her own childhood through them; not reliving it, but living it for the first time. She enjoyed their toys more than they did. She loved playing dress-up and hide-and-seek, things she'd rarely done as a girl. She made up stories to go with the picture books, acting out every part. Her favorite was *The Cat in the Hat*.

Marta took to babying Frankie on Sundays, when she missed the children most. She gave him bubble baths, splashed him with violet water, sprinkled his bottom with talcum powder, read to him before bed. Some nights she dreamed that he was an infant journeying past the soft pinks of her insides to her barren female parts. Then she would cry at the emptiness inside her, and nothing consoled her; not Frankie's soothing hand, not praying, not counting her blessings one by one.

"I want you open eyes underwater," Mr. Karpov insisted, submerging his head in the pool. His eyes appeared enlarged, like a toad's.

Marta tentatively dipped her face in the water. No matter

how hard she tried, she couldn't open her eyes. If by some miracle she could see through her eyelids, she might finally learn to swim.

"Okay, forget for now," Mr. Karpov said with disgust. "Just float on back. Lie down on water like bed."

Marta didn't sleep so well in her own bed, much less a pretend one of pool water. She remembered what her mother used to say: Get out of the corn or you'll be covered with *ajuate* pollen. What did this have to do with swimming?

"Float! Float!" Mr. Karpov screamed. "Everybody can float! Not one person cannot float! Watch me!" He swooned backward toward the deep end of the pool.

For a moment, Mr. Karpov seemed content. Had he looked like this as a baby? What was his first name, anyway? Marta laughed to think of his mother calling him "my sweet little Mr. Karpov." Had she inspected his every last inch of skin? The curve of his ears? His every toe?

"Okay, lesson over," Mr. Karpov barked, consulting his waterproof wristwatch. "This won't be snap-the-fingers case. I will tell this to Mrs. Florit. I cannot guarantee."

Marta climbed out of the pool, dripping rivulets of water. Her hands felt stiff and cold. Dark clouds stampeded across the skies. The sun was nowhere to be seen. Pale petals from the tulip tree fluttered through the air. Marta grabbed a towel and dried off to avoid a chill. Inside, she made herself a cup of cinnamon tea to warm up.

As soon as Señora Delia left for her yoga class, the children crowded onto Marta's lap to watch a video. Once Marta had accompanied La Señora to yoga and was surprised to hear the teacher, a turbaned woman in flowing orange robes, repeatedly telling the women to breathe. Did they really need to be reminded? That day Marta went home and asked Frankie whether he thought she breathed enough. Frankie laughed: *¿Estás loca, mujer?* Sometimes Marta forgot that Señora Delia was Cuban, she resembled her American neighbors so much.

Marta fixed salmon and baked potatoes for lunch and put a little of both in the blender for Fernandito. She steamed some spinach, too, though she knew the children wouldn't touch it. Señora Delia was a fanatic about nutrition and hinted that because Marta was fat, her children might also grow fat. Marta weighed two hundred and twenty-three pounds. She was big-bosomed and had shapely legs, like her mother. She didn't know why she was so fat because she ate next to nothing. A single meringue could take her ten minutes to eat.

After lunch, Marta settled the children in for their naps. She sang them the same lullaby: *Había una vez un barquito chiquitito . . .* The twins fell asleep clutching their stuffed bears, but Fernandito wasn't the least bit sleepy. He was playing with the toy rabbit his grandfather had given him. He kept dropping it into a hat, pulling it out, and yelling, "Ta-da!"—just like his Abuelo Fernando had taught him.

On his last trip to Los Angeles, Don Fernando had spent hours trying to teach his grandson magic tricks. "*Por Dios,* Papi, he's only eleven months old!" Señor Enrique complained when he returned home early one day to see his son dressed in a miniature tuxedo and velvet cape. But Don Fernando couldn't be dissuaded. "It's never too soon to introduce my grandson into the great mysteries of magic. Who else will condition his little hands for illusions?"

That same night Don Fernando kept Fernandito up past midnight so that they could watch the Ching Ling Foo Magic Kit commercials on television. "*Mira, mira!* There's your *abuelo*!" Don Fernando shouted, pointing to himself on the screen. Fernandito looked back and forth between his grandfather and the TV, confused that he could be in two places at once. Then, suddenly afraid, Fernandito screamed and bit his grandfather on the cheek. Don Fernando was on the verge of making the boy disappear (temporarily, he swore) when Señor Enrique showed up and separated them.

The next day Don Fernando told Marta the story, more

wounded than chagrined. He petted his bandaged cheek as if it were an injured bird. Marta felt sorry for him. It didn't surprise her that women still found him irresistible. Even in his Chinese disguise, he oozed a Cuban charm. Each time he saw her, Don Fernando found an excuse to reach behind her ear or inside her apron for a gift. Last time, it was a pair of beaded earrings; the time before, a refrigerator magnet of La Virgen de Guadalupe. When Marta marveled at his tricks, Don Fernando said, "My dear, a wondrous show of illusion can be created with a few simple elements."

Marta finished tidying up the house and waited for La Señora to return from her yoga class. She turned on the soap opera *Pobre Gente*. The name was misleading because the show wasn't about poor people but about rich people whom you grew to feel sorry for because they were always so unhappy. It seemed to Marta that the richer people were, the more they nursed their small miseries. Take Señora Delia, for example. She wanted to be a dancer, but nobody would hire her. A luxury, this problem. Since she couldn't agonize over basic things—like no money for food, or medicine for a dying baby— she drowned in a drop of water.

The traffic home was terrible. Marta was in no mood to take the overnight bus to visit her brother in Nogales. To distract herself, she tuned in to the rush-hour edition of *Pregunta a la psicóloga*. The topic of the day was sex, as if there was ever any other subject on the show. Anyone listening in for the first time would think that the only thing human beings did was fornicate, and usually not with their spouses either. Why was everyone so obsessed with sex?

At the house, Marta found Frankie settled in his leather recliner (she'd bought one on sale from that discount furniture clerk on *¡Salvado!*). Frankie was listening to one of his Korean operas, a fly swatter in each hand. Despite the screeching and pounding drums, the operas relaxed her husband, transported him far away. Frankie showed Marta the dragon's blood he'd procured at an herbal shop. It was supposed to tighten his gums and bind fast the roots of a troublesome molar, his very last. Why was he clinging so desperately to this tooth?

The chickens were loose in the backyard, pecking at invisible specks. Marta reached into a sack of feed and showered the hens with dried corn. Feathers drifted skyward in slow motion. A squabble broke out near the coop. The chickens were getting crankier by the day, old ladies every one. Marta was partial to her newest, a bluish bird she called Miss Penelope after a character in one of the twins' picture books. Miss Penelope flaunted her beauty, tormenting the local cats from the safety of the wire-mesh enclosure. Now and then, she shot Marta a conspiratorial look.

The phone rang after dinner and Marta had half a mind not to pick it up. She wanted an hour of peace to herself before Frankie drove her to the bus station. But she was afraid to miss a call from her brother. He'd been sounding so miserable lately. Last time they spoke, Evaristo had complained that the light in the prison yard was brutal. *The sun is reducing us to ashes. There isn't a tree for miles around.* Nothing Marta said comforted him. Last week he was put in a cell by himself for fighting with a fellow prisoner, a gunrunner from Jalisco who banged his head against the metal bunks all night long.

The static from the long-distance connection made it difficult to hear the voice on the other end of the line. Marta guessed that it was her Tía Matilde in San Salvador, dialing from the corner grocery store, the one that charged exorbitant long-distance rates for terrible service.

"*Bendito sea Dios, ¿quién se murió?*" Marta shouted. It took another minute for the connection to clear. "Is Mamá still alive?"

"*Sí, niña.* Everyone is fine here except for me." Her aunt wasted no time telling Marta the news: she was pregnant and couldn't keep the baby.

Marta held her breath and listened. Tía Matilde said that

she'd had an affair with a fifteen-year-old delivery boy. Yes, it was his child because she and her husband hadn't had relations in years. His thing didn't work anymore, although Tía Matilde suspected that it worked fine elsewhere, just not with her. She was keeping the pregnancy a secret, hiding it under a big gingham smock. She had a premonition that the baby was a boy and would be born on Christmas Day. Would Marta come down to receive him?

By the time she hung up, Marta was in tears. She rushed over to Frankie, asleep in the leather recliner, and kissed his eyes until they blinked open.

"Listen to me." She brought her lips to his, a perfect fit. "You're going to be a father."

Frankie boxed the air with his fly swatters, swept up in an opera-inspired dream. "I'll teach you to defile my family's honor!"

"*Cálmate,*" Marta crooned, holding down his arms. "I have important news."

"*Coño carajo, ¿qué pasó?*" he sputtered awake.

"My aunt called from El Salvador and is giving us a baby!" Marta sat in Frankie's lap, catapulting the recliner into a horizontal position. Then she peppered his face with kisses until he begged her to stop. "I'm going to be a mother at last!"

"Will I still get my bath on Sundays?" Frankie teased.

"Of course, *mi amor*! I'll bathe the two of you together!"

It was the middle of the night and Marta wasn't halfway to Nogales yet. She was dizzy from the diesel fumes and the sagas of everyone around her. If this Greyhound bus were the world in miniature and the people on it typical, then Marta could say with some assurance that humanity would never be satisfied. Dreams and frustrations were meted out in equal measure, ensuring that things stayed pretty much the same.

The Mexican dressmaker next to Marta was going to El Paso for her stepfather's funeral. Behind them, two redheaded sisters were returning to Louisiana after failing to become movie stars. The plump one was expecting her therapist's child. The Vietnamese man across the aisle recounted how he'd been forced aboard a Thai pirate ship as a boy and ended up adopted by a family in Mobile, Alabama. His every word stretched and snapped like a rubber band.

Marta had three dozen tamales packed in a duffel bag for her brother. She was hungry and decided to snack on just one. She thought of the foolishness that had landed her brother in prison. He and his girlfriend had been driving around South Central when they were pulled over for running a stop sign. It wasn't enough to get a ticket. The policemen decided to search the car and found a pistol wedged under the driver's seat. Rosita claimed to know nothing about it. No harm was done. Nobody was hurt. But when Evaristo couldn't produce identification, they arrested him.

The lawyer Marta hired for the case wasn't much help. So far it had cost her five thousand dollars in legal fees and her brother was still behind bars. It didn't matter that Evaristo was innocent. Millions of people like him were in El Norte, working and minding their business. Now chances were that he would be shipped back to El Salvador right in the middle of a civil war. After all her sacrifices! Marta blamed that no-good Rosita. The *putita* had found a new boyfriend in record time, too. Marta didn't have the heart to give her brother this news.

The wind blew hard, rattling the bus as it sped along the invisible road. Marta looked out the window at the vast blanket of stars. She'd forgotten what it was like to be away from the lights of the city. It'd been years since she'd seen a real night sky. It was her second time in these borderlands. The first time she'd come over the mountains on foot, with only her pink rosary for company.

Every passenger on the bus was asleep except for her. Marta

cracked open her window. A sharp smell of sage seeped into the bus. She longed to see the desert flowers, the little purple ones with petals thick as her thumb. Soon she would arrive in Phoenix and change buses for the one that would take her to Tucson and on to Nogales. Evaristo said that half the men in prison spoke Spanish and would be deported, like him. No wonder so many women were raising children alone.

Few reliable men were left in her own neighborhood, Marta thought. The best of the bunch was Pedro Nieves, who worked as a janitor at the Marquis Hotel. Pedro had two wives and seven children back in Tegucigalpa (he sent them the bulk of his salary every month), but he hadn't seen them since 1975. Marta invited Pedro over for dinner whenever she made tripe stew. He'd helped her paint the kitchen and repair the chicken coop, and he was handy when the plumbing gave out. Frankie suspected that Pedro was in love with Marta, but she pretended it wasn't true.

Marta checked to make sure her zippered money pouch was safe around her waist. When she returned home, she planned to burn a dozen votive candles for her baby's good health. Marta leaned against the headrest and ticked off the ingredients that went into sweet baths: rose petals, honey, cinnamon, spearmint, *contramaldeojo*—what was she missing? Nine straight days of the baths, Dinora said, would jump-start good luck. For extra protection, Marta would wear the shielding yellow necklaces of motherhood.

She thought of naming the baby Evaristo, but quickly rejected the notion. Marta loved her brother but she didn't want her son following the same hopeless path. Suddenly the name of her baby came to her: José Antonio, after her father. Papá had always wanted to come to the States. Now his grandson would take his place.

The bus sped forward and Marta drifted into a light sleep. She dreamed a new dream altogether. In it, she climbed a smooth-trunked tree and settled on a slippery branch. On the branch was a silk nest with a single egg inside. Marta lifted the egg to her ear and was surprised to hear the ocean; not a big crashing sound, just the gentle lapping of waves. Then she pressed the egg to her heart and held it there.

It was daybreak when Marta woke up and looked out at the desolate stretch of desert. The wind made the bus shudder harder. There were burnt red cliffs in the distance, and the cacti looked like preachers with upraised arms. Tumbleweeds did a tangled dance across the road. Marta doubted she could ever adjust to a life here—to this landscape watered by nothing, to the winter sun stripping everything bare.

Evaristo

There's a man here who would make me a woman. I blinded him in one eye, then grew a beard. Now a bird is building a nest on my chin. It's the color of cinnamon with white-striped wings. I tell my sister this on the black stinking phone but I can tell she doesn't believe me. Nobody does. Rumm-rumm, *the bird sings. Soon it will lay an egg, but it won't be safe. Everything is moving toward darkness. I know this for a fact. I must invent a window, convince it to fly. I will be held accountable. It's time to get going, little birdie. That's what I'll say. One, two, three, listen to me: we must find a place with a more visible blue. Yes, that's what we need, little birdie. Blue, too much more blue.*

(1986)

Enrique Florit

The moon was still low in the sky, pale and full, hardly visible in the morning light. It sifted through the blinds, grazing Papi's skin. For a moment it illuminated his head, giving him a saintly air. It was difficult to watch him just lying there, a man who woke up bristling with an appetite even for ordinary days. Enrique approached his father in the hospital bed. The scars on his skull looked like railroad tracks except that they twisted and turned and went nowhere.

Enrique took some coconut oil from the nightstand and traced the path of the scars. Then he tapped his father's head, as if this might stir his consciousness. He was convinced that Papi was living deep inside his body, in a place he struggled to escape from. At times he gestured gracefully, reflexively, as if extending an invitation to the air. What could he be feeling?

Since the accident, Enrique had come to the hospital every morning to massage his father with oils and rubbing alcohol. It was important to stimulate Papi's circulation to prevent blood clots. Enrique couldn't count on the overworked nurses doing much, not even the shapely Polish one named Ula, who would've incited Fernando's courtliness. Patiently, he kneaded the withering muscles in his father's arms, his pudgy hands with their bony protrusions, his astonishingly flexible fingers.

Papi's ex-girlfriend Violeta Salas showed up most afternoons with pamphlets about Communist movements in the Third World. She climbed into bed with Fernando, stroking his head and whispering endearments. Now and then she punctuated her reading with a terse "*¡Venceremos!*" No wonder his father had broken up with her. She was gorgeous but it was impossible to ignore her politics. Besides, Papi couldn't stand much of anything that wasn't directly related to him. Violeta, though, proclaimed they were getting along better than ever.

Fernando's legs were atrophying faster than the rest of him. Enrique took extra time massaging his father's calves, which were thickly netted with varicose veins. He bent Papi's knees, rotated his ankles, lifted his legs, then pushed hard against the balls of his feet to stretch his muscles. "Well, you're finally getting some exercise," Enrique teased. "When you wake up, you'll be in better shape than ever."

The remains of the Great Court Conjurer's costume were in a cardboard box near the bed, the detritus of his public persona for over a decade: his bald rubber wig and queue, his embroidered pajamas, the silk slippers that curled at the tips, all smelling vaguely of gunpowder. Mixed in with these were his velvet cape and magic wand and the six garish rings he'd taken to wearing in recent months. Enrique laid his head against his father's massive chest. It was barely moving but he could hear the faint ticking of his heart. His brain might be dead, but his heart was too big to ever stop.

The night before last, Enrique had moistened Papi's lips with a few drops of scotch and swore that his father had tried to smile at him. "That's impossible," Dr. Kleinman said when

Enrique reported this to him the following morning. "There's no brain activity whatsoever." But what did that mean exactly? Wasn't his heart still beating? Couldn't he feel his own son's hands? Enrique knew that Papi wouldn't surrender to death so willingly.

Today, he'd brought along a few music tapes to play for his father: the boleros of Beny Moré, the warbly voiced Olga Guillot, his favorite American singers, Vic Damone and Tony Bennett. Over the years, Papi had gotten to know Vic and Tony personally, taking a little steam with one, talking show business or women with the other. As their stages grew smaller and their audiences older, the world beyond Las Vegas seemed increasingly out of their reach.

Enrique couldn't remember when he'd last eaten. He wanted to bring his son to the hospital and have them share a pot of hot chocolate, the way he and Papi used to do. Fernandito looked like a miniature version of his grandfather, so much so that everyone started calling him Papito. Enrique recalled the old days with his father: eating lunch at the Flamingo coffee shop, poring over the newspapers for macabre crimes, Papi's flamboyant recitations of Martí.

It was the twins' fourth birthday. Delia had come with the girls to Las Vegas to celebrate. But what sort of celebration could they have in their grandfather's hotel suite? For starters, the room was devoid of furniture. Papi had replaced the sofa and bed with mountains of pillows and tasseled silk cushions, living in what he imagined to be the style of a nineteenth-century Chinese lord. The children loved the pillows, especially Fernandito, but Enrique's back was killing him from trying to sleep on the floor.

In the television cabinet he'd found an old video of *Black Fear,* the teen horror film Papi had acted in years ago. Enrique watched the movie every night after Delia and the kids went to bed. He replayed the scene of his father as the janitor over and over again, following Papi as he dragged himself past the haunted school lockers (he would soon be dispatched by their contents), trying desperately to look over his shoulder at the camera. This broke Enrique's heart more than anything.

On Monday night, after watching the scene for the hundredth time, Enrique decided to sort through the mountains of papers in his father's closet. He hoped to find more photographs of Mamá but there weren't any he hadn't seen before. What he found was a love letter from her to Papi on his thirty-fifth birthday. *Amor de mi vida,* it began in her close, neat handwriting. *Eres el hombre para mí, ahora y por siempre.* Her love wafted off the page, saturated every word. It pained Enrique to read it. Who had ever loved him like that?

Then he searched for a will or anything else that looked quasi-official. Amid the candy wrappers and bar bills, the piles of IOUs and credit card receipts, Enrique found an unopened letter addressed to him from Leila in Iran. It was dated over two years ago. Why hadn't Papi given it to him?

Enrique slipped the letter in his pocket and reread it every chance he got. Leila wrote that she was curious about his life, that she had regrets about him and wanted to visit. But what was there to tell since they'd parted? He was twenty-seven years old, married, the father of three. Most days he wasn't too unhappy. His work wasn't as exciting as gambling but it was steady and satisfying and people, by and large, respected him. Things weren't terrible with Delia either. She cared for him and she was a decent mother, especially with the help of that saint of a babysitter, Marta. Above all, she was familiar. What other family did he have?

On average, he and Delia made love twice a month. That was twenty-four times a year or, if the pace continued, another nine hundred and six times before he retired. This depressed Enrique more than he cared to admit. To think that he would probably make love less than a thousand more times in his life, to the same woman. Enrique couldn't help wondering what it would be like to see Leila again. Would she still captivate him with her voice, with the intensity of her stare? He decided to write back to her. He wasn't packing his bags yet but he wouldn't refuse to see her either. No, he wouldn't rule anything out.

Enrique walked down the long corridor of the hospital to the lobby. He put a quarter in the vending machine and picked up a copy of the *Las Vegas Review-Journal*. The headline story was about a ghost town that had been discovered deep in the Nevada desert. According to anthropologists studying the site, the town was called Wings Without Feathers and the main occupations of its inhabitants had been drinking and gambling. That sounded like Nevada all right.

Also on the first page was more news on the Wonder Bread truck scandal. The police were reporting that the shiny white truck was now implicated in the theft of seven female bodies from the Las Vegas county morgue (the previous count had been five). Just yesterday, the truck had been sighted at a heist of sapphires from the Mirage Hotel. Papi would have loved this story. He appreciated anything that illustrated the lengths to which human beings went to satisfy their strangest longings.

There was a chapel in the hospital and Enrique stopped by on his way out. He hadn't set foot in a church since his days in Jamaica but it comforted him to believe, even fleetingly, that God might dwell in such a small place. Enrique got on his knees and prayed that his father wouldn't die over some stupid trick. Papi's childhood nemesis, Padre Bonifacio, used to liken evil to a chicken hawk gliding in the wind—*clerk! clerk!*—waiting to prey on those whose vigilance flagged. But there was no evil here, Enrique thought sadly. Nobody to blame. No victim, no enemy. Only bad luck.

The fact was that his father had been shot while performing his bullet-catch trick. It'd happened on the main stage of the Flamingo Hotel before a sold-out holiday crowd. It was supposed to have been Papi's big comeback (yet another one). According to eyewitnesses, after the gun went off the Great

Court Conjurer—his face bright with alarm and spattered blood—shouted dramatically: "Close the damn curtains! I'm dying!" It took the audience another minute to realize that Fernando Florit was seriously wounded. Then all hell broke loose.

Enrique got a retired firearms expert to examine the muzzle-loading musket that Papi had used for his trick. It turned out that due to the age and corroded condition of the weapon, grains of gunpowder had been seeping from the barrel into the cylinder. After years of use, the charge in the loaded barrel—which had never been intended to be fired—exploded, along with the charge in the cylinder. This meant that with every performance, his father, unknowingly, was drawing closer to tragedy.

Outside the hospital, a couple of scrub jays were making a racket in a date palm tree. The morning was growing hotter. Enrique got in his car and drove to a toy emporium on the outskirts of Las Vegas. He picked out talking dolls for his daughters, a starter telescope for Fernandito, a Winnie the Pooh piñata, and five pounds' worth of candy to fill it with. Then he passed by the supermarket for a gallon of ice cream and a ready-made cake. They would have the twins' party poolside, invite any children who happened to be there.

Enrique settled the purchases in the trunk of his Buick and maneuvered his way back to the city. The road was deserted. The sky was rapidly turning over with clouds. Tumbleweeds came out of nowhere and bounced off the hood of his car. Enrique slowed down and turned on his headlights. The old-timers liked to recall the windstorm that took off the roof of the Kit-Kat Lodge years ago, exposing the hookers and their johns inside, most notably the visiting mayor of Sacramento.

By the time he returned to the hotel, the winds were dying down and the sun was back in charge. There was an urgent message waiting for him from Dr. Kleinman. Enrique rushed to a pay phone in the lobby, already knowing, but needing to hear the news for himself. Dr. Kleinman told him that with his last breath Fernando Florit had opened his eyes, attempted a bow, and died.

❧

There was an astonishing number of tuberoses at the Desert Rose Chapel in Las Vegas, each tolling their scent like a bell. A Cuban bolero played on the sound system, just like Papi would have wanted. The velvet lining of his coffin matched the flowers' ivory shade precisely. Dozens of burning candles stole most of the air in the place. Enrique studied his father's face before closing the lid. It looked pink and puffy, like a crying baby's. Papi's eyes were sealed shut but his mouth was half-open, as if snapping a last gasp of air. Enrique pictured what his father must have looked like as an infant. Could anyone have guessed that fifty-eight years later, his end would so resemble his beginning?

Enrique sat in the front pew of the chapel and felt the heat rising from the overflow crowd. He recognized a number of faces from the magic world: the Australian dwarf who levitated blocks of concrete; the turbaned Germans who were dominating the magic scene with their Bengal tigers; the New York daredevil who'd once extricated himself from a steel box on a flaming raft as it sped down the Niagara River toward the falls. No mere funeral could dampen their razzle-dazzle.

The Germans were going on about how Las Vegas was one of the navels of the universe (there were supposed to be nine altogether), a holy place where the earth met the heavens and inexplicable occurrences were common. Why else would Schätzi, their baby Bengal, walk on her hind legs nowhere else? Magic refuted the senses, denied logic and convictions about reality. His father's death gave Enrique the same sense of disbelief.

The gang from the Diamond Pin gathered on the far side of the chapel. Next to the magic world's glitterati, the Texans looked ragtag, lost and blinking in the blaze of candles. Enrique felt fortified by their presence. As a boy, their encouragement had meant the world to him: Son, they'd said, just tumble into the world and deal. Last year they'd attended the funeral of Jim Gumbel's wife, who'd suffered from a long mental illness. In her final months, Sissy Gumbel used to appear at the casino dressed as Catwoman, hissing and scratching at the blackjack dealers.

Despite the evidence, rumors continued to rage regarding the manner and timing of Fernando Florit's death. Had one of his lovers tried to murder him in a jealous rage? (He was known, still, as an incorrigible ladies' man.) Had he arranged his own suicide to escape his debt? (Close to a hundred thousand dollars, according to reliable sources.) Or had a competitor, in a fit of professional envy, done in the Great Court Conjurer? Certainly no one could say that Fernando Florit hadn't lived robustly.

One by one, the men and women who knew and loved him best took their turns at the podium. Violeta Salas, dramatic in a black caftan, declared to her dead lover, "I'll forget everything about you, except you!" Enrique watched the Texans scratch their heads over that one. The old waitress from the Flamingo coffee shop showed up in a wheelchair. Doreen was suffering from Parkinson's disease and boasted to everyone that she'd just had her nipples pierced.

Even the bartender from the Flamingo was there, bolstering himself with an occasional swig from a silver flask. Jorge de Reyes mopped his face with a handkerchief, looking paralyzed by misery, and read from a battered leather book: "It has been said that it is fortunate that we do not have two right hands, for in that case we would become lost among the pure subtleties and complexities of virtuosity."

Camille and Sirenita behaved themselves but Delia held tight to Fernandito, who was squirming in her lap. The children had been having a lot more fun outside the chapel with the magicians, who competed fiercely to entertain them. These world-class performers weren't about to let anyone, much less a dead man at his own funeral, upstage them. Enrique wasn't sure how to explain death to his children. Nobody they knew had ever died, except for their rabbit and two guppies at pre-school.

What bothered Enrique most was that his children would grow up without their grandfather. For Camille and Sirenita, his funeral was largely a grand and boring spectacle. And Fernandito, who finally fell asleep on his mother's shoulder, would have no memory of it at all, or of the man he was named after. Enrique's eyes watered to think of how his son had stolen his father's heart.

The last time Papi had visited, Enrique had found the two of them in the kitchen making scrambled eggs for breakfast. Papi had every condiment known to man on the table—ketchup, relish, hot sauce, jalapeños—and he was teaching Fernandito to pile them high on his plate. "You must maximize every bite, *hijo*! More is always better! Don't let anyone tell you otherwise!" Maybe there was a reason why Enrique ate everything plain.

Soon it was his turn to deliver a eulogy. Enrique hadn't prepared anything formal. His throat was parched and his tongue felt thick and useless in his mouth. He thought of his father's chronic optimism, his refusal to give up, his loyalty to Mamá in spite of his love affairs, his unceasing generosity. There weren't many people like him left. Enrique coughed into his fist and began to speak: "My father used to say that when a man fell, he was also flying, that to fail spectacularly was better than never trying at all—"

Before Enrique could continue, a man in knee-high boots and a brocaded cape strode down the center aisle of the chapel. He announced that he was the deposed Prince of Samarkand and was there to pay his respects to the Great Court Conjurer, a distant cousin by marriage. Then he removed a pistol from his holster, dramatically pressed it to his temple, and let out an archaic howl.

Delia covered the girls' faces but Enrique was transfixed by the sight of him (the tip of his tongue was, oddly, blue). Whoever this intruder was, he certainly had a rapt audience, the greatest names in magic and poker all under one roof. The prince pushed the pistol harder against his temple and recited part of a poem that Enrique recognized as Martí's: "And love, without splendor or mystery, dies when newly born, of glut. The city is a cage of dead doves and avid hunters! If men's bosoms were to open and their torn flesh fall to the earth, inside would be nothing but a scatter of small, crushed fruit!"

Enrique closed his eyes. He heard the rhythm of dried seeds and the thunder of a thousand wings and pictured the deranged prince slowly floating to heaven. When he dared look again, the intruder had disappeared and a dozen fluttering doves had taken his place in the chapel. Then a storm of orange blossoms trembled down upon them, divinely, like rain.

Marta Claros

W hat had come over her husband lately? No matter how tired he was, Frankie mounted her with the regularity of that metronome La Señora had on her upright piano. Tick-tock, back and forth, for what seemed an eternity, until he shuddered with relief. Then after he finished his business, he would settle on her breasts and suckle them for another hour. This made her sore, too, but Marta didn't mind as much. It was what she liked best about making love with Frankie—closing her eyes, pretending he was an infant, the gentle stirring inside her.

Frankie credited his zest in bed to his new heart medicine. Dr. Meyerstein had him participating in a study for a drug that was supposed to combat angina and increase blood flow to the heart. Marta guessed that somewhere along the way, the blood was making a wrong turn and heading for Frankie's thing instead. How many other women in Los Angeles were suffering like her?

At six in the morning, Marta went into José Antonio's room. *Mi hijo, mi hijo, mi hijo.* She loved saying this, had dreamed of saying it for so long that she could hardly believe it was true. Marta tried to wake him up, but José Antonio only shut his eyes tighter. At breakfast he refused to eat anything. How could he reject his scrambled eggs and tortillas? Two whole fresh eggs just for him, not thinned out with water to share with anybody.

"I'm not hungry," he whined. When Marta was a girl, she'd gone hungry every day. She and her brother used to pretend to order steaks at La Mariposa restaurant. "Rare, medium, or well-done?" Evaristo would ask in his best imitation of a first-class waiter. Now José Antonio ate meat at least twice a week.

Across the street, a flock of seagulls gathered on Mr. Haley's roof. What were they doing so far from shore? In El Salvador, people used to predict the weather by the appearance of birds, especially ones they didn't ordinarily see. But Marta couldn't figure out what these seagulls meant.

On the way to her son's day care, Marta turned on the radio. *Pregunta a la psicóloga* was on the air, with its usual parade of lovesick women. One caller complained that her husband had run off with the plumber who'd come to unclog their drain. Another had a crush on her teenaged nephew. The drama never stopped. Marta suspected that she must be missing some essential element of femininity. Maybe sex was like cooking. You needed a touch of spice for the dish to turn out. Dinora envied Marta all the sex she was getting from Frankie—"He stays hard for how long?!"—and jokingly offered to relieve her burden. Marta didn't find this the least bit funny.

José Antonio asked her why the women on the radio were crying but Marta only said that they'd burned their tortillas. What could her son learn from these women? She didn't want him picking up any philandering tips either. As they exited the freeway, a well-spoken gentleman telephoned in. Marta turned up the volume. It wasn't often that a man called the show for advice. He said that his name was Jorge de Reyes and that he was in love with a Las Vegas showgirl who couldn't keep secrets.

"She talks to her friends about everything, even our love-making," he lamented.

"You mean she tells everyone your business?" Dr. Fuertes de Barriga asked. "And you don't like that?"

"Of course he doesn't like that," Marta sniffed.

"Why do you feel you need to control what she says about you?"

"For heaven's sake," Marta shouted at the radio. "What man wants his business spread around town?" She couldn't hear the rest of the conversation because they pulled up to Little Dolphins Day Care. It was only six minutes after eight but the monitor gave them a late slip. Marta didn't understand this gringo fixation with time. She consulted clocks only out of necessity. To have a watch on her wrist like a pretty time bomb ticking away toward eternity—why, it made her nervous to think about it.

Marta stopped by the park before heading to the Florits'. None of the other babysitters were there yet. Not even that single father who'd asked her to dinner was around. Dinora had urged Marta to go out with him at least once. What could it hurt? "The candles say he's a wonderful lover *and* loaded." But Marta declined the invitation. Who had time for romantic capers? Frankie might be a handful but he loved her. Hadn't he proved it by marrying her?

It'd happened so unexpectedly. One morning Dinora had called from a pay phone and told her that Frankie's Korean wife was in town snooping around. The next day, Marta took off work and waited outside the dress factory. Just as Dinora predicted, Mrs. Soon arrived at noon in a chauffeured black sedan. She was petite and very elegant. She wore a jacket with gold chains connecting the buttons. A part of Marta wanted to introduce herself, to pay Mrs. Soon the respect she deserved. After all, how could they be enemies? Didn't they both love the same man? But she was too ashamed to say anything.

Inside the factory, Marta slipped onto the sewing line next to Dinora and pretended to work. The other women greeted her with their eyes but said nothing. They knew what was going on. Marta noticed Mrs. Soon scrutinizing her from afar. Had she recognized her from a photograph? Then *la coreana* walked over to her and with great dignity announced in Spanish: "I return to Seoul this evening and will not come back to Los Angeles. You are free to marry my husband, if you wish."

The women on the line cheered but Marta was speechless. She managed to cross herself before taking Mrs. Soon's hand and bowing deeply. *"Gracias, Señora."* Now she would have Frankie to herself. That same afternoon he took her to City Hall and they got married, just like that. (Frankie surprised her with a new dishwasher from Sears as a wedding present, too.) Afterward they went out for Korean barbecue, to the same restaurant where they'd had their first date. Maybe married life should have begun with a fancier dinner, but Marta didn't care.

Camille and Sirenita were waiting at the front door when Marta arrived. "Marta!" they shouted in unison. "Marta's here!" Señora Delia was in the family room exercising to an aerobics video. The instructor was an actress Marta had seen in movies when she was a child. She must be in her seventies by now, Marta thought. She suspected that it was plastic surgery, not exercise, that kept the actress looking so good.

In the playroom, Marta helped the girls build a castle with expensive wooden blocks. In the toy district, she could've picked up a set for one-tenth the price. Last week she'd bought the children a book that cost ninety-nine cents and made animal sounds when you pressed its buttons. Señora Delia's books cost fifteen dollars each and did nothing at all. Everything at the Florits' was like that, including a steel refrigerator that cost the same as Frankie's down payment on their house. Marta couldn't imagine wasting so much money even if she had a million dollars.

She earned a good salary, ten dollars an hour, and with that she was able to do what she wanted and still send money back to El Salvador. If only she could secure her son's citizenship papers, she would sleep better at night. Her next appointment at the immigration office wasn't for months. On Marta's last visit, two officials had tried every which way to catch her lying. They'd brought up her brother's deportation, too, but Marta maintained that his case had nothing to do with hers. The man was understanding but the woman, Officer Stacey Rodríguez, accused Marta of wasting the government's time.

Marta stuck to her story: that she'd been eight months pregnant when her godmother was hit by a watermelon truck on the corner of Calle Arce; that she'd flown to El Salvador to see her; that in the days of anguish that followed, Marta had given birth prematurely to her son. If she'd waited the time necessary to get his papers in order, she would've lost her job. This was why she'd crossed the border illegally. Marta had a notarized letter from her employers, Mr. and Mrs. Enrique Florit, attesting to these facts.

The truth was that José Antonio had been born the day after Christmas, weighing barely four pounds. When Marta first held her tiny brown bundle of a son, it was as if someone had said: *Marta Claros, we have decided to give you the Pacific Ocean.* That was how big it felt.

Tía Matilde had almost changed her mind about giving Marta the baby, but La Virgen intervened. In her final moments of labor, Tía Matilde prayed loud enough for the midwife to hear: "*Virgencita,* forgive me for breaking my promise to Marta but I can't give her this child." After a long silence, the midwife whispered, "I'm very sorry but he didn't make it. He stopped breathing." Tía Matilde quickly crossed herself and took back her words. Then the boy miraculously opened his mouth, swallowed a gulp of air, and howled to high heaven.

What other proof did Marta need that José Antonio was meant for her?

For five weeks, she and her son traveled through Guatemala and Mexico, taking one bus after another, bribing inspectors, buying diapers and formula along the way. A friend from church had given birth to a baby boy in December, too. Marta convinced the woman, Lety Sánchez, to meet her in Tijuana with the birth certificate. The border guards wouldn't be able to tell their boys apart, Marta urged her, especially *morenitos* like them. The plan worked perfectly: Lety ended up taking José Antonio across the border as her own child.

❧

Camille and Sirenita had colds and couldn't go to swimming practice. Their favorite stroke was called the butterfly, though there was nothing light or graceful about it. The girls churned up so much water doing it that they nearly emptied the pool. Marta was relieved that they were skipping practice today. Watching them made her feel guilty. After many expensive lessons with Mr. Karpov, she'd never learned to swim. Señora Delia hadn't fired her, though, despite the Russian's complaints.

Her *patrona* was in a bad mood again. Lately, she fought with her husband over inconsequential things—the temperature of the house, the amount of television the children watched. If only a fraction of what Marta heard on the radio was true, then it was likely that one of them was having an affair.

"I could shoot him sometimes," Señora Delia complained over a cup of herbal tea. She was still perspiring from her aerobics workout.

"I did," Marta said.

"Did what?"

"Shoot my husband."

"You killed Frankie?" Señora Delia nervously set her cup in its saucer.

"Of course not." Marta straightened up. "I meant my first husband, in El Salvador." She saw the fear growing on Señora Delia's face. "But I didn't aim to kill. I only shot him in the foot so he'd leave me alone."

"Did it work?"

"Actually, it did." Marta laughed, and her *patrona* joined her.

It was dark by the time Marta picked up José Antonio from day care. The shadows from the trees patterned the sidewalks in lace. How the days flew by when she spent them with children. At La Doctora's house in Beverly Hills, this had been her loneliest hour. Marta wanted to stop and pick up some fried chicken at the take-out place on Olympic but it had become too dangerous, a gang hangout. Last time Frankie was there, one of the *cholos* had tried to break a bottle over his head.

José Antonio was asleep in the backseat and snoring comically, one long snort followed by a couple of short ones. Marta hoped her son wasn't coming down with the twins' cold. Marta couldn't bear it when he endured the slightest discomfort. One day they would visit El Salvador together and bring twenty suitcases filled with presents for everyone, especially Evaristo and Tía Matilde. She wanted to track down her father, too. How surprised Papá would be to meet his grandson. Wasn't José Antonio proof that she hadn't forgotten him, that she loved him still?

Marta found it difficult to keep her eyes on the road. She kept glancing in the rearview mirror at her son, who had one hand draped over his forehead like a TV starlet. His limbs were relaxed and easy, his dreams sweetly peaceful. To have a child, Marta thought, was to hope all over again. *Mi hijo, mi hijo, mi hijo.* She rolled down her window and let the words drift into the breeze.

Leila Rezvani

Leila tentatively entered the beauty salon in northern
Tehran. It was hidden behind the courtyard of a curios
shop that sold gold and coral jewelry. She'd gotten the
name of the place from Yasmine, who'd gotten it from an
actress friend who performed with an underground theater
company. The salon was simple, with fake flowers and worn
furniture, but it was welcoming and warmly heated on this
chilly day. Inside, a dozen women without head scarves were
chatting and smoking heavily.

The owner, Farideh Sadhrapoor, greeted Leila with an
embrace and offered her melon and pistachio cookies. "We've
been expecting you, dear."

Leila hoped to visit California next summer and she was
determined to look good when she arrived. Since Enrique had
written to her (he said that he hadn't received her letter for two
years), Leila had started working out at a private aerobics stu-

dio near her home. She avoided starches and sweets, and swam for an hour every night after Mehri went to bed. So far, she'd lost twelve pounds. She'd begun stockpiling new lingerie, too, sexy bras and panties from France that she bought on the black market for a hundred dollars a pair. They were the opposite of the industrial-strength Iranian bras sold by the street vendors, who punched the cups with their fists to show how sturdy they were.

At the salon, Leila opted for the full bridal treatment. It cost a fortune—two months of an office worker's salary—but in five or six hours, the owner assured Leila, she would be fully coiffed, depilated, moisturized, massaged, manicured, pedicured, and given a stimulating multigrain facial. In a word, she would be transformed.

"Our motto is 'Kill me, but make me beautiful,'" Farideh smiled, shaking a bangled wrist. "So what's the special occasion?"

"I'm going to Los Angeles," Leila said quietly, "to visit a friend."

"A *friend*?" Farideh teased, raising her eyebrows until they nearly merged with her flaming red hairline.

"No, it's not like that." Leila was embarrassed, but she was pleased that Farideh would think her capable of having an affair. Maybe all was not yet lost. She had to fight the urge to tell her about Enrique's tattoo, a pair of dice on his left biceps entwined with her name in Persian lettering (he'd sent her a picture of this). But she couldn't risk crossing the line from daring to outright scandalous.

"And your husband has given you permission to travel?" Farideh asked incredulously. "By *yourself*?"

A few women drifted over, trailing smoke from their cigarettes. They were in various stages of beautification—highlights here, half-tweezed eyebrows there, mustaches and facial hair awaiting removal by thick sewing thread. Everyone wanted to hear about Leila's upcoming trip.

How could she tell them that she was barely sleeping from the anticipation? Enrique had written that he was married and had three children—three!—but he was eager to see her again and hadn't stopped thinking about her. He'd quoted a line from a Cuban poet: " 'Love happens in the street, standing in the dust of saloons and public squares: the flower dies the day it's born.' " Then he'd added, "I look forward to resurrecting our flower."

"I'll be taking my daughter with me. Mehri was born in the States, but we moved back home when she was a baby." Leila could feel the envy and excitement in the room. "We're going to Disneyland."

"Ahhh!" the women exclaimed. They knowledgeably compared the merits of the original theme park in California with the vast Florida compound. Every woman at the beauty salon had relatives in America. They told of uncles and cousins who'd gone there to study and had stayed, or returned for visits only to criticize life in Iran. Often, the men changed their names to Mike or Fred, short names like the bark of a dog. How could these compare to their beautiful Persian names?

"There's no respect for women there," the wife of a wealthy bazaar merchant complained, stubbing out a contraband cigarette. "College girls go drinking and whoring with no one to look after them. Where are their fathers and brothers?"

"I hear so many lies I don't know what to believe anymore." A middle-aged woman frowned, her head rattling with foil packets of highlights. "But everything they hear about us is also untrue."

"Things have changed so much," sighed a thick-browed woman with shimmering nails. "We used to drink in public and pray in private. Now we pray in public and drink in private."

Everyone laughed, although the joke was familiar.

"Now, ladies," Farideh interrupted. "We need to get started on our new customer. *Eshkal nadare?* Come this way, dear. Some tea, first?"

"Yes, thank you." Leila sat on a flowered sofa and accepted a steaming cup from the samovar. She noticed a woman at the far end of the salon, her hair done up in braids and pink ribbons. She wondered if her husband liked her this way.

It hadn't been easy convincing Sadegh to let her go to California. She had had to agree to his conditions. In fact, he'd had a lawyer draw up a contract, with a smattering of seals and signatures. Above all, Sadegh wanted an unlimited number of temporary wives for the duration of their marriage. Leila pretended that this was a great sacrifice on her part. Of course, she knew her husband wouldn't have the nerve to do it. He would be too embarrassed by his impotence.

Sadegh demanded that Leila go to California for no longer than seventeen days, that she was not, under any circumstance, to visit Disneyland—referred to in the document as "a cesspool of American degeneracy"—or to wear shorts or bare her arms above the wrist. Leila was also contractually obligated to purchase for her husband a long list of American products, including boxer shorts, chunky peanut butter, Pop-Tarts, and instant mashed potatoes with packaged gravy.

At first, Sadegh hadn't wanted to let Mehri travel. He said he would miss her too much and didn't want her corrupted by Western ways. Leila knew that Sadegh loved their daughter. Not once did he mention Mehri's weight (she was growing quite plump) or her increasingly unsightly nose. He brought her chocolate ice cream every night and took her for visits to his nuclear facility, where Mehri got to wear what they affectionately called her "space suit." Leila was worried about radiation contamination but her husband dismissed her concerns.

Sadegh tried bribing Mehri to stay with him in Tehran instead of going to the States. He promised her a brand-new rifle and a trip to a shooting range (something she was longing to try) but in the end, the chance to go to Hollywood proved too alluring. Leila wished they could leave Iran for good, but this was impossible. Sadegh would track them down in California, kidnap Mehri back. Then he would make certain that Leila lost all maternal rights.

Her husband didn't discuss his years in the States except to say that they were the worst years of his life. "Nobody should live with their enemy" was his only response to questions about his studies abroad. When Sadegh referred to America at all it was as that ruined country, *mamlekat-e-kharabshodeh*. He never mentioned their trip to the Grand Canyon or returning home to find his twin brother dead in their dining room. Sadegh had stuck to his lies for so long that the lies had become the truth, even for him.

Leila secured a sugar cube between her teeth and sipped the scalding tea through it. Sugar was not on her diet, but surely one tiny cube couldn't hurt. In the United States, she would need to remember to drop the sugar cubes *in* her tea. She looked around and felt a kinship with the women here. Why hadn't she sought them out before? Trying to look good in this country was a radical act. To show a bit of ankle or a polished nail was the height of subversion. Unfortunately, this obsessive preoccupation with appearance left little energy for more serious pursuits.

Who would she miss, Leila wondered, if she left the country? So many of her relatives had already fled—to Germany, Sweden, Switzerland, France. Her Uncle Kazem and his second wife, an Italian biologist named Claudia, had shocked everyone by declaring themselves Marxists and moving to the Soviet Union. Aunt Parvin had left, too, after Uncle Masood died. Nowadays she was living in London off the largesse of her former archenemy, Leila's own mother.

Last year, Maman had finally married the horticulturalist, in a wedding that made the society pages of every British newspaper. She and Mr. Fifield owned a town house near Hyde Park and a country estate in Sussex with award-winning gardens, a showpiece for prospective customers. Maman continued painting her watercolors, distributing them among her friends and family as gifts. Even Mehri had received one of a basset hound for her birthday.

Leila worried about her daughter learning to become a woman in Iran. Once she'd overheard Mehri praying to God to change her into a boy. Who was she to discourage her? Worse still, she feared that her daughter was turning into a younger version of Sadegh—serious, impatient, forever dissatisfied. Mehri revered her father and wanted to be just like him. If she wasn't the best at everything she did, she threw a tantrum. Her teachers had sent her home from school on numerous occasions for fighting with her classmates. Leila suspected that her daughter shared her father's disdain toward her.

Besides Mehri, there were only two people Leila would miss if she left: her father and Yasmine. But Yasmine wasn't long for the country either. Since she'd been caught drinking and dancing at a private party (the local *komiteh* had been summoned by a jealous neighbor), she was plotting her escape. Yasmine had been charged with decadence and spent a week in jail. Her friend was lashed so viciously that her back looked like a butcher's display of ground lamb. And she was one of the lucky ones. Hundreds like her disappeared every day and were never heard from again.

Only Baba remained steadfast in his support of the country. He was like a stubborn captain who would go down with his ship. It was a question of loyalty, not to the government but to the land, to *his* land, which he refused to abandon. Dr. Nader Rezvani was condemned—yes, that was the word—to Iran like thirst to a desert. Leila decided that there was something self-serving about her father's stance. Hadn't Baba always done what he believed without regard for the consequences to his family?

When Leila had confided to him that she was thinking of divorcing Sadegh, he'd joked, "Elizabeth Taylor has nothing on my daughter!" Then Baba had grown serious. "Here, my light, real virtue is admired but not practiced. You must do what you believe. Whatever your decision, you can count on my support." He hadn't said another word about it. Why hadn't he asked her more questions? Didn't he care how she felt? Her father, she concluded, was a man first. One man didn't interfere in the marriage of another.

After Leila finished her tea, Farideh led her to the masseuse. Leila stripped off her clothes and let the sinewy woman—she introduced herself as Bita—coat her body with an amber oil that smelled of oranges and mint. Bita massaged Leila's neck and shoulders, then methodically worked down her spine, popping two vertebrae. As Bita pushed against her lower back, Leila's nipples tightened. It had been so long since anyone had touched her with the slightest intention of pleasure that she began to cry.

"I'm so sorry. Am I pressing too hard?" Bita asked.

"No, no. It's fine."

"The body is intelligent," Bita said softly. "It tells you what it needs. *Eyb naðare.* Cry all you want. This often happens the first time."

"Please continue," Leila said, wiping her eyes.

She tried to imagine Enrique seeing her naked again after so many years. Would he still find her beautiful? Trace his hands along her waist? Gently rest his head on her breasts? What did his wife look like? Enrique had written that Delia had been born in Cuba, like him, but grew up in the States. Leila knew all too well the pull of the familiar. In a contest for his love, who would win?

"Now breathe deeply and we'll have you relaxed and ready for the rest of your treatments. When you leave here today, nobody will recognize you."

"Motashakkeram," Leila said. *"Kheyli mamnum."*

Recently, Sadegh had been acting more kindly toward her. Not warm or loving, just less angry and violent. He hadn't hit her since the day before New Year's. That beating had left bruises that took nearly a month to heal. Leila attributed the change in his behavior to his health worries. Her husband wasn't old or overweight but at his last checkup Dr. Banuazizi had told him that his blood pressure was a little high for a thirty-four-year-old. Now Sadegh was convinced that a heart attack was imminent.

Since then he'd stopped having sex with Leila, claiming that it overtaxed his circulatory system. His bluffing about temporary wives hadn't diminished, a contradiction Leila found amusing. At least she was no longer forced to embrace him. More and more, Sadegh dispatched her to their villa on the Caspian Sea on the pretext that he needed a few days' peace. She welcomed these retreats from the city. Sometimes she stayed away for weeks.

Leila settled on a squeaky swivel chair to get her hair dyed chestnut brown. She'd been using a packaged coloring product made in Austria, but it turned her hair dry and brittle.

"You're too young to be all white," the hairstylist said, picking at Leila's roots with the long handle of a comb.

"It's hereditary," she lied.

Would her brother's hair have turned prematurely white if he were alive? It was impossible to picture him any older than he'd been on their last day together. She still visited Hosein's grave and felt his presence beneath the rotting figs. But she was no longer comfortable speaking to him aloud. There was no privacy at the cemetery. With the war still raging, people were paying respects to their dead day and night.

A customer wearing cropped pants and a bright orange top waved around a cassette that she'd bought from a Turkish vendor in the alley behind the salon. "He told me it was the latest hit in Ankara," she announced, slipping it into Farideh's tape deck. A lively pop song filled the air. Several customers clapped along to the rhythm.

Last year, the prayer leader in Tehran had denounced all forms of music as evil. Leila had been forced to stop Mehri's piano lessons on the grounds that Mozart was too provocative for a good Muslim girl. In the ensuing confusion, Sadegh had managed to buy a Steinway grand piano for next to nothing. (He easily rationalized breaking the government's rules when it suited his interests.) But it wasn't just the musicians who'd become refugees. In Iran, nearly everyone was a refugee in one way or another.

With a mischievous look, Farideh turned down the lights, thrust out her small breasts, and threw back her shoulders. She began to dance, eyes hooded, lips parted, hands twitching and sweeping like a pair of butterflies. As she undulated her way among the customers, her bangles tinkled and her prominent buttocks lifted and dipped. The women hooted as if she were a belly dancer. Two more got up, including the *bazaari*'s wife, who sensuously shook her round belly. Leila longed to join the women, but she couldn't force her body to move.

When the music stopped, the women clapped and cheered. But the sound of a distant explosion stopped their merriment. The war with Iraq was dragging on. So many young martyrs were dying with "keys" to heaven—cardboard cutouts, in fact—pressed to their chests. Thousands of ordinary citizens were also dying. Funeral processions ensnarled the already nightmarish traffic in Tehran. People were moonlighting as professional mourners to make extra money. (There was no shortage of this type of work.) Red tulips, symbol of the martyrs, were planted everywhere.

Others lost their minds from the blasts. One bomb had leveled an apartment building in Leila's father's neighborhood. Baba's colleague and close friend Dr. Ali Houshmand had been killed, along with his entire family. Baba was inconsolable. A week after the attack, their dog, Zozo, who'd been lost on a trip to the mountains, reappeared. Zozo stood guard at the rubble, whining and growing thinner, waiting for the Houshmands to return. Nobody had the heart to take the dog away. Leila didn't understand its persistence. She understood much better the pull of the grave.

Silence fell over the beauty salon like the sadness of winter. These past few days, the winds had blown red dust everywhere, upending trees and knocking out the electricity in the southern part of the city. Odd blue centipedes were infesting the flowering trees. People nervously predicted an earthquake but the winds kept howling and the earthquake never came. Leila looked around at the other women in the salon, partly obscured by the cigarette smoke. By next summer, she decided, her life would be nothing like theirs.

(1987)

May 25

Marta

Marta changed the bandage on her son's forehead. Part of the oozing crust of the wound was stuck to the gauze, but at least it wasn't bleeding anymore. Yesterday José Antonio had fallen in preschool during a game of hide-and-seek and broken open his forehead. The nurse showed Marta how to change the dressing and bandage his forehead, not too tightly or it would cut off the circulation. Marta took her son home early and put him to bed. She wanted him strong for today. Today of all days, because José Antonio was becoming an American citizen.

"Does it still hurt, *mi amor*? Let me get you some breakfast. You hardly had any soup last night."

"I'm not hungry."

"You have to eat something. I don't want you fainting in front of everyone. What will people say? That I'm a bad mother and don't feed you breakfast?"

The swearing-in ceremony was at ten o'clock. For the occasion, Marta had bought José Antonio a linen suit, two-toned shoes, and a miniature Panama hat. The outfit had cost $61.34 with tax. Exorbitant, but Marta decided it was worth it because from this day forward they could live their lives in peace.

Marta had gotten permission from Señora Delia to take the day off and Frankie planned to close the factory early to prepare for the festivities. The women from Back-to-Heaven were coming over with casseroles (Vilma Colón was making her famous beef-and-plantain stew) and Dinora had promised to bring along her collection of records from the 1940s and '50s. With a couple of drinks in her, she might be persuaded to serenade them with a bolero. Marta had invited everyone she knew to the party: the Florits, José Antonio's classmates, the nannies from the park, her neighbors, the many vendors she'd befriended over the years. This would be a celebration that no one would soon forget.

A breeze stirred the kitchen curtains. Marta made herself a cup of coffee, sweetening it with a wedge of sugarcane. For breakfast, she fixed quesadillas and served them to her son with black beans and cream. For a while, they'd tried those overpriced American cereals but they turned out to be made of nothing but sugar and air. An hour later, they were hungry again. The same went for that Wonder Bread, which left them all constipated. So much of the supermarket food here was like that—colorful packages with only emptiness inside.

"Hurry up. We need to go to church before the ceremony." Marta yawned as she pinned an evil eye charm inside her son's jacket. It was important to take precautions against any possible misfortune. Though she'd slept soundly last night, Marta still felt tired. No doubt all the emotion from yesterday had left her spent.

"I want to watch *Mary Poppins.*"

"We don't have time now." Marta loved the movie as much

as her son. After renting it twice, she'd finally bought a copy of the video. She finished dressing José Antonio, then rubbed lightening cream onto his neck.

Señora Delia disapproved of Marta using lightening cream but how could she understand what a difference a few shades of brown might mean? There was no hiding the prejudice in Los Angeles. At school, one of her son's playmates had told him that nobody but maids spoke Spanish. Then his teacher had instructed Marta to speak only English at home so José Antonio wouldn't get confused. It surprised her that a teacher could be so ignorant.

Outside, the neighborhood was quiet. The German shepherd had trapped the same alley cat up the oak tree. That crazy Mr. Haley was painting his porch a bright yellow. A bird Marta hadn't seen before fussed on her gate. It reminded her of the *tortolitas* back home, cinnamon-colored with their white-striped wings. They liked to flutter in the tamarind trees, making a *rumm-rumm* sound like a motor running, calling to each other from great distances to warn of danger.

On the eight-block drive to church, Marta let her son sit in the front with his seat belt fastened tight. "This is a special day, *hijo*. Don't ask to sit up here tomorrow, or the police will put me in jail."

On *¡Salvado!*, the tearful testimony of Evangelina Huerta, a former Costa Rican beauty queen, was under way. Evangelina confessed that she'd tried to hold up a doughnut shop with her young son's toy gun. In the middle of the robbery—the clerks were so scared that they gave her all the money in the cash register, plus a sack of chocolate glazed doughnuts—she heard the voice of the Lord ordering her to put down the gun. Evangelina fell to her knees in fear and remorse. After handcuffing Evangelina, the arresting officer, who was also Costa Rican, asked for her autograph.

Marta and José Antonio crossed themselves with holy water before entering Saint Cecilia's church. It took a moment for their eyes to adjust to the dim light. The same *viejitas* occupied the front pews: Doña Filomena, whose eldest was awaiting trial in Houston for killing his girlfriend, and Doña Anselma, who, though childless, prayed for everyone else's wayward children. Nearby the three widowed sisters — Leoncia, Eugenia, and Saturnina — sat in their identical black shawls. The sisters had been married to carpenter triplets from Tegucigalpa who, tragically, had been killed on Highway 60 when their truck was hit by an eighteen-wheeler filled with porcelain sinks.

A scent of sandalwood incense filled the air. Marta nodded to the women, who blinked with astonishment at their fancy clothes. Then she led José Antonio to La Virgen's alcove, where they offered her red tulips from their garden. Marta wound her old rosary around her son's clasped hands and together they prayed for the great blessing of José Antonio's impending citizenship. "We couldn't have done it without you, *Virgencita.*"

José Antonio pointed to the stained-glass window showing a distraught Saint Cecilia imploring God for salvation. Saint Cecilia had made a vow of chastity as a young girl, Marta told her son, and she'd kept it in spite of her parents marrying her off to a nobleman. "I want you to think of Saint Cecilia when the girls start coming around and wanting you to do this and that."

"I don't like girls," José Antonio said, sticking out his tongue.

"That's right. And remember that nobody but Mami is allowed to touch you down there or give you a bath. *¿Me entiendes bien?*"

"*Sí, Mami.*"

"Whenever you're tempted to do something bad, you'll feel the hot breath of the devil on your neck. Do you know what to do then?"

"Step on his tail!" José Antonio shouted and stamped his foot.

"Just like that. Then if you're very quiet, you'll feel the flutter of your guardian angel on your cheek, just like a butterfly. That's the brush of his wings, letting you know that you're safe again."

It pleased Marta to see the votive candles burning so cheerfully. She gave her son a dollar for the offerings box, seventy-five cents more than her usual. José Antonio stared at the flames. His eyes looked translucent, as though light were shining through them. How could there be enough room in her heart to hold all the love she felt?

Frankie adored him, too. He was teaching José Antonio to speak Korean and cut his steak into tiny pieces so he wouldn't choke. Each day their love grew, embroidered with tender efforts. What would it be like to love their son five years from now, or ten? Marta felt sorry for the women who expended all their emotions on husbands and lovers. Men came and went— this was a law of the universe—but children were forever.

Marta lit a candle and watched the gray, petaled smoke rise to heaven. As she pulled the stick from the flame, a drop of wax landed on her thumb. She thought of Dinora's candles, stuck with straight pins, foretelling the future. A single red-hot pin meant unrequited love. Wax that melted into the shape of a foot warned of a straying husband (no surprise there). A cascade of wax on the candle's right side signaled a windfall of money.

Confessions were under way on the other side of the church. Marta left José Antonio sitting with the widowed sisters and entered the booth of Padre Ramón, the young priest recently ordained in Guatemala. Everyone said that Padre Ramón was understanding, certainly more so than that doomsday Irish pastor, who warned every penitent that they were on the brink of eternal damnation.

"This is embarrassing for me to admit, Padre, but lately I've been thinking of another man when my husband makes love to me."

"Who do you think of, *hija*?"

"Well, you know that actor Félix Curbela? The one who plays the evil brother on *Mala Sangre?*"

"I'm afraid I don't."

"*Ay,* he's very, very handsome. All the women love him. *Bueno,* every time I picture him smoothing his mustache, I feel something inside me I can't explain. Is this adultery, Padre?"

"No, *hija.* But perhaps you can try to think of something less, shall we say, inflammatory?"

"I'll try, Padre."

"Now, is there anything else?"

"I lied to the immigration officials so that my son could become a citizen."

"Have you prayed to our Lord Jesus Christ for guidance?"

"*Sí,* Padre, but I haven't received an answer yet."

"Has the matter been settled?"

"*Primero Dios,* this morning he becomes a *yanqui.*"

"Then God's will be done."

Outside the immigration office, a jacaranda tree was in full bloom. Marta took this as a good omen. A cluster of aloe plants girded the entrance of the building. With her pocketknife, Marta cut off a thick leaf. A bit of aloe sap would help heal her son's forehead better than any nurse's ointments, and the cut wouldn't leave a scar.

A woman wearing the traditional apron of Oaxaca sold chicken tamales and churros from her cart. Marta was hungry again, but she didn't want to risk staining her clothes before the ceremony. Instead she bought an American flag from a Chinese vendor and gave it to José Antonio, who waved it as if he were in a parade. With the little flag and the bandage on his head, he looked like a tiny war veteran.

In the government building, over three hundred people were gathered in their Sunday best to take their vows of citizenship.

The air was close and thick as wool. Marta removed her son's Panama hat. She looked around and recognized a few faces from her previous visits. She was glad to see that Willi Piedra, the composer from Veracruz, had made it this far. And Cresencia Ortíz was here with her two teenaged sons, whom she'd managed to bring over from Chiapas. They were handsome boys, quiet and malnourished looking. A year from now, they would be fluent in English and each twenty pounds heavier.

A sense of excitement pervaded the hall as the judge entered. Everyone was trying to stay calm until they were sworn in. It wasn't an easy thing to become an American citizen if you were poor and came from a little country like El Salvador. It took lawyers and more money than anybody had. It took patience and prayers and a willingness to wait and wait and possibly still lose everything. Marta rubbed the evil eye charm pinned inside José Antonio's jacket. When he became a citizen, it would be a matter of public record that he was Marta's son. Then they could shout to the skies: "We belong here!" And nobody, nobody could take that away.

June 20

Leila

It was a hot summer morning near the Caspian Sea. Leila stood on the balcony of her villa and looked out over the blue water. In the eaves, a mourning dove was cooing over the fledglings in her nest. The winds were shifting south, ruffling the sea. A patch of clouds was darkening like a slow stain across the skies. A man stood by the edge of the sea gutting fish. Leila had read in the local paper that the number of sturgeon in the sea had shrunk by twenty-five percent. Thousands of seals, turtles, and migratory birds were also dying. What decided these natural catastrophes?

The kitchen was nearly empty. Leila had given away most of the villa's contents to the people in town. Only the chandeliers, the grandfather clock, a side table, and two chairs remained of the furniture. Her husband knew nothing of this because he hadn't been to the villa in a year. Leila made herself a cup of tea and set out her breakfast: flatbread with cherry preserves and dates. Then she served herself a dish of coffee ice cream, crushing a few walnuts with the flat of a knife and sprinkling them on top. It cheered her up to have a little ice cream with breakfast.

Today was Leila's birthday. She was twenty-nine years old. Nobody had remembered it—not her daughter, not her husband, not her father or friends. The grandfather clock in the dining room chimed nine times. She'd listened to it every hour for the past two days. Every minute weighed on her like a tiny sinker, dragging her to an airless place. It was worst after midnight, when the glaze of another day seemed unbearable and the stars looked so shockingly white.

Leila felt guilty leaving her daughter in Tehran with a sore throat but she knew the servants would take good care of her. All Mehri had to do was call and someone would be there to sharpen her pencils, or bring her a cup of tea, or pick up one of her blue exercise books from the floor. Already, she'd forgotten the dream of going to California.

The water level of the Caspian was rising an average of eighteen centimeters a year for reasons that were mysterious to scientists. Was it the clearing of the local land for agriculture that had increased the runoff? Were the underlying movements of tectonic plates responsible? (Seismologists were detecting an unprecedented amount of activity below the sea.) Was it the increase in rainfall? Nobody knew for certain. The Caspian was thirty meters below sea level. Leila studied the graceful curve of the coast and thought it only a matter of time before they were all underwater.

It was confusing to organize the day's pills. Dr. Pezechpour made certain not to give Leila enough at any one time to kill herself, but she'd still managed to collect quite a few. (He'd told her that Iranians killed themselves with stunning infrequency. Was this supposed to be encouraging?) The silver bracelet Enrique had given her was tucked next to her peach-colored pills. Leila slipped it on. It felt heavier than she'd remembered.

There were few psychiatrists left in Iran. Baba had inquired discreetly among his colleagues until he'd found Dr. Pezech-pour at the University of Tehran, teaching anatomy and willing to see Leila on the sly. Dr. Pezechpour could be trenchant but he was annoyingly fond of maxims. "Iranians are like wheat fields," he said. "When the storm comes, they bend; when the storm passes, they stand up again." He never considered abandoning the storm altogether.

Behind the villa, the Alborz Mountains shone blue-black in the sunlight. The cypress trees formed a protective ring around her house, giving off a sharp, medicinal scent. What would she give to go running naked into the sea? Men were judged by the risks they took. And women? By how few. In April, Sadegh had changed his mind and forbidden her to leave the country. No amount of begging would make him relent. *Do you think I'm stupid, Leila? A fool with no eyes in my head?* It was her own fault, she decided, for losing weight and getting those beauty treatments. Her husband knew she wasn't looking this good for him. *Tell me who you were planning to see in California! Tell me, whore, or I'll have you locked up for adultery!* Leila retreated to her room and stayed there for days.

New hatcheries were rising up along the Caspian. Breeders were releasing millions of sturgeon fingerlings into the waves. The hope was that the fingerlings would grow and produce more of the roe that was selling for hundreds of dollars per kilo on the world market. How many lives, Leila wondered, depended on this caviar? She pictured herself slowly entering the sea, surrounded by fingerlings, her chador snatched by the wind like a lost, dark kite.

What would Enrique remember of her then? And Mehri? Would she join forces with Sadegh to vilify her? Sometimes Leila looked at her daughter and knew she was raising a girl who would end up hating her.

Others had managed to find a sense of purpose. Maman was happily married to Mr. Fifield, who'd just bought the biggest landscape architecture firm in Great Britain. Yasmine had left the country and was studying engineering in Munich. (In her last letter she'd quoted some German: "Every hour moves through your heart and the last one kills.") Uncles and aunts and cousins were forging new lives overseas. But Leila merely had the sensation of no sensation, of being outside her body, of watching it from a faraway shore that was already vanishing.

Her bathrobe slipped off one shoulder and Leila gazed down at her body, sheathed in its soiled nightgown. She'd grown flaccid again, heavy with gravity. She was what she couldn't have imagined becoming: a matron, a housewife, a nobody. Was this, too, written on her brow? There were two cigarettes left in her pack. She secured one between her lips and lit it. How satisfying to feel the hot smoke filling her lungs. She smoked and swept the apartment to calm her nerves. Sometimes she read poetry. *The birds have gone in search of the blue direction. The horizon is vertical, vertical, and movement fountain-like and at the limits of vision shining planets spin.*

The same dream plagued Leila night after night: peasant women, their faces veiled, gathered around her in groups of three or four, unraveling mountains of fine thread for hosiery factories. Would they use the untangled strands on the spindles, idle in the dim corners of the room? Would they make something beautiful and new? When she told Dr. Pezechpour her dream, he said: "No matter how fast you run, your shadow keeps up."

Leila went to her bedroom and extracted the tan suitcase from the closet. It contained the wet suit that Enrique had sent her for her birthday seven years ago. She unfolded the rubbery legs, creased from so much time in storage. They looked as if they might crawl around on their own. The flippers were faded but still sturdy and good. She set everything down by the front door of the villa.

This afternoon she would write to Enrique on her best stationery and apologize to him for raising his hopes. She would say that it wasn't enough anymore for the seasons to turn, for the mourning dove to tend to her fledglings. Everything was a copy of something else, unoriginal, uninspiring. She would tell him that all she wanted now was to follow the birds in a blue direction, learn more than she knew before. (Last night she'd seen an owl swoop past her window, its eyes swathed in white like gleaming bandages, and she'd imagined it was her brother.) Maybe the end was like the beginning, she would say, all loneliness and nothingness.

Leila lit her last cigarette. Outside her window, wooden boats methodically plowed the sea. How much sturgeon would be harvested from the Caspian today? Leila no longer cared. She didn't believe in the sea anymore. With the French doors of the balcony shut, the villa was, at last, completely silent. Even the leaves of the cypress trees were mute. Leila extinguished her cigarette in the crystal ashtray and watched the smoke drift through her fingers. She noticed the veins in her right hand, the way they wound around her wrist. Her pulse was surprisingly steady, like the strokes of the clock announcing the hour.

July 4

Enrique

The Fourth of July started out promisingly enough, pure and hot. The neighbors trickled in with their children and fruit pies, cole slaw and ice cream. Marta arrived to help with the party and brought her son along. Soon the kids were clamoring to jump in the pool. The boys from down the block insisted on holding a swimming contest but Camille and Sirenita won every race. Enrique knew it was petty, but he loved that his daughters beat every boy in the neighborhood. Those expensive swimming lessons had really paid off.

Enrique offered his guests beer and wine coolers. Everyone was drinking heavily but nobody seemed the worse for it in this sun. He felt a slight buzz himself, which made him blandly anxious. Enrique looked around at his life—the children in the pool, his wife tossing a salad, the solidity of his house and his neighborhood (they didn't have an ocean view but they were a short walk to the ocean), the hummingbird whirring near his newly planted jasmine. Did any of this really belong to him?

Things weren't ideal at home but they were still better than he could've hoped for growing up. The hotel rooms and cheap apartments that he and Papi had lived in had seemed normal at the time. Nobody they knew would've told them differently. The truth was that there was no logic to their existence, but it existed all the same. And they'd been happy in their own way. What Enrique worried about most in those days was that his father would die before him. Now that the worst had happened, what else did he have to fear?

Maybe his childhood had ruined him for any ordinary life. He never trusted when things were good, at least not in any calculable way. He wasn't even sure what "good" meant. In any case, it probably wasn't how most people defined it. Besides, what did "good" matter when it could so easily disappear? Since he'd begun corresponding with Leila, he'd been tempted to walk away from his life every day. It scared him that he might be capable of this.

Enrique wanted to go to Las Vegas for a while and clear his head. Nothing else focused his attention like a high-stakes poker game. He missed the twenty-four-hour neon, and the crowds on Fremont Street, and the endless sunsets at Red Rock Canyon. And he could always count on a good table at the Diamond Pin. Last he'd heard, Jim Gumbel had remarried and Johnny Langston had shot up the giant cowboy at the Pioneer Club that repeated, *Howdy pardner, welcome to Las Vegas.* How else was he supposed to get any sleep?

Enrique planned to take his son with him this time, show him where Papi used to perform. Already, Fernandito could do a few decent magic tricks, including one with fake blood and a stuffed vampire bat that made his sisters scream. For his birthday he'd asked for a fine top hat and a magic wand just like his grandfather's. It unsettled Enrique to think that Fernandito might follow in Papi's footsteps. How was it possible to both encourage *and* protect his son? It pained him to think of leaving his children. No matter their troubles, Papi hadn't abandoned him.

The barbecue was sizzling with burgers and prime cuts of steak. The women, slightly sunburned and wearing pastels and plaids, were bunched together in a far corner of the patio. Their husbands settled around the picnic table for a poker game. Enrique had known most of the men for years — several were regulars at the Grand Casino — but nobody ever exchanged anything more than a few pro forma complaints about the Dodgers.

The afternoon whistled with early fireworks. The kids climbed out of the pool, towel-wrapped and shivering, and ate their cheeseburgers and chips, except for Fernandito, who was busy practicing a trick with brown eggs and pennies. One of the mothers, a preschool teacher, read a story to the younger children about a lonely circus elephant. Enrique remembered the poster from Varadero from his and Papi's first apartment in Santa Monica. In the poster, an elephant with a jeweled headdress stood on its hind legs warily eyeing the ringmaster while a tiger roared behind them. No animals — humans included — were meant to be domesticated, Enrique decided. It took away their fire for survival.

At about four o'clock, Delia sent Marta out to buy more wine coolers at the liquor store on Entrada Avenue. She was supposed to buy sparklers for the kids, too, if she could find any. The doorbell rang and a postman handed Enrique a special delivery letter from Iran. A delivery on a holiday? His last letters to Leila had gone unanswered for months. He didn't know what to believe anymore. A part of him was giving up on her entirely; another part still wanted her to make him hope. Who was it that said the devil tortured men by keeping them waiting?

The letter was postmarked two weeks earlier, on their birthday. The stationery was thick and cream-colored and her hand-writing was perfect, as if Leila had written a draft before copy-ing out what she wanted to say. Enrique couldn't focus on most of what she'd written. He tried to slow down his reading, but none of what she said made sense. Why was she apologizing to him? Why couldn't she visit him? Had her husband found out about their affair?

Leila's letter only went round and round with incompre-hensible sorrow. There were no specifics, no promises, no explanations, just this one fact: she wasn't coming to California. Enrique felt like overturning the damn barbecue, uprooting his jasmine vines, anything to relieve his frustration. Why couldn't he convince her to trust him? Why couldn't he convince him-self? He read the letter for the tenth time, looking for a clue. Miserable, he jammed the letter in his pocket and returned to the backyard party.

Just then everything happened so fast that he couldn't have related it with any coherence. In retrospect, every piece of the sequence might have been anticipated, recognized for its importance, for where it could lead. Accidents didn't happen all at once. He had to believe that. What could be more pre-dictable than a barbecue on the Fourth of July?

Yet it seemed to Enrique that everything did occur simulta-neously: the girasoles' faint lace in the sky; Marta gone off to the liquor store with forty dollars in her purse; the arrival of Leila's last letter, with its sad, circular language; the kids crowding into the twins' room to play Monopoly; the adults so busy with their card games and conversations that nobody— not one of the twelve of them—saw Marta's son slip into the deep end of the pool.

Enrique returned to the backyard party and spotted the boy floating facedown in the water, his shorts ballooning a bright red. For a second he thought it might be Fernandito, and his heart jumped up his throat. As he raced toward the pool he saw that it was the babysitter's son and immediately dove in after him. After the shock of the cold water, time slowed to an impossible degree. Enrique swam as hard as he could, terrified that he would run out of breath before reaching the boy.

José Antonio was unconscious, his skin sallow and cold. Enrique tucked him under one arm and pulled him to the edge of the pool. Gently, he settled the boy on the lawn. José Antonio's head flopped to one side. Water poured from every orifice. Enrique pinched the boy's nostrils, pressing his mouth over José Antonio's. It tasted, disconcertingly, of potato chips. Above them, the palm trees rustled.

The children raced downstairs when they heard the commotion and started screaming, convinced that José Antonio was dead. But Enrique could feel the boy's pulse and knew he still had a chance. José Antonio's chest rose and fell with every breath. Then his jaw began moving from side to side. Suddenly, his eyes opened wide and he stared straight at Enrique. His pupils fanned closed like dark petals. Enrique leaned the boy forward and patted him on the back until everything in his stomach came up pale yellow.

"There's still time for you," Enrique whispered and held him close.

In life there was a before and an after, Enrique believed, a gap between what you wanted and what you got, between what you planned and what actually happened. There were no advance warnings, no billboards advertising a tragedy to come. The moment before always seemed so ordinary, like any other. Pink programs and straw hats whirling through the air. Wayward storks landing in a confusion of feathers and legs. It hurt Enrique to remember this.

There was no convincing "why" to anything, no answers, just good luck or bad tilting life one way or another. Enrique didn't put faith in odds, or statistics, or reason anymore. Some things just couldn't be outrun. Odds might be calculated, inattention focused, reasoning torn apart. But luck, he thought, luck was something else entirely.

By the time Marta returned from the liquor store, José Antonio was warmly wrapped in a beach towel and drinking hot chocolate. The soft stems of his legs jutted out from the white terry cloth. Fernandito tried to cheer him up by performing a magic trick but ended up dropping an egg on his foot instead. After checking his vital signs one last time, the ambulance crew packed up and left.

Marta was inconsolable, provoking defensiveness in the guests. "It could've happened to any of us," the preschool teacher said. But Enrique could tell that Marta didn't believe her. Meticulously, she checked her son for bruises and kissed him all over. At the liquor store she said she'd imagined wings on his back, like the ones Salvadoran women made for sick babies, the ones who couldn't be saved. She'd rushed back to the house frightened to death.

Without warning Marta handed Enrique her purse, picked up her son, and started walking purposefully toward the sea. Enrique followed her, still soaking wet from the pool. What else could possibly happen this afternoon? Soon the whole party was following Marta to the beach—a half-dressed parade of his neighbors and their children holding Fourth of July sparklers (Marta had brought back a sack of them) and paper flags. A propeller plane hovered above the shoreline. A couple of miles to the south, the Ferris wheel on the Santa Monica pier turned. Enrique longed to hear its carnival tune.

The coast curved in both directions, looking as though the ends might eventually meet. Only the horizon was straight, two distinct shades of blue. The sun was so bright, it made everything glitter. Seagulls drifted overhead, calling to one another and shedding feathers. The beach was sticky with seaweed and tar. Enrique wasn't sure what to do. Around him, people were jogging and picnicking and playing volleyball as if nothing bad ever happened. The children, led by his daughters, begged to go swimming but Enrique held them back.

Marta strode to the ocean's edge, set José Antonio down in

the sand, and instructed him not to move. "Watch me," she ordered. Marta plunged into the cold water—to her hips, to her waist, to her chest and neck. A wave rolled over her, soft and enormous. She sputtered and rubbed the salt water from her eyes but quickly turned and waved to her son. Enrique watched her in silence from the shore. He was afraid that Marta might sink but instead she rose with the very next wave. Then in a synchrony of arms, legs, and lungs, Marta swam.

Epilogue

Evaristo

Evaristo had a difficult time remembering things. He was only twenty-six but it seemed to him that he was forgetting many lives' worth of detail and incident. Perhaps it was this forgetting that was congesting his skull, splitting it with pain and dizziness. If he didn't remember what he'd seen, nobody would. There were countless dead without anyone to speak for them, without anyone to say: *I am your witness.* But it was no good for him to sit by himself in the mountains. His silence was killing them all over again.

Evaristo lived alone on a remote hilltop with the money Marta sent him monthly from Los Angeles. She'd given him enough to build his wooden house, too: one room painted blue as the winter sky, with a tin roof and a door for each of the four walls. He'd built the house himself with help from a maguey spinner who lived downvalley. Evaristo had wanted each door to face precisely north, east, south, and west and so he'd bought a compass for this purpose.

After the house was finished, Evaristo hired a photographer to climb up the hill and take a picture of it. The portly man set up his tripod, slipped under a mysterious black cloth, and fainted. Evaristo had to revive him with a splash of river water. "Dear Marta," he wrote on the back of the photograph in shaky block letters. "See how you help me find peace. Your loving brother." Marta wrote back with the subsequent month's fifty dollars: "My dearest Evaristo, May God bless you and your little piece of sky. Forever yours, Marta."

It was unusual for a man in the mountains of Morazán to live alone, without family or farming skills, but nobody ever asked Evaristo why he was there. Rumors sprang up about him, none of which he tried to dispel. People said that he'd come to the mountains to escape a witch, that he was dying of a liver disease that blackened his blood, that his heart was broken by an ill-advised love. Who couldn't see this in his eyes? Still, his neighbors understood that the less they knew about him, about any stranger, the safer they were.

Each dawn Evaristo set his cane-backed chair outside the east door and slowly, dragging his chair inch by inch along the swept dirt girdling his house, followed the slow course of the sun. During the rainy season, he stayed inside with his doors wide open, lying in his hammock and watching the clouds descend on the mountains. He got up only to eat: tortillas and beans with eggs or a wedge of cheese. At night, he spent his time reading the hourless stars.

Over the summer, a businessman had opened a boot factory in Gotera and convinced the young people to abandon the fields and work for him. One evening he showed up at Evaristo's place. "*¡Qué vergüenza!* A strong ox like you sitting around doing nothing. I'll see you tomorrow at sunrise." But the following morning, Evaristo arranged his chair for another day of minding the sun.

When the pain in his head subsided, memories taunted him like sharp filaments of light. The priests with sticks up their asses. The schoolgirls taken away by the *guardias* and raped. The year in the border prison awaiting deportation. A fat-bellied gunrunner from Jalisco had tried to force himself on Evaristo (the *pendejo* had climbed into his bunk in the middle of the night) but Evaristo had gouged out the man's right eye. For this, he'd been put in a cell by himself.

It was noon and the mountains shone in the clear air. Not a shred was left of the morning fog. Evaristo traced the outline of individual pines with his forefinger, the arch of an abandoned church, its bell silently tolling for the dead. The barren mountaintops rose above the pines like a row of balding monks. To the north, directly over the sorghum fields, a flock of vultures circled. If only he could be like them, Evaristo thought, unhurried and free of anger.

The corn on the hillsides was almost ripe and Evaristo planned to help his neighbors with the harvest. The farmers joked about his uncalloused city hands, but they appreciated his strength. So many of them had been idled by the war, left with only leg stumps or half an arm, stripped to uselessness like that military jeep down the road.

If he listened closely, Evaristo could hear the river, an hour's walk away. Last month, a *curandera* had come to visit him, smelling of bay leaves and mint. After her invocations and a sprinkling of purifying water, she'd advised him to bathe in the river every Sunday. Only regular baptisms, she said, could make him forget the evil he'd seen. But Evaristo didn't want to forget, and he refused to go.

Today the river seemed to whisper the names of nearby villages: Cacaopera, Jocoatique, Meanguera, Arambala, Perquín. In Los Angeles, Evaristo had heard many beautiful names, too; Spanish names that had nothing to do with the places they described — El Monte, Sierra Bonita, La Cienega — names chewed up like gum in the Americans' mouths.

A few yards from Evaristo's house, a canary made its nest in a banana tree. It sang to him at dusk, sad songs, each one different from the next. As Evaristo watched the skies, he imagined that the canary was his sister come to his side. He laughed to think of this, and the sound of his own voice startled him. The canary stared at him until he grew quiet again. Then it fluttered to a lower leaf of the tree and began another woeful song.

ACKNOWLEDGMENTS

To my kind, unwavering friends and generous readers,
thank you: Chris Abani; Wendy Calloway; Bobbie Bristol;
José Garriga; Micheline Aharonian Marcom; Alice van
Straalen; Bobby Antoni; Scott Brown; Richard Gilbert;
Shideh Motamed-Zadeh; and, most especially, Ernesto
Mestre; my sister Laura García; and my husband, Bruce
Wood. Special thanks to Won Kim for ongoing support,
to Ana Sánchez Granados for continual inspiration, and
to Erika Abrahamian for her linguistic expertise. The
biggest thanks of all, of course, goes to my daughter,
Pilar García-Brown, for her irreverence,
her humor, and her love.